PISTOL PASSPORT

PISTOL PASSPORT

Eugene Cunningham

Chivers Press ● G.K. Hall & Co.
Bath, Avon, England Thorndike, Maine USA

This Large Print edition is published by Chivers Press, England, and by G.K. Hall & Co., USA.

Published in 1995 in the U.K. by arrangement with the author's estate.

Published in 1994 in the U.S. by arrangement with Houghton Mifflin Company.

U.K. Hardcover ISBN 0–7451–2381–3 (Chivers Large Print)
U.S. Softcover   ISBN 0–8161–7418–0 (Nightingale Series Edition)

The text of this Large Print edition is unabridged.
Other aspects of the book may vary from the original edition.

Set in 16pt New Times Roman.

Printed in the U.K. on acid-free paper.

British Library Cataloguing in Publication Data available

Library of Congress Cataloging-in-Publication Data

Cunningham, Eugene, 1896–1957.
    Pistol passport : a novel of the Texas border / by Eugene Cunningham.
        p. cm.
    ISBN 0–8161–7418–0 (alk. paper : lg. print)
    1. Texas — Fiction. I. Title.
[PS3505.U428P57 1994]
813'.54—dc20
                                                                94–2967

For
IRENE

CONTENTS

CHAPTER ONE

'THE JACKLINS LIED!'

Leandro County had turned out almost in a body, for this last day of the Drago murder trial. The shabby district courtroom was crowded with men and women waiting patiently through the afternoon for the jury to bring back its verdict. They had packed the room during the days of the long-drawn trial and now the climax was being prepared in the little jury room down the corridor.

At the table with his counsel sat Drago, a lean, swarthy, handsome six-footer, with dark mustache seeming almost black against the jail-pallor of his close-shaved skin.

He saw the rows of faces on his left without focusing dark eyes upon any there. He had known these people all his life. He had worked and played with the younger men, and danced with most of the younger women. The older ones had been friends of his father and uncle. But now they were not Smiths and Joneses. Because of the murder charge against him, they were no longer individuals who liked or disliked him. They were massed and marshaled into something called *The People*, and when they stood that way he did not know them. And in their eyes *he* was changed. He was no longer a person. He was a branded killer, for nobody doubted—nobody *could* doubt—what verdict 'Red' Coops's jury would bring in.

Two hours, now, the jury had been out. The prosecutor's staff was outside, somewhere. Old Judge Watson was in his chambers next door— probably dozing.

But the audience only shifted position on rickety chairs. The feud between Dragos and Jacklins, coming to this tense ending in a Leandro courtroom, was not to be missed.

Drago shifted slightly in his hard chair and old Theo Attley, his chief counsel, leaned toward him:

'Pretty soon, now,' Attley whispered.

Drago nodded. He took the Duke's and brown papers from the table and began to roll a cigarette.

'I wish they'd come back and get it over,' he said tonelessly. 'We know it'll be conviction— with *that* jury!'

He brushed yellow flakes of tobacco from his gray trousers.

'I'm afraid so,' Theo Attley admitted. 'The Jacklins lied. All their principal witnesses were perjurers. And there are no friends of yours on the jury. But don't worry, son! We'll start the wheels as soon as this sentence is in. If only your uncle hadn't pulled away from you—'

Drago nodded. But he hardly heard. For the hundredth time, he thought of the shooting which had brought him here.

2

He and Nevil Jacklin had quarreled, almost from the moment that Drago had resigned from the Rangers and come back to Leandro County to work for his uncle. And sour, pious old Tom Drago had warned his nephew that there must be no gunplay between the Jacklins and the Dragos. Tom Drago had said—

A door opened, behind and to the right of the judge's bench. The district judge came through, a round-shouldered little man in black alpaca coat and cotton trousers striped blue and white. Judge Watson's leathery face was very solemn. He climbed into his chair and looked out over the courtroom. Under straggling mustache, his mouth showed very tight. He was an old cowboy-companion of Drago's father. Drago had eaten at his table many a time; had broken horses for him.

A bailiff came in. Drago watched him steadily. Then there was the shuffling sound of feet in the corridor behind the officer. The jury was coming in. Drago stood to watch the twelve men cross the courtroom and file in behind the little fence that bounded the jury box.

The gavel of Judge Watson fell upon the desk and the buzz of talk which had spread across the audience ceased. There was silence in the courtroom so thick that Theo Attley's breathing sounded very loud at Drago's side. The clerk made the formal inquiry of the foreman of the jury, concerning a verdict.

'Red' Coops was a big man, red-faced, owner of the Leandro Livery Stable. He nodded and swallowed self-consciously.

'Yeh. We got a verdict,' he said huskily. And then, before he could be questioned further, he drew in breath:

'We found him guilty of first-degree murder and we sentence him to be hung!' he bellowed.

Again the gavel fell on the desk. But this time Judge Watson must hammer frantically before the murmuring stopped. Drago watched the jury. Face by face he studied them. One or two looked at him stonily, but the others stared nervously past or over him.

Drago turned a little, then, at the counsel table. He moved the two yards to stand with dark head very erect before Judge Watson.

'You have been found guilty—Have you anything to say before I pass sentence?'

Drago nodded. His cigarette was dead in his fingers. He dropped it on the floor, set his foot carefully upon it, then lifted his eyes again. He faced the painting of 'Justice' on the wall over Judge Watson's head. Suddenly, his hard mouth lifted at the corners. Paint had peeled from the picture. The 'Lady of the Scales' seemed to be peering at him with one eye, through a hole in her blindfold. She seemed to be leering at him one-sidedly.

'If you don't mind, I would like to say a few things.'

Then he turned with thumbs hooked in the

wide brown belt about his lean waist. For the first time that day, he looked directly at the faces of those people sitting stiffly out there.

'This verdict is a bigger surprise to my counsel than it is to me,' he said, speaking quietly. 'I reckon they expected a conviction, all right. But they didn't expect this particular recommendation. I think I did. I watched Red Coops's jury during the trial and—Yes, I think I expected this. I don't think much of that jury. I didn't think much of it when it was chosen. But we couldn't go on challenging forever. We had to take what we could get, it seemed. Red Coops and—the rest of the lot...'

Now he turned to look at the jury. And he surveyed them, beginning with the big red-faced liveryman—whom he had once knocked into a horse-trough for abusing a pony. Red Coops did not meet Drago's dark, sardonic stare. None of the others seemed anxious to face him, either. Drago turned back to the courtroom.

'Most of you people have known me just about since I was born on the D Bar. You knew my father before me. You know that when I resigned from the Rangers I was sergeant. It may even have drifted to you that I was a pretty good Ranger.'

'You shore was!' an enthusiastic voice yelled from the back of the room. 'You certainly was!'

And Judge Watson seemed not to hear the

remark.

'Thanks, Till!' Drago told that one-time D Bar cowboy, smiling slightly. 'Now, all of you know that from the time I came back to Leandro County and went to work on the D Bar again, Nevil Jacklin and I didn't get along. A lot of you, I reckon, said among yourselves that it would have to come to killing, Jacklin and Drago being the kind of men they were. Well, *I* thought so! I didn't like the man and he didn't like me. I didn't intend to buy a trunk—or step off the sidewalk for any Jacklin who ever lived—for all the Jacklin tribe!'

He lifted a wide shoulder, and smiled faintly:

'*I* wasn't worried! I considered myself as good a man as Jacklin. Now, most of you sat here during all this trial. So you've listened to—*witnesses* tell what I said and what Jacklin said; what he did and what I did. *The Jacklins lied!* And, because you've listened to their lies and liars, I am going to tell you as quickly as I can just how Jacklin was killed. You heard the story from me on the witness stand, but because that jury of Red Coops's brought in the verdict it did, I'm going to tell you that story again.'

His smile was a little contemptuous.

'Not because I'm afraid of dying. If I were the kind to be afraid, my whole past life would be a different kind of life. I never would have gone some places that I've been in. The State can hang me, but it can't make me play cry-baby. So, what I tell you here and now happens to be the truth. It's not told with any idea that it can get me out of this. It's told because there's a certain number of you out there that I've known all my life—and liked. One of these days you may tell yourself that you heard my story and it sounded like the truth.'

Someone—the sound came from the direction of Sandy Till, the cowboy who had yelled—began to clap his hands. And across the courtroom swept the scattered sound of other hard palms beating together. Drago grinned sardonically. For the Jacklins and their lying witnesses, he observed, made a grim, silent, almost moveless block in those spectators.

'On the Wednesday night that I killed Jacklin,' Drago continued, when the sound had died away, 'I came in from the ranch. I met Nevil Jacklin in the Gold Dollar Saloon. He surprised me when he came up in the presence of many men—some of you out there—and said that he wanted to call off our feud. I said that was all right with me and we shook hands. We had a drink or two together. Then he told me he wanted my help in examining Juan Mercado, a Mexican cowboy who had worked on the D Bar and also for the Jacklins. It was a business of some cattle being taken. Jacklin thought Mercado was guilty of rustling them. *I* didn't think so.

'Well, we started out of the bar-room

together, using the side door into the alley between the Gold Dollar and the Silverman store. When we got into the alley, there was nobody around. I am the only man alive who knows what took place in that alley. Those *witnesses* of the Jacklins—who *happened* to be at windows above the Silverman store, and in other places—they were lying. They weren't there! They couldn't have heard anything if they had been there. Jacklin began the old row all over again. He told me he was going to settle it once and for all. He didn't make a motion *toward* a gun. *He drew a gun!* And I drew mine just as fast. I shot him before he could shoot me. Then I went back into the Gold Dollar to tell the men there—some of you men who are sitting here now—that I had killed Jacklin because he had tried to kill me. We went back outside and—*somebody* had picked up the pistol that had been under Jacklin's hand not two minutes before! And so, it was said by the Jacklins that I had tolled an unarmed man into the alley and killed him. The Jacklins lied!'

He looked again at the jury before he turned back to the bench.

'And now, Your Honor,' he said quietly, 'you'd better get this over with.'

Old Judge Watson lifted his faded eyes above Drago's head. In a voice that was hardly more than a stammering mutter, he rattled off the set phrases of the death sentence. When he had finished, Drago nodded and turned to the

8

deputy sheriff.

'All right, Gafford,' he said. 'Let's be getting back.'

His little cell in the sandstone jail overlooked Court Square. He took off his shoes when the cell door had clanged shut behind him. Tigerishly, he began pacing the length of the cell. He had done that for weeks, now. As he walked, mechanically he lifted long, muscular arms and flexed them. It had been almost his only form of exercise in the weeks of confinement. But he had hardly softened or put on weight in the jail. He was of the lean, restless breed.

Theo Attley came in after a while, to say what he had said in the courtroom—with the difference that now he planned an appeal.

'Using what for the costs?' Drago inquired. Then he patted the old lawyer on the shoulder. 'We haven't any money, Judge. We used up everything I had, and some of yours, trying the case.'

'If Tom Drago—' Attley began, as he had begun in the courtroom.

'My uncle decided that I had absolutely disregarded all his orders,' Drago checked him grimly. 'He took it for granted that I picked the fight with Jacklin; and I wouldn't be surprised if he believed that I shot Jacklin knowing that he didn't have a gun. Which leaves us—flat-broke. The only thing I've got in the world is that big chestnut gelding of mine, with my

9

saddle and bridle. And all that belongs to you. The whole outfit might bring five hundred dollars from some cowboy who wants to say that he's riding my horse, sitting in my saddle.'

'We'll do something!' Attley said stubbornly.

Drago ate supper, very much as he had eaten all his other meals in the jail, with ordinary appetite. He had two months. Two months before they would build a scaffold against the inner wall of the jail, and take him out to hang him. He went to the barred window and looked out. Court Square was dark, now. Beyond it, on the streets that bounded it, the lights of stores and saloons showed yellow. Two figures came across the square. One was a woman. Her white dress was plain in the Gold Dollar's light, as the two came out upon the sidewalk. Drago thought of Sara. He had heard no word from her since his arrest. And only the night before Jacklin's killing, Sara had told him that she would go anywhere with him, do anything for him—

Someone was climbing the stairs to the cell block. The jangle of keys told Drago that it was one of the jailers. But someone came behind the deputy sheriff. Drago crossed to the door and stood waiting. Johnny Belk moved to the side and began to speak stammeringly:

'It's a dirty shame! A hell of a verdict, even for that big, crooked windbag, Red Coops! It's—'

'Never mind, Johnny,' Drago told him. 'How's—everybody?'

'You can stay a half-hour,' the deputy told the youngster.

The slow fall of his footsteps died away toward the stair.

CHAPTER TWO

'TWO FRIENDS OF YOURS, DRAGO'

'Sara—' Johnny Belk hesitated, then seemed to plunge on irritably: 'I don't know what got into that girl. I've talked to her, but she won't talk back. She acts like—like—'

'Sara's all right,' Drago told him. 'Don't be bothering your head about her. How's that Button horse of mine? You been riding him to keep him in shape?'

'That's a great horse!' Johnny cried enthusiastically. 'Greatest I ever forked. When you see him—'

He stopped short, almost with a gasp. Drago laughed and put a hand through the bars to grip the boy's arm, hard.

'I know! I know! Hard to remember. So don't worry about it. It does look like a pretty complete rooster-act for the Jacklin outfit. They ought to stage quite a celebration on the Cross J tonight. For they managed to do what

11

Nevil nor any of the others could do.'

'Well,' Johnny Belk said, with great ferocity, 'don't you ever think they'll carry out that sentence. No, sir! You're going to get out of this and hightail it into Mexico. It's the dirtiest trial and the worst verdict the State of Texas ever saw. But you've got friends. You've got plenty of friends. And they're not going to take this lying down.'

'Thanks,' Drago said smilingly. 'And how is all this going to be done?'

Johnny stammered. But he shook his fist savagely:

'Never you mind. It'll *be* done.'

Drago paid little attention to the boy's pompous assurances. He was thinking of Sara. One side of his brain was saying that a girl who wouldn't stick to her man when he got into trouble was not worth thinking of. But the other half was recalling other things—Her yellow hair and clear skin. Her large and almost childish blue eyes. The slender body which had become so beautifully rounded, so alluring, during his five years with the Rangers. He held the iron bars of the cell and his long arms stiffened. He felt almost as if he could tear that door away—if Sara waited for him beneath the sycamores on Court Square. But she was *not* waiting for him on Court Square! She was not waiting for him anywhere. He sagged a little and talked of this and that; gossip of the county. At last, when Johnny told

12

him again with youthful savagery that the jail would not hold him long, he thanked him absently, almost tonelessly.

When he turned back to his cot, after the deputy had escorted the boy out, Drago found himself suddenly very weary. There had been a great strain during his time in the courtroom, even though he had been sure from the beginning that the jury would bring in a guilty verdict. As for the death sentence—He had once spent twenty hours tied to a tree in the middle of a Mexican bandit camp, assured by all of them that presently he was to die under torture. If that experience had not been able to break his nerves, this could not.

He lay on the cot and, with big hands locked behind dark head, stared into the blackness of the cell over him. One line of light came through the cell window, from some saloon or store below. He stared fixedly at the golden bar upon the ceiling. The scene in the courtroom seemed to slip away; become unreal. It was not true! He had not listened to old Judge Watson's familiar voice saying in a stammering monotone that he was to be hanged by the neck until he was dead. It was not possible! All that was no more than a nightmare. That had happened to other men, of course. But it could not happen to him. Then he moved on the cot and twisted his head until he could look upward and backward and find the bars on the cell window.

13

'*It is true*!' he said aloud. 'If they can make it stick!'

* * *

He waked the next morning for an early breakfast and Sarkey, the squat, brutal-faced deputy, leaned on the cell door to watch him eat. There was something catlike about Sarkey today. His heavy mouth quivered in a triumphant grin. Drago ignored him, because he had learned during his weeks in the jail that nothing so infuriated the deputy as going unnoticed. Besides, Drago reminded himself, he was fair game now for all the curious staring ones. There was something gruesomely fascinating about any man who had been condemned to hang. Everyone who looked at him—with the exception of a handful of close friends—would eye him so. He had become suddenly a creature apart, different from other human beings—hardly a human being at all. But he was not going to break. He would not, for pride's sake!

So, Sarkey's remarks about Drago's nerve, and the fact that the sixty days of yesterday were only fifty-nine this morning, went unanswered.

'We had a fellow in here once,' Sarkey told him, grinning, 'that made a kind of calendar on the wall. You going to do that, Drago? Check off the days, until—*the* day?'

14

Drago went on eating as if he had not heard. And Gafford Hancock, Sarkey's fellow-deputy, interrupted the inquisition. Hancock was no fonder of Sarkey than was Drago. He came up now and stood beside the other officer.

'Juan Mercado's trial opens today over at Ancho, Drago,' Gafford said. 'And you're on the list to testify right at the first. I ask' the boss and he said—uh—yesterday didn't make no difference he knew of. So, we'll be going over about ten o'clock to Ancho.'

Sarkey's bristly head rolled sidewise to Gafford Hancock.

'Who's going to guard him?' he asked.

'You and me, I reckon.'

'*Uh-uh. Uh-uh.* I'll tell the boss I don't want you, Gafford. Me and Ferd Ingram are the boys to take him over and bring him back. Two good deputies with nice, loose trigger fingers. By God! He won't cheat the rope if Ferd and me take him in tow!'

When Sarkey had hurried away to arrange for the trip to the adjoining county, Gafford Hancock looked after him, then spat disgustedly.

'Watch your step, boy!' he warned Drago ominously. 'Him or Ferd either, they would plug you in the back if you made a quick move to get your tobacco sack. Me, I'm going to pull out of this damn' job, soon as fall roundup starts. *I'm* not going to side two killers like

15

Sarkey and Ferd Ingram, not a bit longer'n I can help. But while you're on the road, and while you're in that Ancho courtroom, *watch your step!*'

At ten o'clock—handcuffed, and flanked by Sarkey and the tall, Indian-like Ferd Ingram—Drago marched down to the back door of the jail to a buckboard that waited. Drago lifted his head and drew in a great, slow breath. To a man who had slept so much out of doors, who spent so many days of his life in the open, the very idea of a cell was like the click of a trap. He had himself held grimly in check while in the jail. It was only in a moment like this, when he was briefly outside again, that homesickness swept over him with the force of a physical blow.

He wanted to be on Button, his tall chestnut gelding, riding down a long trail that led away and away to some far hill—and over it. He felt that he would have cheerfully traded five years of his life for a year of freedom—freedom such as he had always known—and had taken so for granted.

Sarkey pushed him impatiently.

'Well, get in, get in!' he snarled. 'We got to get over and let you do your yard of lying for Juan Mercado. Reckon it's fair enough—the way Juan come to testify for you. But Ancho juries ain't likely to take a convicted murderer's word for much. It's just a lot of foolishness, taking you over.'

16

Ferd Ingram said nothing; merely walked around the buckboard and got in, to take the reins of the sheriff's team. But he turned his long, narrow head slowly, and his murky, dark eyes swept up and down Drago. Ferd Ingram said much less than Sarkey, but Drago knew him to be by far the more dangerous man.

Sarkey amused himself, along the fifteen miles of road, by asking Drago if he would not like to try an escape. Ferd Ingram smoked endless cigarettes, and for the most part stared straight ahead between the horses. When he did turn, it was for careful surveys that took in every detail of the prisoner. And he rode with a pistol conveniently under his right leg, away from Drago's hand, but close to his own.

Ancho was only a smaller edition of Leandro. They were there before two o'clock in the afternoon. A deputy sheriff, coming out of the courthouse, informed the Leandro men that Drago's turn on the witness stand would hardly come within an hour; might very well be delayed until the next day.

'State's taking more time with its witnesses than we allowed for,' he said. 'Reckon they found more witnesses about Mercado than they expected. Defense, too, is got quite a smear.'

'How does it look for Juan?' Drago asked him.

'Well, now, I wouldn't want to do no betting. But from the talk around, the defense is a little heavier than anybody believed. You won't be the only one to say Mercado was in Leandro County at the time them Lazy M steers was run off. Yeh, I wouldn't be a speck surprised to see the jury acquit Mercado.'

'Got anything we can eat, up in that jail of yours?' Sarkey inquired. 'We missed our dinner.'

'Nothing but a little bit of mighty cold leavings,' the Ancho officer said apologetically. 'Sorry!'

'I've got some money,' Drago said generally to his guards. 'I'm not fond of cold leavings when I can get better. If you want to go down to the Ancho Café, I'll buy the dinners.'

He had turned a little. Now, he almost let surprise show in his face. For at the corner of the courthouse Johnny Belk stood close to the building wall, watching, listening. And beside the boy was Sandy Till, that one-time D Bar cowboy who had been so enthusiastically pro-Drago in Judge Watson's courtroom. The two seemed intensely interested in the conversation.

Then Sarkey, grinning at Drago, said:

'And why not? *I'll* eat a murderer's dinner!'

As if the words were a signal, Johnny and Till vanished around the corner of the courthouse.

The buckboard moved deliberately around the courthouse and into the principal thoroughfare of the county seat. The Ancho

18

Café was a one-story brick building, almost at the end of Ancho Street. Horses were tied to hitchracks before it. Buggies, buckboards, and wagons were hitched along the buildings. For court sessions in Ancho—particularly when a well-known cowboy stood charged with rustling—brought in county people for miles around.

Ferd Ingram drew the buckboard to a halt before the café. Getting out easily, despite his manacled hands, Drago half-turned. There, before the hitch-rack, and within thirty feet, was his big chestnut gelding. Upon Button were his saddle and bridle. Even the stock of the Winchester carbine protruding from a saddle scabbard looked like his!

'What's all this?' he wondered inwardly. But his face was blank as he crossed the plank sidewalk ahead of Ferd Ingram and Sarkey, to enter the eating-house door.

Terry O'Donnell, the squat, red-faced proprietor, greeted Drago cordially and courteously, and did not so much as glance at the glinting steel at his wrists.

'Hi, Terry!' Drago answered him. 'How's tricks?'

'Tol'able. Tol'able,' the Irishman shrugged. 'You're testifying for Juan Mercado, I reckon! Well, I can't be believing that Juan's a horse-thief, nor yet a cow-thief—Not on any wholesale scale. Juan'd beef a steer, or sell a hide—along with the big cowmen. But not

19

sixty-seventy head, like they're saying. I hope you clear him.'

'I'll do my best,' Drago assured him. 'Where'll we sit? I have got a couple of guests with me. A nice table for three, Terry.'

He felt an odd sense of lightness—like that coming with the third drink of an evening. For on the left of the long, somewhat dusky, room, sitting over coffee cups, he saw Sandy Till and Johnny Belk. They seemed not to have noticed the entry of the party.

Terry O'Donnell motioned to a table which had been cleared. Drago observed that most of the other tables which lined both sides of the room were littered with dishes, as if recently occupied.

Ferd Ingram went around and sat down.

'Get in there next to the wall, Drago,' Sarkey demanded.

'How about taking off the jewelry until I get done eating?' Drago inquired.

Ferd Ingram shook his long, vicious head. But Sarkey, after hesitating briefly, reached into a pocket and drew out a handcuff key. He grinned:

'The only difference between my plugging you here, or in the street,' he told Drago, 'I'll be kind of good-natured about it in here, after I get done eating. Only reason you get 'em off is because you pay the dinner-bill.'

Drago took the chair next to the wall and sat with arms upon the table. He could see Sandy

20

Till and Johnny Belk looking steadily across the room at him. Sarkey's roving eye found them. He scowled for an instant, then his grin returned.

'Well, just looky!' he cried. 'Two friends of yours, Drago. And, likely, the *only* friends you *got* for many a mile. Reckon they come over to do some fancy lying for Juan Mercado, same as you.'

Drago made no answer. He was watching an odd maneuver of Johnny Belk. The boy put his hand under the table, clear under the dropping edge of the tablecloth. He withdrew it and, meeting Drago's eyes, made a little sign with his head, then repeated the motion.

And Sandy Till, also, watched Drago and nodded as if to draw his attention to what Johnny was doing.

There was nothing wrong with Drago's comprehensive instincts. He had been in far too many tight places, during his years of Rangering, not to have learned how to play up to any lead, however small, that was offered him.

He looked toward the kitchen. Terry O'Donnell was not now in sight. Ferd Ingram was making a cigarette. Sarkey was settled comfortably in his chair, a thumb hooked in his shell belt over the Colt he wore, butt-front, on the left side.

'The question is'—Drago was thinking—'what does all this mean? A note, or something, under the table? Well...'

CHAPTER THREE

'THEY'LL NEVER GET ME BACK—'

Three elderly cowmen and their wives got up from a table in the rear of the room, to come past Drago and the Leandro deputies. Now the room was empty—except for Belk and Till and Drago's party. Ferd Ingram sat like some drowsing rattlesnake, with unwinking, cloudy eyes fixed on some point between Sarkey and Drago.

Sarkey bellowed at the two across the room. He asked Johnny Belk and Sandy Till if they had their stories together. In the kitchen was the rattle of dishes. Terry O'Donnell appeared in the serving door to announce that meals would be forthcoming quickly.

Drago got tobacco and papers and began to build a cigarette. He let his right hand sag to his lap, then slide beneath the tablecloth. He felt metal—the barrel of a pistol. He moved his hand a little, and touched a second gun, hanging like the first from a nail driven in the underside of the wooden apron. He held the tobacco-laden cigarette paper in his left hand while he leaned across to Ferd Ingram.

Automatically, the tall deputy bent toward

22

Drago. The loose tobacco in the cigarette paper went into his eyes, then Drago flicked the two Colts from beneath the table. Sarkey's chair squeaked loudly as he swayed away. Without looking at Sarkey, Drago smashed out with the left-hand gun, while he lunged across to rap the blinded Ingram over the head with his other gun.

Sarkey was falling when Drago came to his feet and pivoted. But the Colt had struck only glancingly. He was clawing at his own gun. Grimly Drago stamped on Sarkey's gunhand, then stooped to strike flailingly at his temple with a Colt barrel.

Johnny Belk and Sandy Till were on their feet now. Drago rammed the pistols into the waistband of his trousers. He looked flashingly down at the two unconscious men. Then a small, satanic grin lifted the corners of his mouth and eyes. He caught Sarkey by the shoulder and dragged him near enough to Ferd Ingram to permit linking their right wrists together with the handcuffs Sarkey had taken from him.

'Thanks a lot, you—you *sidewinders*!' he said briefly to his rescuers.

Then he turned. Terry O'Donnell stood with both huge hands holding up his paunch—laughing soundlessly, but with tears streaming from his little blue eyes.

'As for you, you wild-eyed Irishman—Well, I only hope you get your tail in a big, deep crack, one of these fine days. So I can ride across the State, if necessary, to pry you out!'

He ran lightly up the room and stopped at the door, to look out at the street. People passed up and down, but none seemed interested. He was not too well known in Ancho, these days. He went deliberately across the sidewalk, to where the big gelding waited. The reins were knotted in forethoughtful slipknot. He jerked them loose and passed them up over the neck.

When he settled in the saddle, the temptation was very strong to yell triumphantly. But, instead, he turned Button and walked him sedately to the corner. Once around it, he kneed the tall chestnut into a trot. He kept Button at that gait for fifty yards, before letting him slide into an effortless lope.

Ahead was the dark line of woodland marking the Leandro River—a mile and more away ... Drago stared at it. He was free. He found that hard to understand; harder to believe. After weeks of close confinement in a cell, and no more than moments of passage between jail and courtroom, it was incredible that now he sat a horse in the open again.

He twisted in the big saddle and looked behind him. But from the county seat came no plunging riders, no shrill yells, even, to tell of pursuit roused. He turned again. The road before him was empty at this hour. He drew a great breath, leaned a little forward and kicked

Button with unroweled heels. The chestnut grunted and jumped into a racing gallop. So they went thundering down toward the Leandro and the swaying wagon bridge that spanned the 'bottoms' of the deep narrow stream.

Drago whirled the gelding at the bridge and sent him down a trail that led to the stream itself. And now he *knew* that he was free. Once in the dense wilderness that bordered the Leandro, no posse was likely to find him. He knew almost every foot of the bottoms, where before his day outlaws had harbored.

'One thing!' he promised himself grimly, aloud. 'They'll never get me back in a cage— whatever the other thing may be that I have to do. *Nunca! Jamás!*'

He rode on until Button hesitated upon the bank of a tiny creek that flowed over limestone into the Leandro. Drago had fished with bent pin and linen string in that clear creek. He grinned faintly as he sent Button into it and up its shallow course. Then out they went, upon a great shelf of rock. From the water to a rugged height, cedar-crowned, there was little chance of leaving trail. And from that hill to the edge of the Belks' small ranch he was on D Bar range.

By nightfall he had covered more than a dozen miles and had seen nobody. The moon rose and he rode alertly. He could have wished for darkness, for on that familiar ground he needed no light, and the hunters—who by now must be spreading over both Ancho and Leandro Counties—would have their search for him made easier in the brilliant light.

Button went at trot and lope toward the Belk house. For Drago had one call to make before he could bring himself to leave the Leandro country. He had to hear from Sara Belk her decision about him.

As he rode with the Winchester across his lap, he argued with himself about the girl. After all, he had doubtless been too harsh in judging her. If his own uncle—who had been also his employer—had turned upon him, doubted him, a girl of eighteen who knew very little of men might very well have wondered about him. She would have heard enough to his discredit, Leandro County being divided as it was, so violently between Jacklin and Drago partisans.

He told himself that when she heard him give his version of Nevil Jacklin's killing she would believe him. After that—Mexico was the place for him. He knew the Border country and its ways; spoke Spanish fluently.

'I can make my start all over again down there,' he thought. 'There are plenty of big ranges below the River, and a Texas cowman who really knows his business won't be long out of work. I can look toward owning an iron of my own. If Sara really meant all the things she said, about being so desperately in love

26

with me, she'll be willing to take Mexico with me. We can forget Texas and a murder charge. Johnny can bring her down to me and—'

His castle-building was halted by sight of the cottonwoods ahead, the motte of huge, gaunt trees beside the Belk homestead. A light burned in a window as he rode quietly up to the corrals. He could hear Aunt Rebecca Mullen, the Belks' old negro cook, singing in the kitchen. He got down and left Button behind a harness shed with reins trailing.

'When Israel was in Egypt Land,
Let my people go!
Oppressed so hard they couldn't stand,
Let my people go!'

He grinned as he passed the door. It was so familiar, the every intonation of Aunt Rebecca's voice, the odors of cooking from the kitchen. He went on along the side of the house, toward the front gallery. Voices sounded in the dusk there—and the sudden, light sound of Sara's laugh.

He stood at the house corner, wondering who sat with Sara tonight. And a man not three yards from Drago said:

'Darling! You know I always did love you. And I think you loved me. That business was just foolishness. So—'

Drago recognized Sam Mays' voice and he stiffened, waiting for Sara's answer to

Leandro's leading young storekeeper. When the reply came, he had to think of the ancient proverb, about eavesdroppers hearing no good of themselves. For she laughed:

'I thought I was in love with him, Sam. You went to St Louis and left me. And then he came back and made me believe I was in love with him. But after he shot poor Nevil Jacklin the way he did—I think I was always a little bit afraid of him. You know what they say about the Dragos—they're dark and probably part-Indian; *like* Indians, anyway. I'm glad something happened to break us up, before I married him! Even if I didn't love you, I'd still be glad. Johnny thinks the sun rises and sets in him. But he's just a baby!'

Drago grinned one-sidedly and turned. He walked steadily back along the house wall. So, that was over. She had always been afraid of him, had she? And even without Sam Mays, she was 'glad that something had happened' to free her of the engagement.

He came to the corner and stopped there mechanically, to listen for an instant. Then, hearing nothing to alarm him, he moved around the corner—and almost stepped upon the feet of a tall man who leaned like a brooding statue against the house, arms folded, plain in the moonlight.

Drago recoiled with a sound, half-oath, half-grunt. The pistol which had been under his hand came up.

'It's all right, son,' Keats Tucker reassured him. 'I knowed Johnny and Sandy aimed to try to git you clear. I 'lowed you'd be drifting this way, once you was loose. I—had a good notion what you'd find, after you got here. So, I come along to wait for you.'

For perhaps ten seconds Drago glared at the angular face, half-shadowed by the wide hatrim. The T Circle's owner met his eyes steadily. Drago laughed shortly and returned the Colt to his waistband.

'You gave me a jolt,' he said. 'And after the other jolt—'

'You mean Sam Mays,' Keats nodded. 'Yeh, Sam is a young man nobody can say a thing against. And Sara, *she* ain't the kind to go around dying for her man, or her country. Sam is just about what she'd ask for, if she was to set down and write out an order to Sears, Roebuck. Well! You're free and I doubt they'll ever put you in another jail. So—What do you aim to do?'

'Mexico,' Drago shrugged. 'At least, that's what's been on my mind. They'll hunt Texas over for me, of course. The Jacklins will see to that! But, once across the River, I'll be able to hold my own.'

'Bawdeh is right,' Keats Tucker nodded. 'Tell you! You know where Bellero is, down on the River?'

'Heard of it,' Drago said, after a moment of thought. 'Pretty tough place, if I'm thinking of

29

the right spot.'

'Likely, you are!' Tucker said dryly. 'I ain't been down in five-six years. But it was plenty tough the last time I was there. And I ain't heard of no missionary societies sending a party down. Well, suppose you head for Bellero. And when you hit the place, look up Saul Black. He's a good friend of mine, and he runs his cattle on both sides the Bawdeh. I'll give you a note to him. He'll set you riding.'

'Thanks! Thanks a lot, Keats,' Drago told him gratefully.

'*De nada!* For nothing!' Keats checked him irritably. 'Little enough for *me* to do, for Steve Drago's boy. Anybody with a grain of sense would know *you* never took a shot at Nevil Jacklin when he didn't have a gun on. I was talking to Attley about it today. We made up our minds to the same notion: Somebody out of that crowd that swarmed around in the alley stole that gun out from under Nevil's hand. If we could find out who done it—'

'Well, while Attley is looking for that man, and that gun, *I'll* feel a lot safer across the River at Bellero!' Drago said grimly. 'I'll be riding, now. Is that T Circle camp in Shady Cove still pretty well supplied? I'd *hate* to try to rob an empty camp...'

'There's plenty of grub at Shady Cove. Shells, too. Help yourself. I would hack off that mustache, too. Let your beard grow and git yourself pretty dirty. You always had the

30

name of being pretty much the dandy. That will be on the reward notices, you can bet. Plain saddle-tramp—that's your play, now. What'll be your go-by?'

'Jack Smith,' Drago decided. 'Why?'

'Likely you'll find a letter from me, waiting for you at Bellero. I can send it in an envelope to my brother Davy Crockett at Fort Worth and he'll mail it on to you. Tell you the news. Luck *to* you, son. Your pa and me—and Xavier Watson—we went up the trail together a dozen times.'

'So did Uncle Tom Drago,' Drago recalled dryly. 'But you help, and Xavier Watson nearly broke his heart in the courtroom because he had to carry out an oath he'd taken. While Uncle Tom—Ah, well, there's no use going into that. In his own peculiar left-handed way, he was doing what he thought was the right thing, I suppose. I'll be looking for your letter and—thanks again!'

CHAPTER FOUR

'WHO YOU WORKING FOR?'

Drago ate at the T Circle line-camp and rode on—his mustache a knife-hacked stubble—with canned goods and shells in his saddle pockets. In a patch of brush that crowned a

31

hill, miles beyond, he spent the next day.

Johnny Belk had thoughtfully put his excellent field glasses in the saddle bags and with the powerful lenses Drago watched the surrounding country during the hours of daylight. Occasionally he saw horsemen, but there was no way of telling whether they were looking for him, or merely riding about range business.

He was done with supper when dusk came. He saddled and swung up. Then he left T Circle range as secretly and as fast as if old Tucker had been an enemy, not his father's old friend.

Sleeping days and riding through the nights, he left hardly more trail than if Button had owned no feet. He spoke to nobody; met nobody in his wolfish travel. He was like some old, gray *lobo*, he thought, changing the range. He was not the man he had been, when riding as sergeant of Rangers or foreman of the D Bar. He could never be the same more or less happy-go-lucky and kindly man again. There was a brand upon him—

'The mark of the trap,' he said aloud, time after time. 'Once it's on your hide, you're a dangerous animal. You can't help being wary and dangerous.'

In the beginning, he found himself rather puzzled about Sara; or about his feeling. He examined himself carefully and was surprised that he suffered none of the symptoms he had always believed a deserted lover felt. His principal reaction was something like disgust—and that was directed at himself, for being so fooled by a pretty girl.

Later, as he rode through darkness or across moonlit and empty prairie, he found Sara's face coming less and less frequently to mind; found himself looking forward to whatever might lie ahead at Bellero on the Rio Grande—the 'River.'

He saw the lights of Harz City on his right, several nights after leaving the T Circle. And it suited his sardonic mood to ride quietly into that little settlement of German folk and loaf for a while in the store of a smiling little man, eating greengage plums and bargaining for a pair of fringed leather leggings and shell belt and holster. The storekeeper also sold him a shirt of gray flannel, and waist overalls to replace his dirty gray trousers; and a shoulder holster with cylinder-spring, to carry his second gun.

Past Harz, the open range was wild and empty, as he angled toward the River. He rode across the Flats of Doloroso and up to the great pines of the Sierra Negrita, then down into the *malpais* named for the Devil's Wife, and up again. Now he ventured to ride of days, and from cowboys and sheepherders and occasional wanderers like himself—men quiet and non-committal and watchful of eyes—he got his directions.

From the *malpais* to the River, the trails

were those seldom ridden by honest men. They led across the scorched cañons and cactus-spiked divides of the Three Stooping Soldiers Range; followed the crests of releases usually; and sometimes led him to cabins where men as heavily armed as himself sat about, with nothing visible in the way of occupation.

Ranger that he had been, used to the ways of the hunted, he admitted that he had really known nothing of the *buscadero*—the wanted—clan, until now. He said nothing, for he was asked nothing, in any of these stopping-places. The people gave him food and showed him where to put his blanket at night. They said 'So long!' in the morning and he rode on south.

Perhaps his twentieth campfire was built on the rim of Picacho Cañon. The next day he rode through buttes and sandy flats toward Bellero on the Rio Grande. And here he found his soiled, wrinkled envelope from Keats Tucker.

'We are wurkin,' Keats wrote. 'Still huntin the man thatt stole Nevil Jacklins gun ande Attley says tell you be cairfull ande do nott gitt took befour we finde the man they are notices outt for you son $2500 rewarde ded or alive be cairfull. Juan Mercado gott cleer in the tryal in Ancho.'

And Saul Black was dead. The bar-tender at the Manhattan Palace told Drago circumstantially of Saul's going, ringed about

34

like a grim, gray old wolf with corpses of Mexican horse-thieves. Drago leaned on the pine counter in the shabby, one-room 'dobe and scowled. An El Paso bank had foreclosed on B 70 range and was operating the ranch—according to the man of drinks—'like a cross between a pore farm and a gals' seeminary.'

Drago grinned, in spite of his disappointment. It was his last gold piece that he was breaking, now.

'I reckon you come down looking for a job?' the bar-tender inquired. 'Well, there ain't much head-quartering in Bellero neighborhood to give a man his cakes. Not if he's too particular about what he'll do for a living. Of course, lots drift in with somebody raising the dust on their back-trail. I take it you ain't that kind. So I ain't going to tell you that Buffalo Lopez will use a fast gun down in San Leon. Say! Just happened to remember: Man was through here, couple weeks ago, from up in the Camel Flat country. I remember him saying he rode for the 6 Prod outfit and they was not too full up. Know that country?'

Drago said that he did not.

'Well, I never been up that way, either. But it's beyond Taunton Basin. Lot of outfits up there. Big and little. I reckon it's crowding three hundred miles.'

Drago considered the situation during the remainder of the day and, even while he played his own particular and profitable version of stud poker with the hardest group he recalled ever having seen, he wondered whether he would be wise to cross the River. Getting up from the table near midnight with exactly three hundred dollars of enemy-money, he walked out to the dusky quiet of the single street and looked up at the starry sky.

'I'll call it an omen,' he decided. 'Three hundred miles to Camel Flat and three hundred dollars to travel on. Yes, I'll give that 6 Prod outfit a whirl. Nobody up there is apt to recognize me. I'll try it.'

As he rode toward Camel Flat, the chance-met riders who pulled in to yarn with him began to speak more and more often of what they called the 'Taunton Basin War'—and to look at him rather speculatively. He understood that any man going toward the Basin must seem a possible recruit for one side or the other.

Nearing Taunton, the county seat, the road became more thickly peopled. Drago observed how the riders encountered now approached him with hands very near to weapons and watched him steadily from the moment he was in sight. For all that he intended merely to ride through and go on for the hundred miles to Camel Flat and the 6 Prod, he could not help being interested in all these signs of war.

In Taunton, when he had stabled Button in the Lone Star Corral and rolled shell-belt around holstered Colt and shoved the gun into a saddle pocket, he felt the tension as if it had been some emanation rising from the very ground. It was in the manner of the little one-eyed corral owner; in the walk of the men he passed on the street. And, in watching these warriors of rival factions, Drago almost forgot his own status.

To a fighting man such as he had always been, the atmosphere of Taunton was somehow pleasant. He had no thought of becoming a part of this action. He had not yet learned exactly who were the principals in the war, and least of all did he know what were the reasons for the feud.

He saw the long, dingy sign of the Cattlemen's Bar ahead and, because more men seemed to turn in there than elsewhere, he stopped when he came to the door and looked about him. After a moment of staring around, which showed him nothing that was alarming, he pushed the swing doors back and went inside.

The Cattlemen's bar was almost as long as the big room. When Drago came in from Court Street, for another sharp and interested, if veiled, study of his surroundings, the bar was lined almost solidly with cowboys and freighters and merchants and cowmen; and with a sprinkling of men like Drago himself, with less about them to show their occupations. More men were packed about the gambling layouts in the adjoining room, visible

37

through the arched opening in the partition.

A good many there returned his blank regard with equal steadiness—and faces as expressionless as his own. Softly, he beat his hand upon the dust-grayed leather of his fringed brown leggings. He saw a narrow opening at the bar and moved that way.

The clump of his boot heels, the clink of his spur chains, were almost drowned by the rattle of glasses and click of chips and steady murmur of talk. But the two men between whom he stepped turned instantly to face him.

Drago stared straight ahead at the array of bottles on the back-bar. But he felt their level, probing stare upon him. He kept dark face, dark eyes, expressionless. It was no more than he expected, to be studied carefully by all he met here in Taunton. Doubtless, there were few in the Basin like himself, lined up with neither faction. He knew that any wanderer must conduct himself very discreetly, if he wanted only to pass through quietly on his road elsewhere.

So he ignored the stares still trained upon him and, catching the eye of a bar-tender passing him, he spoke courteously—and tonelessly:

'That *Four Roses*, there. That's just about the right amount of roses, I would say. I'll back that belief.'

The bar-tender stopped short and looked at him, wiping thick hands that were the exact

38

white of a fish belly upon a soiled apron. He had heavy-lidded green eyes and they rested for seconds upon Drago's face. Then they shuttled sidelong, in a glance at the man on Drago's left which had inquiry in it. He made no move to furnish either bottle or glass.

Drago sighed and turned to look, in his turn, at the man beside him. Even in tough Taunton Basin, there were limits to discretion and the avoidance of clashes which might focus attention upon him. He smiled faintly as he studied the man whose word the bar-tender so obviously waited for.

He placed the man instantly as someone of importance; in this bar-room, at least; probably a man of weight in the Basin. He had the look of hard efficiency of head and hands. He was bat-eared and dark—darker than Drago. His face was knife-scarred. Though he stood six full inches shorter than Drago, his shoulders were broader, and his arms were gorilla-like, for length and thickness. His hands were enormous. Now, he stared through slitted lids, murky eyes belligerent.

'Who you working for?' he demanded.

'Nobody,' Drago answered indifferently. He turned back to the bar-tender. 'About the *Four Roses*, now—'

'Ah!' the bat-eared man said mockingly. 'Ain't working for nobody—in Taunton Basin.'

'That's right,' Drago agreed. 'Nobody. In

39

Taunton Basin.'

He had not turned. He was still looking at the bar-tender. But he did not miss a certain air of tension that seemed now to grip the men to right and left of him. It was something electric in the bar-room's atmosphere; it told him that he had not said the right thing to the bat-eared man. So he moved his elbow a little. His right hand hung limply from the wrist near his chin, as he leaned on the bar. It was very close to the open throat of his shirt; close to the butt of his invisible, shoulder-holstered Colt.

'About that drink, now,' he said again to the bar-tender.

He was smiling faintly, with something satanic about the lift of mouth and eye corners. The man of drinks seemed not to hear him. For 'Bat-Ears' was talking again:

'What'd you come into the Basin for?' he was inquiring slowly. 'Where'd you come in from?'

Drago turned back to him. The unpleasant smile deepened.

'Some folks might tell you that was none of your damn' business,' he said levelly. 'In fact, *I* might.'

'In Taunton Basin, you'd tell Wyoming Dees that?'

'And why not?' Drago's tone, now, was one of simple wonderment. 'I certainly would, if he asked me. I wouldn't tell him any lies. Wouldn't take the trouble! Oh, this hairpin,

40

Dees, that's from the single-barrel country, is he supposed to *amount* to something hereabouts?'

There was something like a concerted gasp from the drinkers within earshot. As if twenty-odd men had suddenly drawn in their breath amazedly, all at once. Drago was watching the scarred face of 'Bat-Ears'—of Wyoming Dees. He saw the loose, cruel mouth tighten; saw the furious blood come up under the swarthy skin. He saw, also, the telltale twitch of Dees's gunhand. At that, he grinned widely.

But interruption came. It was the bar-tender's twin brother, by the look of him. But a more prosperous twin. The yellow diamond in his shirt bosom was three times the size of the stone the bar-tender wore. He had the same sleek, wavy hair, parted in the middle. But there was another difference—this man had the broken nose and cauliflower ears of the fighter.

He stopped behind Dees and grinned generally at everyone before him. Dees turned a little to look at the newcomer.

'New man of yours, Wyoming?' the latter inquired.

He jerked a big thumb toward Drago, rather as if he indicated a horse just bought.

Before Dees could speak, Drago answered for himself:

'No, not any. In fact, I'm not wearing any brand, here or anywhere else. I belong to that

41

grand old fraternity known as Saddle-Tramp. No brand a-tall,'—he grinned at Wyoming Dees—'even in Taunton Basin!'

'Did you maybe come in for Hinky Rust and Silent Wade?'

Drago looked thoughtfully at him, before shaking his head. For the man's voice had become a rumbling snarl, with mention of those two names. Drago knew Rust and Wade only as two of the ranchers fighting in this Taunton Basin War. But now he knew them for something else—for enemies of this broken-nosed man and Wyoming Dees. So, evidently, he was in the headquarters of the other faction. He looked solicitously at the broken-nosed man:

'You have a sort of trouble with your ears, now, don't you? Sort of buzzing, when a man speaks to you? Seems to make it downright hard to understand what's said to you. I told you that, so far as Taunton Basin is concerned, I'm a plumb maverick. Now, I'm going to tell you something else: If that bar-tender of yours doesn't make a fast move with a bottle, and give me the drink I ordered, I'm going to feel it necessary to climb the bar and show him the error of his ways!'

'Oh! Like *that*, huh?' the broken-nosed man grunted.

Suddenly, he began to grin. Up and down the bar men laughed outright.

He moved in a little closer to Drago who,

42

with both elbows on the bar, watched without expression. He had his bullet head down between his shoulders. His big, flat-knuckled fists had come up to waist level. He moved his feet slidingly.

Drago leaned with negligent air upon the bar, watching blankly. He had the sudden amusing thought that one thing well-learned at V.M.I. served him now—some smattering of boxing. He stared at the other's shoulders waiting...

When he saw the telltale tightening of the man's shoulder-muscles, he moved like a striking snake. Both his elbows came off the bar and he lunged forward to drive his fists in terrific alternation between the other's hands—straight to the belly. He shifted his feet and whipped his right in a furious hook to the angle of the heavy, undefended jaw. Then he stepped back, to let the man fall.

As the big figure came down with the slackness of a pole-axed bull, to sprawl with his face in the sawdust covering the floor, from an eye corner Drago saw the movement of Wyoming Dees.

He whirled and caught Dees's wrist. That hand held a Colt and Drago bore viciously down so that the gun pointed at the floor. Dees swore furiously and let the hammer drop. With the roar a slug rapped the floor all but at Drago's foot. He smashed his left fist into Dees's face and twisted his gunhand savagely,

43

making him drop the pistol.

Dees staggered and his scarred face was twisted. Drago snatched at his other wrist, then turned. He brought both of Dees's arms up over his right shoulder. Up, he heaved him, and flung him to crash head first into the iron belly of the cold stove near a wall. Dees lay as motionless as his broken-nosed friend by the bar.

There was still the man who had tripped him. Drago whirled back, but found only an empty space where that one had been. He grinned contemptuously at that, then looked at the bar-tender. That worthy was gaping at him. He moved uneasily under Drago's regard.

'The *Four Roses*,' Drago said. 'Or else—'

CHAPTER FIVE

'HOOLIHAN WILL DO'

The bar-room was very quiet. So the slap of quart bottle and glass upon the bar seemed a loud sound, as the bar-tender moved jerkily— and fast.

Drago kept his side-face to the room, and watched both victims, while he poured a drink and lifted the glass. He used his left hand. The right was hovering near his open collar.

From a leggings pocket he brought a silver

44

dollar. This he spun across the bar. He looked down at the man at his feet who was now beginning to twitch feebly.

'Give him the change for court plaster!' Drago told the bar-tender.

He walked to the door through thick silence. He pushed the swing doors apart and went out. Button stood at the hitchrack. Drago looked at him, but went on past. He walked along the plank sidewalk until he came to an eating-house. It was nearing five in the evening, and he had not eaten since dawn. He turned in and found the place empty of customers. The proprietor was a peg-legged man, with only a fringe remaining of what once must have been a noble head of red hair. His eyes were blue and slightly bulging. His heavy underlip was outthrust.

Drago grinned inwardly. He knew the earmarks of a belligerent man. Here was a fellow who would argue with you over the quality of the weather, if you told him it was sunny on a sunny day.

'Steak and eggs and—what *passes* for coffee,' he said gravely.

'What passes for coffee?' the peg-legged man repeated, glaring at Drago. 'Say! I do'no' what short-horn range you decorated last, but it don't take much figuring to see what range you'll look your last on. *What passes for coffee!* You'll drink *Arbuckle's Ariosa* in this place. You'll drink it and you'll *like* it! I swear! *I*

45

do'no' what this county's coming to. Bunch of would-be hoolihans riding the chuckline and kicking about ever' bite of grub they put into their bellies—'

'All right! All right! Arbuckle's goes,' Drago said hastily, with the meekest of expressions. 'Are you'—he waited until the indignant clump of the peg had stopped before the range at the far end of the counter—'a Western man?'

A skillet clattered upon the range. Around on his peg the man whirled, to gape unbelievingly at his customer. He swallowed noisily, then drew a long, gusty breath.

'Well—Well—' he began in a thick voice.

'No offense,' Drago drawled placatingly. 'I didn't know. It was just that—Well, you—you sort of talk like one. But I reckon you've been hanging around cowboys and Western men awhile, and you've taken on a little of their ways. I didn't mean anything.'

'If my old hogleg was handy, I *swear* I'd shoot you in the middle of the seat of your breeches!' the peg-legged man bellowed. 'I reckon there wouldn't be a speck of use shooting you in the head. You'd never feel it. Me, Dennis Crow, hanging around cowboys! Taking on a li'l' bit of their dumb ways! Me—that was born on the middle fork of Little River. That drove herds up the Trail till I lost this-here off-leg under a bronc'! That won the gold spurs at El Paso for steer-roping—'

A man came through the door while Drago

labored to keep his face conscience-stricken. Mechanically, Drago looked sideways at him. He seemed to be a townsman. At least, he wore shoes instead of boots. He stared furtively at Drago, then came on down the room and around the far end of the counter. He whispered buzzingly in Dennis Crow's ear. Crow whirled away from him to stare at Drago. The steak was smoking in the skillet. Crow came clumping up the counter, reddish bald head lowered a little between heavy shoulders, fierce blue eyes on Drago's face.

'You—*you* laid out Wyoming Dees and Olin Oge at the Cattlemen's,' he said slowly, incredulously. He stopped with both big hands on the counter, face a foot away from Drago's. 'You laid them two tarantulas out on the floor, then came in here to eat?'

'It was the first place I came to,' Drago shrugged. 'If you don't want my trade—'

'I ain't talking about that! What I'm meaning is—Man! Are you plumb ignorant, like you look and act, or—What do you call yourself, anyhow?'

'Hoolihan will do,' Drago said thoughtfully. 'You could even make it *Mister* Hoolihan.'

For a long minute, Dennis Crow stared at him. Then he shook his head and turned away. He clumped back to the range. He came up the counter with a steak and fried potatoes and two eggs. He went back and poured a cup of coffee. He put it before Drago. Suddenly he grinned.

'*Arbuckle's Ariosa*. And, by God! you can't tell *me* you ain't used to it. But you had me hoorawed for a minute. I swear, I thought I had hold of some mail-order cowboy that was trying to learn the difference between a cow and a critter. But'—his red face was abruptly turned solemn—'most men that'd run foul of Wyoming Dees and that scoun'el saloon-keeper, Oge, they'd be leaving here in a mile-high cloud of dust, trying to keep the news behind 'em!'

Drago ate placidly. As rangeland cooks went, Dennis Crow was thirty-third degree. It was the best meal he had eaten in a month. Crow grinned pleasantly at the compliment. Then he began to sketch the picture of Taunton Basin and the two sides of the bitter war that was entering upon its sixth month. Drago listened interestedly. The little citizen hung upon the counter and stared fascinatedly, if furtively, at him.

'So, it's Hinky Rust and old Silent Wade, a-bucking Gano Gotcher and Lige McGinsey. Both sides is hiring fighting men. Hiring 'em regular, too! For this-here war has used up twenty. More, likely! For they naturally ain't publishing it when a man's downed. And all come of that one miserable bunch of dogified long yearlings of the Lazy R and the Half Circle W that Rust and Wade lost, and claimed Gotcher and McGinsey took from their

48

cowboys. When Hinky Rust and Silent got a bunch of their boys together and raided the LL and the Walking M, a blind man could've saw what was coming. Lord knows, a *deef* man could've hear the racket they been raising...'

'And don't forgit the train robbery,' the citizen interjected eagerly. 'Nobody caught for that, yet. Both sides says the other ones done that.'

'Yeh,' Crow nodded. 'Month back—uh—*Hoolihan*, the westbound passenger was stopped at Mesquite Hill jist inside the Basin. Two trees was throwed across the track. Five men done the job, the crew says. Right slick job, too! They robbed all the passengers and took the way-safe apart with giant powder. Made the messenger open up the car. I don't think they got much; not over a hundred apiece for the five of 'em. But that was just because it wasn't in the safe for 'em to take out. And after the job the bunch got clean away. Like Sam, here, says, both sides is accusing each other of the stick-up.'

'*You* kind of put your foot into things today,' Sam grinned wisely. 'I tell you, Hoolihan—and you can't hooraw me, because I know that ain't your real name—in Taunton Basin, you're on one side, or else you're on the other. When you landed on Wyoming Dees, that's head-gunfighter for the LL and the Walking M, you just throwed yourself right over the fence onto the Lazy R and Half Circle

49

W side. Yes, sir! Ain't that the truth, Dennis?'

'Can happen,' Crow said, in an absent tone. 'Jist two sides in the Basin, nowadays. Two sides and—maybe three things to do.'

Drago stood up, putting the cigarette he had been rolling into his mouth. Absently, he fished in a pocket of his leggings and got out a dollar. From his hat-band he took a match, and scratched the head with a thumbnail.

Sam shook his head with terrific solemnity:

'Ain't nobody ever come in since Wyoming Dees hit the Basin, talked to him like you done—like he never amounted to nothing. Much less stopped his draw and flung him into the stove as if he was a sack. He has killed five men everybody knows about, in less'n six months. And likely some we don't know about! He'll be on your trail. But he slid out of sight after he come to. I think he rode out of town awhile back.'

Drago looked with his faint, satanic grin at the voluble little man. He placed him as that terrible and dangerous creature, the talkative fool. But even fools have their uses, when properly handled. So he nodded gravely to Sam and said that he was glad to hear of Wyoming Dees's going.

'I gather'—he was addressing Dennis Crow—'that I just about walked into LL and Walking M headquarters, when I happened to go in the Cattlemen's?'

The restaurant man nodded:

'Yeh, Oge's place is their camp, in town. The other side mainly uses around the Longhorn. And both sides scatter around the li'l' saloons and the stores.'

'Be seeing you,' Drago told him.

Dennis Crow seemed to be pondering something. His belligerent blue eyes were speculative as they met Drago's. But whatever it was that weighed upon his mind, he did not reveal it. He only answered:

'Well, now, I certainly *hope* I'll be seeing you some more, Hoolihan. Yeh. I sure do.'

At the door Drago looked again at Sam, who had followed him there, apparently eager to give out more information. And he had no desire whatever for Sam's company—not in Taunton!

'Do you think it's plumb safe for you to walk down the street with me?' Drago inquired. 'Of course, you know the town and probably you'll be able to dodge if I get shot at. But—'

The little man's lifted foot came hastily down without taking him over the threshold. His face turned gray. He swallowed with a sticky noise.

'I—I—I wasn't going to go. You see, I—I ain't had my supper yet,' he said quickly, stammering.

'Ah, go on, Sam,' Dennis Crow drawled sympathetically. 'I'll be open hours and hours yet. You can git your supper later on, any time.'

51

'No. No, I—I won't have time, later on. I'll eat now.'

Drago nodded sympathetically, also. He went out and looked swiftly down the street toward the Cattlemen's. But there was no sign of activity there. Nothing but a bunch of cowboys standing under the wooden awning around the door. He glanced across the street. Another saloon was there, with a knot of cowboys loafing along its front. It was not so large as the Cattlemen's of Olin Oge; not so bright in appearance. In peeling paint upon the false front was the dim likeness of a steer with unusual spread of horns. He felt safe in considering this the Longhorn of which Dennis Crow had spoken; headquarters of the Lazy R and Half Circle W warriors when in Taunton.

He grinned slightly as he regarded it, then stepped into the street and went at loafing gait across.

'I've seen one faction,' he thought. 'As well take a look at the other side while I'm here.'

The men outside the Longhorn looked at him without apparent interest. And when he pushed through the swing doors, nobody in the bar-room seemed concerned by his entrance. Even when he came to the bar and leaned an elbow upon it, to order a drink, nobody turned to study him, as had been the case in the Cattlemen's. He poured whisky into a glass and stood with hand cupped about it, staring absently at the faded mirror in which he could watch the door behind him. He wondered if he should not swing up on Button, now, and ride on out of the Basin.

Nothing that he had heard from Dennis Crow was interesting. He could find no sympathy in his mind for either faction in this war that ripped the Basin in smoky halves. It seemed to have degenerated into a series of battles between hired warriors on both sides. Professional killers of the Wyoming Dees breed, ready to do any brand of murder for ten dollars a day, were killing each other. That was all. No particular principles were involved, on either side. He wondered if riding out of the Basin had been the third thing which Dennis Crow had mentioned as a possibility for a stranger in Taunton.

'Two sides and three things to do,' Dennis Crow had said.

Looking sideways, Drago noticed a battered piano against the end-wall. He stared at it while he had his drink and poured another. But the piano pulled him. He finished a second drink, then carried bottle and glass back with him. He tapped the keys experimentally. The piano was not badly out of tune. When he pulled the ancient stool up, some men turned, where they stood at the bar.

Drago played wholly by ear. A tune once heard he could never forget. It would run in his head as might the image of a man he had known. It was *La Cucuracha*, 'The

Cockroach,' now. He had heard that one in Bellero on the River. He played it with a swing and added frills of his own to the bass. A cowboy up the bar yelled enthusiastically. Drago stared blankly at the ceiling. *Susanna* came to mind.

CHAPTER SIX

'NEVER DREAMT OF GUNPLAY'

For half an hour he played old ballads and cow-camp choruses. Around him the drinkers were packed. Above their yells, at last, he heard the bar-tender's voice:

'Drink up that bottle, feller. *Your* liquor's on the house. All you can tote.'

Drago grinned and swung around on the stool. He accepted the full glass that someone poured for him and turned back.

'Last one,' he told his audience. 'The old *Cowboy's Dream*:

> 'Last night as I lay on the prairie
> And looked up at the stars in the sky,
> I wondered if all us poor cowboys
> Would drift to the sweet bye-and-bye—'

'Where you from?' a cold voice interrupted him.

He ignored the question and continued to play. But the heavy voice rasped in his ear insistently:

'What you doing here?'

'None of your damned business,' Drago answered evenly, without turning.

His right shoulder was caught in a hand that was like a great clamp. It was the most terrible grip that he had ever experienced. It numbed his shoulder; threatened to snap the bones. Left-handed, he reached flashingly for the bottle just beyond him.

'No damn' pianner-pounding dude—'

Drago twisted half-around and stopped that chilly snarl with a smash of the bottle into a square, red face from which two pale eyes glared. The bottle broke upon the man's forehead. The grip on Drago's shoulder slacked. He came swiftly to his feet and, as he stood up, he saw that the faces behind the huge figure that was staggering back were not those of the friendly cowboys he had seen two minutes before. A little clump of hard-eyed men were there, now. They were gaping incredulously at sight of the great hands clawing at whisky-drenched eyes. Then, with an oath, a lithe, black-haired youngster jerked a gun from the waistband of his overalls. He stepped a little forward as he drew the Colt.

Drago flung the jagged remnant of the bottle at this one's face. His hand snapped inside his shirt. As tail to the motion there appeared his cocked .45. He had his eyes steadily upon that dark youngster. There was no use saying 'Hands up!' or trying to dodge the issue. That lean, dark, cowboy's thumb was on the hammer of his Colt. Drago let his own Colt-hammer fall as the muzzle came to cover the other. With the roar of it, the crowd surged back and away, but the dark cowboy, shot through the heart, made one last jerk of the hand before he dropped.

Drago's second shot was directed at a freckled, middle-aged cowboy who had stood at the dark youngster's left. This man dropped a pistol with an agonized oath as the slug tore through his gunarm.

Drago lifted his pistol a little, then:

'Next man reaching for a hogleg is going to get his dose somewhere besides the arm,' he snapped.

They were motionless for an instant, staring at him. Then they began muttering to each other. Drago heard a thumping of footsteps in the alley beyond the door behind him. He stepped over until the piano covered his back from a shot, and waited. His faint smile was deadly, as he stared down the eyes of most of those before him.

'What's—what's the shooting about?' a shaky and querulous voice demanded, well behind him. 'Who's doing that shooting?'

'Who's doing the talking?' Drago countered grimly.

'Berry Nicks, the sheriff!'

'Then come on in and take charge. I don't turn over my gun to anybody but an officer.'

The shrieval footsteps were almost dragging. But he appeared around the end of the piano, a tall, very thin man, with narrow face overshadowed by an enormous hat. His mouth worked very much like a rabbit's and his bulging eyes roved fearfully to right and left. Drago laughed—a harsh, unpleasant sound.

'Two of your would-be hard cases got too free with deadly weapons that they weren't able to handle. One of 'em's dead. The other has a broken elbow. Oh, yes! The would-be hard case who started the trouble, trying to yank me off the piano stool, is still trying to get the whisky out of his eyes. I reckon that's about the story.'

He looked first at the group belonging to the huge, pale-eyed man, then at the other faces in the gaping crowd. The sheriff made a vague noise, clearing his throat.

'You—I—Put that-there gun away. I got to look into this legal, stranger. You—Gi'me that gun!'

Drago shook his head faintly. He rammed the Colt into the waistband of his trousers, instead. The sheriff's watery eyes followed the motion, but he did not see fit to make an issue of the refusal. Instead, he looked at the cowboy who was wrapping a bandanna about his bullet-torn arm.

'He got to shooting at The Breed,' the wounded man snarled. 'Missed Breed and hit me. Breed was watching—wasn't doin' a damn' thing. Me, neither. Never dreamt of gunplay.'

'That's why your gun is now on the floor, I suppose?' Drago inquired blandly. 'It was just loose in the holster and fell out. And the Breed, not *dreaming* of gunplay, fell dead with his gun in his hand. Goodness, gracious, but this is a suspicious country! I suppose if you really *did* expect gunplay, you'd show up with a cannon!'

'He's lying!' the huge man who had snatched at Drago's shoulder snarled, taking a step forward. 'I asked him a question and he slammed some whisky into my face, yanked his hogleg out and started shooting up the whole crowd. I tell you, Berry Nicks, when he downed The Breed, it was plumb murder. Now, git busy.'

'Ah, The Breed, he had his cutter out and coming up at this feller's belly before *he* ever went for a gun,' a scornful, drawling voice announced flatly.

Drago looked flashingly that way. It was a miniature giant—a man no more than five-four, but enormously thick of shoulders and arms. And he wore his hat over one eye and thrust out his square chin in the you-be-damnedest fashion Drago had ever seen.

'I seen it all, Berry! So did Charley here! Hinky Rust is a-dreaming—as per usual. First

58

place, he *couldn't* see nothing. He was too busy a-pawing at them eyes of his'n. Second place, *he* never seen anything straight in his life when he was looking straight at it. This feller done just what anybody'd done. He seen The Breed and Silent Wade with their guns out, so he yanked his and he smoked the two of 'em to the queen's taste!'

Now that the little man had broken the stiff silence, others nodded. Berry Nicks put half-hearted questions. But the balance of the testimony was against Hinky Rust and Silent Wade.

'I reckon I got to let the justice make the inquest and do the deciding,' the sheriff mumbled. 'Don't you move, feller. Judge'll be along soon's I can git him.'

He moved through the crowd toward the swing doors. Drago leaned negligently upon the piano. He was very alert to any move of the Rust-Wade faction. But they merely glared at him sullenly. The little man who had come to his defense, with the shambling and shabby cowboy he called Charley, stood at the other end of the piano. Neither made any move to speak to Drago. He could hear part of their mutterings as they spoke to each other. Charley was talking in a worried tone. The little man shrugged.

'Can't help that, Charley. We got to stick till this is settled. She can wait. She won't like it, but 'twon't hurt her.'

The sheriff came back with a white-haired, thin-faced, distinguished-looking man. As they passed Hinky Rust, the Lazy R owner put out a huge hand and touched the old man on the shoulder. Drago guessed that this was the justice of the peace. He watched narrowly while Rust mumbled in the old man's ear. The old man nodded:

'Why, if that's so, Rust,' he said in clipped, precise English, 'our examination of witnesses will surely discover it.'

He looked at Drago without expression, then down at the sprawling figure of The Breed. Without formality he began his examination of witnesses. Peel was the little giant's name. He gave his testimony with the same belligerent side-glances at Rust and Wade that had marked his first statement. Charley told the same story. Rust and Wade denied The Breed had pulled first. The old justice stared blankly at the wall. He questioned others, then shrugged.

'It is my finding that the deceased, known as The Breed, came to his death at the hands of—what's your name? Hoolihan? Hmm!—at the hands of Hoolihan. The man Hoolihan was acting in the defense of his own life. I'll handle the affair officially tomorrow, Sheriff.'

He stood staring at Drago. Then a corner of his firm mouth twitched upward. His blue eyes narrowed. He turned away without saying anything, and went through the crowd toward the swing doors. Drago looked thoughtfully after him. Then he was jerked back to thought of the present by Hinky Rust's voice.

'You can tally that one on your stick,' he said grimly. 'Yeh, that one! The next one—'

Drago grinned at him and looked for Peel and Charley. But they were gone. He missed Silent Wade, also. He went quietly to the door and looked up and down before stepping out upon the sidewalk. As he stared absently at the front of Dennis Crow's restaurant, he heard from some little distance on his left the flat rap of shots. They were close together, three or four of them. Silence came, to the town outside and to the saloon.

Drago stepped swiftly to the right until his back was against the front wall. Men burst through the swing doors and gaped around. Drago shrugged at their questions. Then Hinky Rust appeared, with three salty-looking cowboys at his heels. He looked suspiciously at Drago, then grunted to his followers. They started down the sidewalk, in the direction from which the sound had come.

But a man was running up the street toward them now. They had taken no more than a half-dozen steps when Drago heard the unmistakable voice of Peel, the little giant. He was talking in a gasping snarl. Drago caught two words—'Charley' and 'killed.'

There was a swift flurry of bodies. Then Peel flung himself at Rust's men. The tight mass

61

reeled back across the saloon porch toward Drago. He had one glimpse of Peel swinging furiously, then a swirl of figures blotted out the shorter man. He came in sight again. He was grinning now as he drove blows with piston-like speed. From a cut over one eye, blood was coming down his face. His hat was gone, and his stiff tow hair was all but standing on end. This business of fighting four men, all outweighing him, seemed to rouse in him a sort of good-humored fury.

He knocked down one of the cowboys with a short punch to the belly. But Hinky Rust was towering over him, both long, thick arms out to close upon the stocky figure. Then Drago went into it with a rush. He smashed a man on the neck under the ear and that man fell against Rust. Peel was grappling, now, with the remaining cowboy. They staggered back and forth across the planks of the saloon porch.

Drago left the planks to swing a looping right up to Rust's chin. The big Lazy R man staggered with the impact, then roared like a mad bull. But Drago, both feet solidly set again, smashed four unguarded-against punches to the belly. He sent Rust staggering backward to bring up against the saloon wall. He saw the huge hand come up to waist level. He crossed the space between them like a racing snake and his own Colt was out. He snapped the long-barreled pistol upward and back—then forward. Rust fell sideways with the crack of it across his temple. Drago reholstered it quickly and turned with back to the wall.

Peel had thrown his man and banged his head against the planks until the fellow lay still. He was getting up now. He looked at Drago and shook his head as if to clear it.

'Feller,' he said. 'Feller, you certainly do pay off your debts mighty prompt! I liked your style when I seen you first. But I'm free to say I like her plumb up and down and from the back, now!'

Sheriff Nicks appeared in the saloon's doorway. He looked highly uncomfortable. When he faced Drago, he did not lower his watery eyes to meet Drago's level stare.

'What's the row about?' he mumbled. 'I swear, it seems like there ain't no such thing as quiet around this damn' town or county no more! What's the idee of you cracking Rust over the head with a gun, huh? I tell you, feller, coming into town and starting—'

'I happened to see it,' a calm, very precise voice interrupted him.

The gray-haired justice moved through the thickening group of men who filtered out of saloon and store doors.

'Peel was being swamped by Rust and these others. This man—ah—Hoolihan, apparently moved by gratitude for Peel's straightforward and valuable testimony at my inquiry, joined the battle. He had rushed Rust to the wall and

63

was easily licking him. Rust pulled at his pistol, and instead of shooting him, Hoolihan merely knocked him senseless. If you're minded to make arrests, Sheriff, arrest everyone concerned for disturbing the peace and I'll be pleased to have a hearing immediately. But arrest *everyone*!'

'Hell! If I was to start arresting these damn' cowboys ever' time they started fighting, jail'd be full all the time.'

Berry Nicks nodded violently, but Drago saw how his bulbous and watery eyes shuttled down to Rust, who was just now moving arms and legs in returning consciousness. It was very plain that Taunton's sheriff had no intention whatever of arresting the huge owner of the Lazy R.

Drago looked at Peel and lifted his dark brows. They moved off together. Peel fell into a sullen quiet as they walked down the plank sidewalk past the Longhorn. Drago dropped into step beside him and said nothing. Mechanically, Peel stepped into the street. As he angled across it, Drago went with him toward a two-story house that had a 'hotel' sign across its porch.

'Downed Charley,' Peel muttered. 'Silent Wade and two of his killing cowboys. Poor old Charley, he was no fighter. He packed a gun, but against competition like that he was the li'l' woolly lamb in a big wolf country. But he *was* a good feller. He worked for us a long time. Ever'

64

way but fighting, he was a Hand. We was all right till this damn' war between the LL and Walking M, and the Lazy R and Half Circle W, bust out.'

'What outfit do you represent?' Drago asked curiously. 'I thought those four were all that amounted to anything in Taunton Basin. Thought a stranger had to fall in line with one side or the other—or do the third thing: Ride away like hell!'

'You would, judging from the racket,' the squat man said gloomily. 'And it ain't Tonto Peel'd say you was more'n a mile off the track, either. That's kind of funny, too. For the 56 is the oldest outfit in the whole Basin. Old Man Theo Littell, he come to Texas in '56 from Tennessee. He wound up here in the Basin when there wasn't no roads but Injun pony tracks. Young Theo, his son, he carried on the 56 outfit; built her up and made the iron mean a lot. Then—'

He shrugged his big shoulders:

'Then he died and left two kids, Marjorie Littell and her useless, harum-scarum kid brother, Clint. And things are plenty different on the 56, these days. Yeh! Different and— heaps skimpier!'

He seemed disinclined to go further into the tale of 56 troubles. When he looked ahead at the hotel, he was sulky of expression. But Drago found it, somehow, interesting.

'What kind of fight was it, when Wade and

65

his bar-room gladiators smoked up Charley? Anything in the business you can take hold of?'

'Ha! With that damn' jellyfish, Berry Nicks, holding the sheriff's star down?' Tonto Peel snarled furiously. 'Hell, no! They downed Charley, then they rode out of town. So far's the law's concerned, that's that. Nobody seen it but a Mex' kid. And if he was to git up and tell it in court, any way but in favor of that gang, he'd git his throat cut. And he damn' well knows it, too. He won't talk about it. But I'll settle Silent Wade for that murder, if it's the last thing I ever do!'

He jerked a thumb toward the hotel—as if indicating something to explain his feeling. Drago looked that way, but saw nothing to make Tonto Peel's disgust any clearer to him.

'You do seem to have a pretty mixed-up state of affairs here in the Basin,' he said thoughtfully. 'I've heard a little about it, here and there. But this is the first I've heard about a third faction in the war.'

'We're it,' Tonto assured him sourly. 'All of it. Well, come on around. I have got some talking to do that I wish somebody else could do for me...'

CHAPTER SEVEN

'ANOTHER KILLER'

Drago hesitated on the step of the wide veranda that half-enclosed the hotel. Then he shrugged faintly, and followed the stocky puncher up. They went around to the side and, with sight of the slim figure seated in a great rawhide-bottomed chair, he stopped short frowningly.

He had not expected to meet a girl here, even after Tonto Peel's remark about 'Young Theo' Littell's daughter.

Tonto went straight up to the chair and, in the rapid patter of a schoolboy reciting something memorized, he said:

'Miss Marjorie, I got bad news and nothing but bad news. Poor old Charley got killed awhile ago by Silent Wade and some of them Half Circle scoun'els of his. Charley left me to go buy some things at the store. I heard the shooting and I kind of had a notion it was Charley in trouble. But it was all over before I got there. It was a put-up job! That gang was sore at Charley and me because we give evidence in favor of this feller, Hoolihan. So they ganged up on Charley.'

The girl came to her feet, with slender, lightly tanned hands clenching and unclenching at her

67

sides. She was somewhat older than Drago had first thought her, he observed when she stared at Tonto Peel. Her gray eyes were widened; her red mouth was slightly open; and the blue linen dress rose and fell quickly with her breathing.

'Charley!' she whispered. 'Ah, no! Not Charley! Why—Why, he never quarreled; never had trouble, a fight, with anyone! You don't mean that, Tonto!'

'What difference does it make what kind of feller he was?' Tonto snarled. 'Of course he never hunted trouble. But you don't reckon them two bunches of sidewinders have got to buy a excuse before they down somebody? We told the truth about the way Hinky Rust aimed to drill this feller, Hoolihan, and—'

Drago was leaning against a post of the veranda, staring down at the cigarette between his fingers. From somewhere down the street, toward the Cattlemen's Bar, there sounded a rifle shot. He took two long steps forward, toward the girl and Tonto Peel, as a slug tore through the square box of the post and ruffled his back-hair. He looked sidelong to see that the adjoining building shielded him from that marksman, then shook his head slightly.

'I wonder—that is I just *barely* wonder—if that fellow mistook me for someone else. But that's all I can do, stretching the point as far as may be: I can just *barely* wonder if that shot was meant for someone else.'

'What'd the LL and Walking M want your

scalp for?' Tonto grunted. 'You never—Say! You never fell out with *that* bunch, too?'

'I'm afraid so,' Drago nodded. His tone was very sad, but his small, satanic grin lightened it—and somehow gave to it a sinister, a threatening, note. 'I'll have to do something about it.'

Marjorie Littell stared fixedly at him. There was no friendliness in her face. She put up a hand to brush a lock of hair back—hair as yellow as corn-silk. Tonto Peel, looking from Drago to her, seemed suddenly to become conscious of an omission. He indicated Drago with a jerk of the head.

'Miss Marjorie, this is Mr Hoolihan. That's all I know about him—except he's a fighting man! He killed that killer they called The Breed—you know, the one that was s'posed to have murdered the two fellers he was bringing into town for Berry Nicks. Killed him slicker'n a whistle, then shot Silent Wade in the arm. That was where me and Charley come in. They was trying to make it out murder, you see, and me and Charley told what we seen. So Judge Bell called it self-defense and—'

'Another killer,' the girl nodded. Her voice was flat, tired. But her mouth tightened contemptuously as she met Drago's dark stare. 'We don't seem to see any other sort of man nowadays. But, Mr Hoolihan, if you came—as you must have come—to bring your guns to the best market, you have rather killed your

69

chances, haven't you? By falling out with both factions, I mean?'

'Looky here!' Tonto Peel broke in angrily. '*We* have been between a brick and a hard place, Miss Marjorie, ever since this trouble started. You know that. It's been nothing but a excuse for both sides to hammer the 56, and the Double Slash, and the Circle Bar, and ever' nester in the country. There's been just me and Charley and Clint—and Clint ain't been doing much. Now—'

He looked sidelong at Drago. His glance was pleading.

He turned back almost desperately to the girl.

'Now, they got Charley. That leaves me. But if Hoolihan *would* ride for the 56—if he would, there'd be *two* fighting men on the spread. Killer, you call him? All right! Maybeso. But let me tell you this before you say it again: he's ex-act-ly the same kind of killer Tonto Peel is! *Por dios!* If you think Charley's chalkmark's going to be rubbed out, without me doing something about it—'

She began shaking her yellow head. The clear, grave face was set in stubborn lines. Tonto's hand came up to his battered hat. He yanked the brim down over one belligerent eye. He thrust out his chin at her.

'All right, then,' he said grimly. 'You can run the 56 without me! I been ten years on it, and I hate to leave. But I ain't going to work for a

70

outfit that won't hit back when it's hit. If you won't see daylight, then I'm not going to git myself killed off when it won't git me nor nobody else a thing!'

'Oh, hire him, then,' she said wearily. 'Hire him by all means. But'—she looked at Drago—'*we* don't pay the wages that the others are paying. Forty a month is the scale on the 56. The others go up to ten a day—and cartridges!'

'Since you insist on my riding for you, I'll buy my own ammunition,' Drago said gravely. 'Out of the forty a month.'

Tonto Peel grinned at him and indicated with a head-jerk that they would go. At the corner of the veranda, Drago heard a rap of heels on the floor. Mechanically, he looked back. Out of a window behind Marjorie Littell's chair had come, with a graceful, panther-like slide and jump, a girl in wide white Stetson, crimson shirt, fawn-colored pants, and half-boots of fancy inlay.

He had one glimpse of her olive-hued face and wide, dark eyes and vivid mouth. He heard Marjorie call her Nita. Then he was around the corner, trailing Tonto Peel. 'Who was the girl in the cow-chasing outfit?' he asked Tonto. 'Nita, Miss Littell called her.'

'Where? Come through the window? Oh, that's Nita Fourponies. Half-Cherokee. Looker, ain't she? Every man in this country has tried to put a loop over her, one time or other. All but me, that is. They all figure because Nita's a breed, she ought to be fair game. *Then* they wake up! Nita's warm people! Her and Clint—Marjorie's kid brother—they're apt to git hitched some time. Nita lives over on the Perdida. Got a li'l' hawse-ranch over there. Couple of Injun young'n's ride for her. She's been to college. Yeh! Warm people. Marjorie likes her fine.'

He led the way into the hotel through the front door, then down a long hallway that had a stair to the second floor on one side of it. He was heading for the stair when Drago stopped him with a short, hissing sound, and went noiselessly past the stair, along the worn strip of hall-carpet, to stand before a door ten feet away.

While Tonto stood at the stair-foot, scowling uncertainly, Drago pressed his ear lightly against the panel of the door. He had heard one word to stop him.

'Wyoming' was that word.

It had sounded as if applied to someone in that room. To Wyoming Dees? He wondered. So he strained to hear now, and the words came clearer.

'That's where they was heading for, anyhow. For Spoon's store. Likely, Silent wanted Alonzo to fix up that hole in his arm that he got from the Hoolihan fella. The other three would stick to guard him. It's the best chance we're likely to git, at Silent Wade. If we take out eight

72

or nine to their four—good-night, Silent! We can sneak up on the store, Wyoming—'

'Yeh. It sounds all right,' Wyoming Dees's rasping voice answered. 'Rust and Wade have been mighty shy of separating here lately. But I wish we could have got ahead of 'em ... That's a neat arroyo that the trail crosses, just before you come to the store. Put a half-dozen men behind the rocks in it, and you couldn't help but git that bunch. Silent and them three he's got with him, they're the saltiest part of the whole double-outfit. Well, we'll slide up careful. You better git together five-six of the boys, Dumpty. Me and Olin Oge and you-all, we'll be plenty. I reckon Olin wouldn't stand for Silent Wade being rubbed out unless *he* was around. We'll slide out, come dark.'

'They'll likely set up half the night playing poker,' Dumpty contributed. He laughed. 'Don't you *hope* they do! They'll show up right plain in the light. We can see 'em from the winders.'

'Rather git 'em coming through that arroyo. Safer,' Wyoming grumbled. 'But we never knowed in time for that. Drag it!'

As noiselessly as he had approached it, Drago ran away from the door. He waved at Tonto, to send him softly on upstairs. They were on the next floor before the door of that room opened and a *clink-clump* of spurred and booted feet sounded on the hall-runner. One man ... So Wyoming Dees was still in the

73

room...

'What was it?' Tonto whispered, leaning curiously to Drago. Briefly, Drago told him what he had heard. Tonto shook his head and shrugged. He opened a door and stepped into a room.

'Well, it ain't a damn' thing to worry about. They'll wipe out Silent Wade and some of them loose-holstered killers of his, and maybe Silent's crowd can rub out some of the LL and Walking M dry-gulchers while they're gitting wiped out. So there you are!'

Drago moved over to the window and stared blindly out. Tonto was fishing under the bed. He brought out a bundle and laid it upon the bed. Drago continued to stare—and to think.

'Poor old Charley,' Tonto grunted. 'He bought him four new shirts and a pair of breeches. Aimed to wear 'em to a dance next month. And now—I reckon I'll take 'em over to the undertaker. They'll bury him in 'em. Damn them slinking killers!'

'Yeh!' Drago drawled, turning now. Tonto stared blankly at him. 'Feel that way? All right. Suppose—just suppose that a couple of ferocious hairpins like—why, you and me!— happened to land at this store of Spoon's? *Before* Wyoming Dees and his killers arrived for their little party, I mean! What would happen?'

'I can answer *that* one without looking at no cards. Them two hairpins'd be shot into

74

dollrags—red dollrags—before a man could begin to get out a lot shorter name than *Jack Robinson!*'

'Yeh?' Drago drawled again. 'You really think so?'

Tonto Peel stared hard at him.

'But suppose these two hairpins—of whom I speak with so much loving admiration,' Drago went on—'suppose that they came to do Silent Wade a good turn: came to warn him and his bunch that Wyoming Dees and a prize assortment of killers were on the way to lay 'em out?'

'Who? Me? Warn that slinking murderer?' Tonto yelled. 'Me? That aims to go down him one-two-three the minute I git a chance? Say—'

Then he checked himself, to scowl at Drago.

'Let go your wolf, feller,' he grunted, in more moderate tone. 'You're hugging something down close to your vest. I'm beginning to listen more careful to what you say. What's it?'

'There wouldn't be much of a fight if Wyoming's bunch could bushwhack Silent Wade's. Of course, you and I, *we* don't give a tinker's dam how many of either side get killed. But if we can stage-manage it for our own base ends, to arrange for a good battle that will account for more on each side—Well! That arroyo Wyoming seemed to be so fond of ... Wouldn't that be fine cover for Silent's bunch? They could hide out and wait for Wyoming...'

'Oh!' Tonto Peel said. Still he stared at

75

Drago. 'Oh, yeh ... There being eight-nine of Wyoming's bunch, they'll likely drop off and get into the fight, instead of running like a littler bunch'd do, when the lead begins to sing out of them rocks.'

'Right-*ho!*' Drago grinned. 'That should account for some empty saddles, and a few stirrups turned hindside-to, on both sides.'

'But why two of us? Just to take word to Silent? Why either one of us! Why not send that Mex' kid that seen Vinson Kymes and Silent Wade murder Charley?'

'I thought we'd send him, or somebody like him,' Drago nodded. His mirthless smile deepened. 'But we'll be around the neighborhood, too, Tonto. It'll save a long ride, later on. You see, after the smoke blows away, and if and when Silent's salty bunch drives off Wyoming Dees's remnants, they'll go back to the Spoon store, to lick their wounds and talk it over. About then, you and I will walk in on 'em. We'll want to ask about Charley's murder, you see ...'

'*Amor de dios!*' Tonto breathed, shaking his head. 'If *you* ain't a hard case and a schemer! I have killed a man or two—or dreamt I done it—but I'm one of them hairpins that gits pushed into a row and goes for it hellbent. I—Well! We'll do it! I'll take Charley's things over to the undertaker, then I'll hunt me that Mex' kid and send him to carry word to Silent Wade. Then—Well, I reckon Marjorie'll have to drive the buckboard out herself.'

He picked up the bundle and they opened the door cautiously. They went, with some effort at quiet, downstairs. Drago heard a low babbling of voices. He craned his neck to look through the open door of the dining-room and, so, through the window out of which Nita Fourponies had come so swiftly and gracefully to the veranda. He could hear her voice now. At least, it was not Marjorie's. There was a throaty laugh running through the breed girl's tone. Marjorie answered with gravity.

Then Nita said:

'Well, I saw him on the street. I tell you, Marjorie, it was foolish to hire him. Damn' if it wasn't!'

'I had to. Tonto insisted and, after all, we had to have someone. You know very well, Nita, that the ordinary cowboy will not take a job on a Taunton Basin outfit nowadays.'

'You have got me wrong, Marje,' Nita protested—and laughed. 'What I intended to convey, darling, is that he's too handsome! You'll be falling in love with him. Then there'll be merry Hades to pay. You take that from Nita.'

'I imagine! I can picture myself falling in love with a killer of that stripe,' Marjorie said bitingly, while Drago, motionless, grinned without humor. 'What do you think I am, anyway, Nita? Some cheap dance-hall girl? Some gaping nester's daughter, to be twisted around the finger of the first ne'er-do-well who swaggers up and around me without splitting an infinitive?'

'No, Marje. No, I don't think you're either one. Neither do I think you're a lovely snow image who can't see—and appreciate—the old *come-hither* in a good-looking man's eyes. We don't need to argue about it, hon'. We can wait and see. But you keep him off my range! I'm not going to have my peace of mind threatened. And *that* reminds me—where has Clint taken himself to? I haven't seen that young hellion for a week!'

'He's probably off gambling somewhere, I suppose,' Marjorie said wearily. 'He doesn't honor me with his confidence, you know. He came in on Thursday—a week ago today. He saddled that black Double-Slash outlaw and rode off. Oh, yes! He *did* wave to me as he went.'

'I'll give him down-the-river when I next see him,' Nita promised grimly. 'If he hasn't got sense enough to appreciate the kind of sister he has, I'll supply the appreciation. I—'

Drago grinned and went on after Tonto Peel. But when he reached the veranda, Tonto was crossing the street. And Nita Fourponies came around the corner slapping quirt against bootleg.

'Hello, you!' she said calmly. 'So you're the new 56 hand. Well—'

'Reckon,' Drago nodded. He looked her up

and down. She *was* a looker! And the man-style outfit, the vivid colors she chose for shirt and neckerchief, were calculated to bring out the blue-black of her hair, the cameo-clearness of her olive face, the depth of dark eyes. 'Yeh, Hoolihan. That's me.'

'Yeh?' she drawled, and put her hand over her mouth. Her eyes shone. 'Consider me holding back a smile of amusement. That's two smiles of that famous order in Taunton, in this one day! You see, Mr Hoolihan, I happened to be standing by Judge Bell—Monroe Bell, who presided at the inquest when you'd finished with that lousy bushwhacker, The Breed—when you passed awhile ago. Says the Judge to me, says he:

'"Hoolihan ... Hoolihan," says he. "Funny how men forget things. For instance—family resemblances. Now," he says, "I have known what you might term a whole passel of *Drago* men in my day and, Nita," says he, "never a one but *looked* like a Drago. Hoolihan!" he says; "trying to hoolihan me!"'

'He's getting sort of old,' Drago said carefully. 'Eyes are going back on him, maybe? But, you don't have to talk about it, now, do you?'

'I? *Have to?* Say, brother! When you know this country better, and know Nita Fourponies better, you'll damn' well know that I don't *have* to do anything! I suppose there's maybe a big cloud of dust rising on your back-trail somewhere? Oh, well, I'm just a pore breed gal. What's white folks's troubles to me?'

'Thanks,' he said, with quick gravity. 'I'd rather have your word than—the bond of most. And—I hope I come to know you better.'

'Don't strain yourself!' she snapped at him—then smiled.

'Oh, it wouldn't be any strain at all,' he assured her. 'I can even think of some occasions when it would be a pleasure. If you don't mind...'

'We won't go into so much detail, right now. It might get us tangled up, you know. *Adiós!*'

'Now, just what,' Drago asked himself as he turned away, 'does she find so all-fired amusing about—everything?'

But to that question—like others occurring to him here in Taunton Basin—he found no answer.

CHAPTER EIGHT

'I WAS INTENDED TO BE A PREACHER—'

He went mechanically back to Dennis Crow's restaurant. At the door he stopped to look in and, finding nobody there but a couple of punchers who seemed intent upon their eating,

80

he loafed inside and sat down at the counter.

Dennis Crow turned at the range. After a quick stare, he came clumping up to Drago. His belligerent face was softer now than Drago had ever seen it. He seemed actually pleased with the world.

Drago grinned at him.

'I have got it figured out that you're wrong about the Basin,' he said. 'There are four things, not three, that a man can do: He can join one side or the other. He can hightail it clean away. Or—he can ride for the 56. Forty a month and buy your own shells.'

'The hell you say, now! I stick to what I told you: Only three things a man can do in Taunton Basin nowadays. If that man's the like of you. And really only one thing if he is exactly like you. I'm mightily pleased you seen it like that. It's high time the old 56 was taking openers in this game that's been stripping it. I reckon it will, now!'

'Can happen! Now, do you reckon you could furnish me with a sheet of paper and two envelopes and a stamp? I'm about to turn educated and do some writing.'

'I can that! And I can see that the letter's mailed so's nobody has a notion who wrote it! Wait a minute...'

He disappeared into his living quarters and came back with a tablet and pencil, envelopes and a book of stamps. Drago wrote briefly to old Keats Tucker, to tell of Saul Black's death and his ride north.

'You can get me by addressing Henry Hoolihan, care of Dennis Crow's Café at Taunton. I appreciate the way you and Attley are working in my behalf, even if I can't expect you to find the man who stole Nevil Jacklin's gun and make him admit it.'

He did not sign the letter, but folded it and sealed it into an envelope. He addressed a second envelope to David Crockett Tucker at Fort Worth, stamped both covers and handed the envelope to Dennis Crow.

'Now, if you'll hold anything that comes for me,' he said, 'I'll very much appreciate it. I am going out to the 56 with Tonto Peel, pretty soon. Maybe, with two of us on the spread, the outfit can make a stab at holding its own.'

'With two like you and that salty little rooster, it ought to do more'n just hold its own!' Dennis Crow nodded. 'Yonder's Tonto, now, across the street. Reckon he's looking for you.'

Drago nodded and got up. He found the short foreman in a store veranda opposite the eating-house and lounged across, thumbs hooked mechanically in the belt of his leggings, keeping watch to right and left and straight ahead.

Tonto grinned and leaned to mutter in his ear:

'That Mex' kid is a-riding for Spoon's store now. And his kid brother is bringing that hawse of yours down to the livery-corral at the far end of Court Street. Mine's already there, along of the buckboard that I'm s'posed to drive Marjorie out in tonight—and won't. But Nita's place is beyond us. She and Marjorie can ride out together. We better slide, huh?'

Drago nodded. They went together to the livery-barn. A negro hostler was rubbing down Button, crooning to the tall chestnut lovingly. Drago flipped him a dollar and resaddled. He got a bag of grain and rammed it into his slicker behind the cantle.

'We're going out to the ranch now, Tup,' Tonto told the negro. 'When Miss Marjorie comes, you tell her I had important business. Her and Miss Nita better make it a team.'

They rode until the county seat dropped over a long rise behind them, keeping to the side of the dusty road. Finally, Tonto turned off to the west, heading for a jagged range of hills. They put the horses to a hard trot and for a couple of miles rode with chins on shoulders. But there was no sign of pursuit; none of anyone interested in their going.

Drago pulled in. Out of the saddle pocket he got his belt and holster, and buckled them on. Tonto watched silently while the buckskin toe-thong was tied about Drago's thigh above the knee; watched while Drago lifted hand to shoulder level, held it so for a split second, then let it drop flashingly to the white Colt-butt. He grunted when the long-barreled .45 snapped out, and he spoke in a meditative tone:

'Used to be a lightning gunfighter over at Carlos. He was acting deputy for Berry Nicks. He was the slickest proposition with the hoglegs ever I seen. I'm certainly sorry he's dead. I would have liked to send your li'l' boy over to Carlos, to show him what a real quick-draw looked like...'

They were jogging on when darkness came. The moon appeared in the black sky above the hill-crests. Tonto led the way with the sureness of a man who knows every inch of his ground. He brought them topping out of a deep arroyo and up a hill until, from its top, they saw a short line of yellow pin-points down-slope.

'That's Alonzo Spoon's,' he grunted. 'I reckon you've seen plenty tough places, feller. But my notion is, you've maybe seen bigger ones, but you never seen a tougher one, than that. It was always tough. Even before this war fetched in all the hard cases for five hundred mile around. But now, with the gang that hangs out around there, it's plenty tough!'

'I take it that we can hear shooting from here?' Drago asked. 'Then we'll stick here and listen for it.'

He fed Button and Tonto's sorrel. They sprawled comfortably, Drago and Tonto, on the close-cropped grass of the hilltop. They smoked and watched the pin-points of light at the store.

It seemed hours later that they heard the

shots. First a faint rattling volley. Then another. After that, for a long time there was intermittent firing—single shots or, at most, two or three close together. Presently that died away.

Drago got up.

'Our cue to ramble down and see what pieces are left,' he grunted. 'It's just possible that Wyoming Dees's bunch wiped out Silent Wade's, in spite of the warning we sent 'em. Well...'

They saddled and went down the slope. The pin-points of light became squares; became windows. The windows were blotted now and again, as by bodies passing them. They pulled in and dismounted. They were fifty yards from the store. They let the split-reins drop and the horses stood motionless with sagging heads, hidden from view of any curious man in the store by a juniper clump.

'Moonlight must have helped Silent Wade's shooters,' Drago meditated aloud. 'It won't be so good for us, in case they're keeping a lookout. Well, it's my own fault. I was intended to be a preacher and I fell by the wayside. I—What's wrong, now?'

'I—I—you oughtn't to have said that!' Tonto gasped. 'I bet it was your ma done that intending. And I bet you she never knowed you any too well! We can make it to that big rock yonder, then to that clump of bushes...'

They went crouching from cover to cover.

85

They made the last dozen yards in a soundless rush that left them flat against the plank wall of the store almost under a window. They waited, one watching to the left, the other to the right. From within they caught the murmur of voices.

'Now, who's next?' a voice was asking. 'Damn, but you did git shot up, fellow! They done everything but kill you. I ain't guaranteeing a thing. But I'll patch you some.'

Drago took off his hat and leaned sideways until with one eye he could see inside the store. A lank, black-clad man stood at the counter with a tin basin, into which he dipped a bloody rag. A man was lying down on the counter. The freckled face of Silent Wade—fiercely triumphant, now—was in range from the window. Somebody else was there, for Drago heard a voice belonging to none of these he could see.

'If Hinky had brought out some of the others, instead of just sending word,' this voice snarled, 'we could've laid out the whole lot of 'em. You know damn' well, Silent, that Wyoming Dees and Olin Oge was leading them fellers. If we could've got them two—'

His voice faded away.

'I wish he'd come out,' Silent Wade nodded. 'I reckon he must've had some reason. Hinky wouldn't pass up a chance at Wyoming—or Oge, neither. Well, couldn't have been more'n nine in the bunch and we fixed five that we know about. Maybe we stitched buttonholes on some that rode back, too. Not bad!'

'I'm going in the front door, like an innocent pilgrim attracted by the light,' Drago whispered to Tonto. 'You stand at the back door and be ready to come in when it sounds right.'

'Hell with you!' Tonto whispered fiercely. 'This shindig is my affair and I don't aim to have you crowding in to buck Silent Wade ahead of me! I'll go in the front myself and ask that lousy bushwhacker if he thought he could git away with murdering Charley—'

'That's no good. Somebody might get hurt,' Drago told the angry cowpuncher in gentle voice. 'Somebody important, I mean—one of us. Let me do this, Tonto. I've been nursing a small idea.'

He went toward the front door of the store without waiting for reply. He looked back, at the corner. Tonto was going toward the back, dissatisfaction plain in the slouch of his walk. Drago stepped up on the end of the veranda that ran across the store's front. He went, with care against squeaking planks, toward the door. He looked inside. Nobody was facing that way. Silent Wade and a cowboy stood watching the storekeeper dress the wounded man. Drago stepped inside and, at the rap of his boots on the floor, Wade and the cowboy whirled, while the lank Spoon looked up from his work.

'What's the matter?' Drago inquired cheerfully. 'Been shooting at somebody? I could hear some shots as I rode out. But, my stars, do they do all that powder-burning in the Basin for just one man—and without killing him?'

Silent Wade's eyes roved to the thumb-hooked hand over the white Colt-butt. So did the eyes of the man beside him. Then they lifted—to study the doorway behind him.

'Who's with you?' Wade snapped metallically.

'Huh?' Drago grunted, half-turning to stare blankly at the door. 'Say, from what I've seen of the kind that runs in Taunton Basin, I don't need, nor do I want, any of the LL, or Walking M, or Lazy R, or Half Circle W, bar-room gladiators with me. I saw the light and headed up. I knew you were ahead of me. So I came in.'

'Yeh?' Wade drawled viciously. 'And what do you want of me? You talk right loud, Hoolihan, but—'

'I wanted to ask you about that cowboy your bunch shot down just before you left town. I didn't know Charley, except from his testimony in the Longhorn when the rest of you were lying to beat four of a kind. But he did me a favor, then. So I thought I'd inquire about what kind of a deal you gave him. It's your talk!'

'Then you're dealing with me,' the cowboy at Wade's elbow grunted. He leaned against the counter, his hands, like Drago's, hooked by the thumbs in crossed shell-belts. 'You're a stranger in the Basin. There's heaps of politics that you don't know about. So I'll tell you. And you better listen close.'

He grinned at Drago.

'Charley had a full-sized killing coming to him for a long time. He knowed, so he walked damn' careful! It was a li'l' business of Who-Owned-the-Calf! He talked some, too—kind of loud—about what he aimed to do to me. Well, I met him as we was coming out of Taunton. He went for his gun and I went for mine. I beat him to it and I plugged him, and—that's about that! Now, if I ain't made everything plain—'

'Sounds clear enough,' Drago nodded, blank of face.

He came over to the counter, letting his hand drop away from his pistol. He looked curiously—or seemed to look—at the man on the counter. Alonzo Spoon was tearing bandages. Out of the corner of his eye Drago saw how Wade and Vinson Kymes looked furtively at each other. Then Kymes half-turned away, so that his right side was invisible to Drago.

'You come out from town, huh?' Wade said slowly. 'You—pass anybody heading toward town?'

'I wouldn't say I passed them. When an innocent stranger in the Basin hears men coming hellbent his way, he's liable to slide off the road and squat behind some cover and let 'em go by. That is, if he's not too innocent a pilgrim! Who was it? The fellows who smoked that boy up?'

Then it happened. Kymes whirled back, his pistol out. Silent Wade's left hand snapped inside his shirt. There was a bulge at the waistband which Drago had not failed to notice. But before the hand could reappear, Drago had taken the short step necessary to reach Wade. He spun him about and sent him reeling at Vinson Kymes. His own belt-gun was drawn with the free hand at the same time.

And with a rush of feet, the back door was thrown open. Tonto Peel sprang through it and fired at the two men before Drago could lift his .45. There was the rattle of return shots. Something seemed to breathe on Drago's cheek and he heard a grunt from Alonzo Spoon. Then he was firing at the two as fast as he could thumb the hammer. So was Tonto Peel.

Almost on top of Vinson Kymes, Silent Wade went crashing down. A hand clawed at Drago's sleeve and he jerked away with an oath. Tonto Peel looked at the two on the floor, then sideways at Alonzo Spoon, who was slipping down the counterfront.

'Looks like a wipe-out,' he observed grimly. 'I do'no' which of us got which of them, feller, but I do'no's I give a whoop either. They're gone and it's a damn' good riddance!'

Drago moved to bend over Kymes and Wade. They were stone-dead. So was Spoon, as Tonto Peel informed him. There remained only the cowboy on the counter. Drago moved back, curious to know why this man had not moved. He stared hard at him, stooped a little and put hand to the cowboy's heart. Then he shrugged.

'Let's be moving,' he said. 'There's not a thing to hook this to us. I'll bet anything you want to suggest that Wyoming Dees and his crowd get all the credit for it. And if it fails to bring a smack from Hinky Rust and the rest of that crowd, you can put me down for a Chinaman. And the Dragos—I mean the Hoolihans—don't run to laundry tickets.'

They ran out to the horses and swung up. For a long while Tonto led the way across the hills. But after an hour of fast going they came to the flats once more. Tonto suddenly bent over his saddle horn and laughed hysterically.

'I—I—was jist thinking,' he gasped, 'about what a great preacher—you'd have made—if you'd listened to your ma!'

Drago stared ahead without expression. Then he lifted a shoulder in a small, grim gesture.

'You think a man picks his own trail every time? Don't let anybody tell you that! I admit that I never had any hankering after a preacher's job. But I did want to do—well, some of the things luck, or life, hasn't let me do. I haven't got to live the kind of life I wanted to live. So, now, I'm just a rattling hard case that's twin brother to the *lobo* wolf. And—How far now?'

'We'll be in around midnight. So I'd better be figuring up a good lie to tell Marjorie. She'll be hotter'n the old kitchen stove because I sneaked out and left her to ride by herself.'

They went on quietly through the yellow moonlight. Tonto seemed to have forgotten about Wade and Kymes. He turned furtively in the saddle time and again, to look at the tall, lean figure beside him. Drago was silent. He wondered if it were wise, to be halted here in Taunton Basin where so many hard cases from all over Texas, Arizona, New Mexico, would naturally congregate.

'So many know me from the days of Rangering,' he told himself. 'Somebody's bound to wander in; to take one look at me and say: "I remember him!" Still, and yet, it did seem to sort of slide up and sit down on my lap, this joining the 56 spread. I did owe Tonto and Charley something. So—'

He shrugged off the doubts, and Tonto, catching the little gesture, said inquiringly:

'*Trabajo?* Trouble?'

'Not a bit!' Drago assured him in a hearty voice. 'I was thinking about something and—Wouldn't you like to be in town when Wyoming's gang reports, licking their sores?

92

There's a science to this business of fighting ...
Never do any of it you can get somebody else to
do for you! Now, tonight, we followed that
rule—and see how happy we are!'

Tonto grunted amusedly at the thought.
They rode on and at midnight came up to a
log-and-stone house with, behind it, a second
house, long and low. A lantern burned in a
stable.

'Marjorie must be home,' Tonto grunted.
'She—Oh...'

CHAPTER NINE

'I'VE WARNED YOU BEFORE'

He spurred into a trot and Drago sent Button
after him. They came up to the stable, pulled
the horses in, and swung to the ground. Drago
looked around. Then the murmur of voices
inside drew his stare that way. Tonto seemed to
stiffen.

A man was speaking in there. Marjorie
answered. Then Nita Fourponies spoke. Tonto
swore viciously under his breath and went with
shoulders pushed forward, long arms
swinging, into the stable. Drago wondered if it
concerned him. But he followed to the door
and looked in.

A man as big and dark as Drago himself, but

blue-eyed, was just leading the team away from the buckboard. He turned with the heavy rap of Tonto's heels behind him. It seemed to Drago that a sort of tightening came over his smooth, handsome face. But if it were tension, he hid it instantly and smiled at the 56 foreman.

'Hi, Tonto. Looks like I'm doing your work for you all the time. Marjorie says you run out on her in town. Left her to get home best way she could—'

'That's her business!' Tonto said between his teeth. He seemed to have trouble with his speech. 'That's 56 business, McGinsey. So it's no business of yours and—'

'Tonto!' Marjorie Littell called sharply, quickly, from where she stood beside the buckboard.

Nita caught her arm. She said something that sounded like:

'Let Tonto alone! He's doing fine!'

But Marjorie ignored the advice. Tonto was standing, very much like an infuriated bantam rooster, with both of his big fists doubled into thick knots, and glaring furiously up at the grinning McGinsey. He did not turn his head when his employer reached his side and caught his sleeve. Marjorie Littell had moved quickly—rather as if, Drago thought, she feared more than angry words, here in the 56 stable. Tonto pulled impatiently at her imperative hand.

'Tonto! Tonto, I'm not going to have this.

94

You let Lige McGinsey alone! This is silly, this way of yours. Lige was very kindly unharnessing the team for me. Certainly, there's nothing about that to get you on the warpath. It happened that he was coming across 56 range—'

Tonto made a snarling sound and pulled the harder at her gripping fingers.

'Coming across our range! Yes, I'll just bet he was coming across our range. I'll even go farther, I'll bet I know the reason he was crossing our range: he was looking for a chance like this one. Looking for a chance to find you here without anybody but old Chin, the cook, wearing pants on the place! I know all about his reasons. Because I've watched him before, more than once, sneaking around the place. I—'

'Tonto,' Lige McGinsey said in a very soft voice, 'one of these days you're going to make it necessary, as well as pleasant, to just rub out your little mark. I've warned you before. Because of some several little things, I haven't got farther than just warning you. But there's a limit to any man's patience and you certainly are crowding up against my limit!'

Tonto snarled again. He glared up belligerently at the bigger man.

'Oh! You think it's going to get necessary to rub out my mark, huh? And so you tell me, like it was something brand-new. Like you hadn't been trying to rub out my mark for Lord knows how long!'

He lifted one of the big fists and shook it furiously at McGinsey.

'I suppose you think that I don't know whose .45–70 used those shells that I picked up, not two weeks ago, on Hogback Ridge? The day after I'd been shot at by somebody hiding at the end of Hogback?'

Drago, still hidden in the darkness just outside the door, inspected the various details of this scene both shrewdly and with a practiced eye. Now, he saw how Lige McGinsey's eyes went shuttling toward Marjorie Littell, then back to Tonto. Particularly, Drago observed how McGinsey's left hand held the bridles of the buckboard team, so that his right arm was bent with the gunhand close to his pistol.

Drago moved his own hand the merest trifle, so that it was over the butt of his pistol. Then he lifted a shoulder in the slightest of shrugs. He could not see Lige McGinsey staging a gunplay with Tonto Peel; not here, in front of the two girls. So he relaxed a little and leaned against the door-facing.

McGinsey turned a little away from Tonto and grinned at Marjorie Littell:

'Be a nice girl, Marje,' he said, in a voice that—to Drago—seemed artificially good-humored. 'He's just about to scare me to death. And I don't have to tell you that I'm not hunting a row with him; that I never have hunted trouble with anybody on the 56.'

He smiled at her, disarmingly, and gestured with the hand that held the horses' bridles.

'And, if you want to tell me that I'm not to ride across 56 range any more, or come up here to the house to talk to you—I'll take it. It's certainly your right to pick your visitors. But, I'm not going to take any such word from one of your hired hands. Nobody but you can tell me to stay off of and away from the 56. Because—It means too much to me and you *know* it means too much to me.'

Still leaning against the door-facing, Drago lifted one corner of his tight mouth in a grin at once amused and appreciative. He had disliked Lige McGinsey at sight. Very heartily he shared Tonto Peel's very evident opinion of the Walking M owner—whatever that opinion might be! But he was not a man to belittle an enemy simply because he was an enemy. Now, he gave Lige McGinsey credit for smooth, fast thinking.

A smooth customer! His words, his tone, his face—even the small gesture of his free hand—all were calculated precisely to impress a woman. Drago nodded sardonically to himself. For what woman can help softening toward that man who compliments her completely by saying, or showing, that he wants her?

Nor was the effect different here. Marjorie Littell nodded to McGinsey. She said:

'I know. I know, Lige. And I am *not* telling you that. You're always welcome on the 56. I think you should know that.'

Her head jerked and her face flushed angrily, with sound of rippling laughter from the darkness beyond the buckboard. But she turned back immediately to her foreman:

'That will be all, Tonto,' she said stiffly to Tonto Peel. 'You told me at the time about finding those shells and about being shot at. I told you then that I did not, could not, believe that Lige McGinsey would dream of shooting at you. And I'll tell you the same thing, here and now, before him. And there are two things for you to remember, Tonto: I own the 56, and it's my business to say who is welcome on it. Also, I count Lige McGinsey as a friend of mine. If you can't remember these things; if you can't treat Lige McGinsey courteously—'

From behind the buckboard there was the exaggerated sound of yawning. Then Nita Fourponies came around a wheel, a lazy, graceful, altogether eye-filling figure.

'Well, Tonto,' she said drawlingly, 'that makes it two and two. No more, no less! Two who claim that Lige McGinsey didn't try to bushwhack you—or have Wyoming Dees or one of his other thugs part your hair with a .45–70—and two of us who are completely sure that he did.'

She looked at Marjorie Littell, and her expression was that tolerant smile one bestows

98

upon a too-enthusiastic child.

'Dear me, dear me!' she said in a sorrowful tone. Then she looked across to where Drago lounged moveless at the door.

'All right, Handsomeness, you can come out into the light now. I'm afraid you're not going to get the chance to kill Lige tonight. But I don't answer for any time hereafter. No, not tonight. For I don't believe that Lige would ever risk a shot at Tonto, or any other man, who was looking him in the face. He takes his shooting very seriously—from behind rocks and little things like that. So, Mr Hoolihan, you can take your hands off that pistol and come to pack in our bundles.'

Lige McGinsey whirled with her words. He faced Drago, and for perhaps ten seconds the dark, handsome face was demoniacal. His eyes were glaring, his teeth glinted wolfishly between loose lips. None could see him except Drago. And quickly McGinsey caught himself. He was even grinning when he turned back to face Marjorie Littell.

'Oh!' he said slowly. 'Hired a new hand, did you, Marje? Well, for your sake, I hope that he's better than the average of the sidewalk cowboys who've been drifting into the Basin lately. I've had to put up with some of them. It would seem that they send to Sears, Roebuck, and get a Buffalo Bill outfit, then come out West to fight Indians, you know.'

Drago came quietly forward with face

inscrutable. But he looked at McGinsey as he passed, and his dark brows, his narrowed eyes, even the points of dark mustache, lifted in a small and entirely understanding smile.

'Is this Wyoming Dees one of that Sears, Roebuck crew?' he inquired very gravely. 'I met him in town. He was hugging the Cattlemen's stove when I went out of the barroom.'

Then he had passed the Walking M owner and was solemnly taking bundles out of the buckboard. But as he passed McGinsey again with a hundred-pound sack of onions in one hand, a hundred-pound sack of potatoes in the other, carrying them as if they had no weight at all, he smiled again at McGinsey.

When he had finished carrying the groceries up to the kitchen door, Drago went to find Tonto. The 56 foreman had unsaddled both horses and turned them into the corral and hung up saddles and bridles. He was waiting for Drago at the corral gate. And when he spoke it was in a tone thickened by fury:

'If it's the last damn' thing I ever do,' he snarled, 'I'll stitch some buttonholes in that big, good-looking son of a dog. And Marjorie! Why, you'd think anybody with as much sense as she's got wouldn't have to do more than look at McGinsey and see him for the particular kind of illegitimate he really is. But no! She can see anybody else. She can see you and me and all the others in the Basin, for nothing but killers! She wouldn't be caught brushing her skirt against us as she passed. She has to put up with us, because that gets the work done. *But* she lets us know how she feels about our kind. But that—that—Lige McGinsey, that started hiring the gunfighters and turning 'em loose in the Basin to do the dirtiest kind of murders—*he's* a friend of hers, he is! Nobody can say a thing about him! If he rides up to one of us on the range and empties his Winchester at us, she'll find some kind of excuse for him. She—'

Drago laughed, a small sound and entirely mirthless.

'She does rather make us understand that between McGinsey and our kind one of those great gulfs yawns, *no es verdad*? Oh! How about her brother? What does Clint Littell think of all this?'

'Clint?' Tonto said grimly. 'Well, I'll say one thing for him. Harum-scarum he is. Just about as near good-for-nothing as anybody you'd want to meet—or *not* want to meet. He ain't worth the powder it would take to blow him to hell. But, for all that, he can look at Lige McGinsey and see what kind of sneaking, two-faced son McGinsey is. No, sir! Clint ain't got a bit more use for Lige McGinsey than I have.'

'Clint's off gambling somewhere, no?' Drago inquired softly. 'I heard Marjorie tell Nita Fourponies that she thought he was. She said he rode off last Thursday. Nita seemed all worked up about the idea and promised to comb his hair when he got back.'

'Yeh, Nita would be,' Tonto nodded. 'But let's go turn in! Nita gives Clint down-the-river every time she gets a chance at him. Which is not too often nowadays. But you can't do a thing with Clint. He just laughs at her and tells her that she certainly did learn a lot of fine, three-cornered words off at college. I reckon Nita's about like the rest of us with Clint. You somehow can't get as mad at the kid as you would at most people who do the things he does—and don't do the things they ought to. I reckon that's what makes me so damn' mad. After he hightails it, the way he did last week, leaving me to do everything on the outfit, I can think of fifty things I ought to call him!'

He led the way into the dark bunkhouse, still snarling.

'And then, he comes back, and he grins at me—'

'Like right now,' a light, pleasant voice drawled, from the darkness somewhere ahead of them. 'Of course, Tonto, you can't see it. But this very minute I'm wearing my biggest, brightest, Number Two Smile. It's trained right on you. I do reckon I'd better start practicing on my Number One, though, before morning. If I'm going to have to face Marje and Nita both, tomorrow breakfast, I'll need all I can loop in the way of winning grins.'

Tonto made an exasperated sound, midway

between snarl and sigh. He went on into the darkness of the bunkhouse, while Drago waited at the door.

'Damn' shame if they don't cripple you,' Tonto said. 'You and your trifling ways, Clint! Where you been, anyway? You sneaked off and left me and Charley to tote the whole load. And now, Charley's dead. Killed in town yesterday afternoon. Vinson Kymes and the rest of that gang of Silent Wade's done the murder. But I reckon you never heard anything about it. You—'

'I didn't know anything about it!' Clint Littell answered. His voice had altered, hardened. 'I've been a hundred miles away from the 56 and I've been—pretty busy...'

Rawhide creaked under him. Tonto had stopped somewhere beyond. Now a match flared in his hand. It touched the wick of an oil lamp and brought light to the long room.

Drago stared curiously at this shiftless younger brother of Marjorie Littell. He was very like her—yet totally different. Just now he was dusty and beard-stubbled, and heavy shadows lay under his eyes—which were large and very blue. He had come to a sitting position on the edge of a bunk. His young mouth was hard. But he looked worried, rather than grimly intent upon vengeance, Drago thought.

'Come on in,' Tonto said to Drago. 'Clint, this is Hoolihan, riding for the 56 now. He was

103

in on the tail-end of Charley's killing. I talked him into siding me.'

'How did Charley get killed?' Clint demanded. 'Just a plain murder, I reckon! You couldn't figure Charley getting killed except like that, or by accident. And if Vinson Kymes ever killed a man by accident, word of it never got to the Basin!'

Tonto began with Drago's trouble in the Longhorn and described briefly the enmity roused by his and Charley's testimony. Clint listened, but he did not seem much shaken by the story of Charley's murder. Rather, he began to study Drago with curiosity barely concealed. At the end of Tonto's account he nodded, continuing to face Drago, who had slipped out of his leggings and sat down upon a bunk.

'Glad you're with us, Hoolihan,' he said. 'Maybe the three of us can manage to keep these two sides from leaking over the edges of their battlefield onto the 56. We've been missing entirely too much stuff—particularly horses. According to my old history books, war is always hell on horses. It hasn't been a bit different here in the Basin, *this* war! But we can talk about all that tomorrow, after I get hell from Marje and Nita. I don't feel too well tonight. I—came back in a hell-and-a-half of a hurry. I got—Well, there's no use going into that tonight.'

'Clint,' Tonto said drawlingly, where he sat

upon his own bunk, pulling off his boots, 'I reckon I couldn't argue with you that it's any of my particular damn' business, where you've been the past week. And I never could set myself up to give out sermons on how bad drinking and gambling and such are for young cowboys, not with a thing or six I can remember about Peel history. I'll even go farther. A gambler that can always make good wages bucking the tiger, like you do, I reckon he'd be own cousin to a long-eared jack, not to gamble. But—'

His straining grunt was punctuated by the thud of a boot upon the floor. He stood, barefooted, and went over to the lamp. Not until he had taken a match from the shelf beside it and lighted his cigarette did he face Clint again. Then his belligerent blue eyes were narrowed and his square chin outthrust.

'All right! All right!' Clint said wearily. 'You wouldn't preach a sermon—but you're going to preach a sermon. So get it over with. I make out, gambling, but still there's something wrong with the business. So—'

Grimly Tonto's bristly yellow head nodded an affirmative. He blew out smoke.

'Maybe not with the gambling. But wrong with the layout!' he agreed. 'Because, if you keep on helling around, letting all the work get itself done on the 56, depending on Marje to do what she don't know how to do, you're going to *have* to make your living flipping pasteboards. You'll have to make a living for Marje, too!'

He drew smoke into his great chest and, with head a little back, watched it lift slowly toward the ceiling.

'That is,' he added almost carelessly, 'if she's not married to Lige McGinsey by that time. If—well—if Lige is aiming to marry her ...'

Drago, lying comfortably upon his side, considered the details of 56 difficulties, while he studied Clint Littell's startled face. He seemed a pleasant youngster. There was a devil-may-care good-humor about Clint that appealed.

'It begins to look like killing,' Clint said angrily. 'I reckon I'll have to kill Lige. But never mind that now. I'm back to stick around now, Tonto. I don't want you passing this on to Marje, or Nita, but it wasn't gambling that took me off this time. It was a girl. Foolishness, I reckon, but—that was what pulled me away last week. It's all settled, and I'll be right here from now on.'

'Lige McGinsey is up at the house now,' Tonto remarked slowly. 'I didn't know whether to tell you, or not ...'

'What?' Clint snarled. 'Up at the house?'

'Keep your shirt on! He's got the cot on the porch. He won't try anything—not, knowing Hoolihan and me's here.'

CHAPTER TEN

'YOU MIGHT CALL IT BASINOLOGY'

Drago was first up in the morning and first outside. There was a spring-fed trough at the side of the bunkhouse which served the 56 hands as bath and laundry. Drago looked toward the house and, finding no sign of activity except a thin column of smoke rising from the kitchen range, he stripped and scrubbed from head to foot.

Still there was no movement in either bunkhouse or the long, low bulk of the *casa principal* built by 'Old Theo' Littell. So he went to the saddle room of the stable and from his saddle bags got razor and brush and a clean blue flannel shirt. He had done shaving when Clint appeared in the bunkhouse door. The boy was not too happy of expression, Drago thought. He grunted a good morning and splashed in the trough, dried face and hands upon the square of sugar sacking that hung on a nail under the fragment of mirror, then seemed to draw a long breath. He moved off toward the big house.

While Drago smoked, a wizened little Chinese appeared in the kitchen door. He stared at Drago, then came briskly out to stand and stare with his head on one side.

107

Drago bore the inspection amusedly. At last he said:

'Hi, Chin! I'm the new cowboy. My name's—'

Chin put up both thin hands and made a pushing motion. His slant eyes glinted between the lids like twin beads of jet. He laughed, and it was a cackling sound as much contemptuous as amused, Drago thought.

'Ne' mind'm name,' Chin grunted. 'Tell'm name next week—you *be* here, next week! Cowboy in Taunton Basin—*pssssh!* All same glasshoppeh. New cowboy come. Gun bang. New cowboy jump—*pssssh!* Gun bang more. New cowboy gone. *Pssssh!* Too damn' much new cowboy. Name no difference. Call'm "Last New Cowboy." All same glasshoppeh. *Pssssh!*'

'Chin scaring you off?' Tonto called from the corner of the bunkhouse. 'He's seen a few come and go, lately, at that. I reckon we ain't had one on the 56, though, just exactly your kind. You can't blame Chin much, account his Oryental experience didn't take in the kind of man that laid Wyoming Dees on the Cattlemen's floor and put The Breed sidepartnering with Old Devil.'

He came loafing across. Unlike Clint Littell, the foreman of the 56 seemed in very good humor this morning.

'Chin,' he addressed the cook, 'this man Hoolihan here, he killed that man that chased

108

you under the water-trough in town. You remember, the one they called The Breed? He's a man to watch and handle like dynamite. He was in your country one time; out in China. Killed him four thousand Chinese and come home. Now, me and Hoolihan we aim to wipe up this Taunton Basin War. We figure to take a week at it, then go on a spree. You better watch your step. You feed him leather for steak, or burn the biscuits, he'll tally four thousand and one Chinese. Better remember the face and the name—Hoolihan!'

'Ahhh! Hoolihan not a name!' Chin said scornfully. 'You think I city boy? Hoolihan not a name; Hoolihan a bang! You ride up by big steer—fast. You fall out from saddle on big steer head—*pssssh*! Knock'm down flat! *That* Hoolihan!'

'Yeh? Well—that's Hoolihan, this Hoolihan! And don't you forget it a minute. Only the steers he'll hoolihan'll be the LL and Half Circle W and Walking M and Lazy R outfits—and all their gunmen! Breakfast, Confucius! Lots of breakfast. And, Chin— Clint's back. He'll eat with the girls.'

'See'm,' Chin nodded. 'Sneak in house. Change clothes.'

Tonto nodded and his grin was twisted when he turned to Drago.

'He'll be all slicked up and sort of you-wouldn't-kick-a-pore-puppy, time he sits down to breakfast with the girls,' he said, with the same helpless, affectionate exasperation which had marked his voice the night before, when talking to the boy. 'I swear, I can't make him out! What do you think about him?'

'Pure cowboy! About enough brains to wad a shot-gun shell. Not enough jawbone to keep him away from things he likes—the liquor and the cards and the women. He's all full of good intentions, right now. But give him a month, maybe a week, of hard work and no excitement, and he'll begin to itch for the cards and that girl—or another one—again. Clint wasn't cut out for work. And the girl, you said, is not much of a manager?'

'Does what she can,' Tonto said sourly. 'But she can't give her foreman a free hand, even when she can't manage the place herself. Makes sales and buys behind his back—and she gets skinned every time. Clint's no better. It was plenty different in the old man's day. And if it don't turn out plenty different pretty soon, they're going to belong to the people that "used to be cowfolks," I tell you! Well, let's eat!'

Chin fed them in the kitchen. From the house dining-room the murmur of voices carried, where Marjorie and Nita and Clint ate with Lige McGinsey. Drago and Tonto finished their meal and Tonto ordered lunches from the little Chinese. On the way to the corral Tonto sketched the run of work.

'I'm going over to our east line,' he finished.

110

'Likely, it'll take me all day to fix our line fence. Charley was to do it. You take a *pasear* north. It'll give you a chance to look at our range. You'll come to a stretch of rocky ground and see a white needle sticking up. That's our line to the north. Ought to be about a hundred head of long yearlings and some twos in that Needle Pasture. Kind of check. I ain't had time lately. Come on back when you want to, any way you want to. Thing to do, now, is get acquainted. You'll need to know our lines and about what's supposed to be on the range. Then—'

'I may sleep out,' Drago told him. 'All right?'

He saddled Button and with food in a saddle pocket rode north. Presently he began to nod with satisfaction. In ordinary circumstances, any near-competent manager could make the 56 pay. It was pretty country. There were shallow mountain creeks, spring-fed, winding down wooded slopes to water little green meadows. There were cañons where cattle and horses could shelter during winter storms, with browse on which they could live where there was no grass.

'A lovely range!' he told himself again and again as Button climbed off the flats.

As he headed into the hills, Drago passed bunch after bunch of white-and-red cattle. They were in good shape, but, to the eye of a man trained on the great D Bar of Leandro County, there were very evident signs of neglect. Drago nodded, recalling what Tonto

Peel had said about Clint 'letting the work get itself done.' Entirely too many unbranded animals were among those 56 cattle. Nor were they altogether calves missed in the roundup. Within five miles he glimpsed a half-dozen big mavericks, and made mental note to come out again with a branding iron.

Near noon, he saw ahead of him, rising almost like a marble monument, that tall white needle of which Tonto Peel had spoken. He began to look for the 56 yearlings and a few broke from the brush ahead, looking at him almost as wildly as so many deer. He tallied twenty, and thirty. He was almost at forty when shod hoofs clattered on rocks ahead.

He pulled in Button, secure in the knowledge that for the past half-hour he had made very little noise. From the sound, a small band of free horses moved ahead of him. Peel had said nothing about any horses running in Needle Pasture. But Drago thought that, on an outfit so short-handed, so carelessly managed, the horses might be almost anywhere.

He rode quietly forward with his carbine across his lap. Presently he sat Button in the brush on the rim of a small cañon. The clatter of hoofs was louder. The horses were in the cañon now, heading straight toward him. Shielded by the brush, Drago got out his binoculars and studied the half-dozen horses which were being driven toward him by a tall and lantern-jawed man. He caught the brands on three of the horses and nodded to himself. They were 56 stock, all right.

He shook his head as he lowered his glasses: 'And that tall hairpin, why, you'd think he was working for wages. Maybe he is, at that! The joker being that the 56 is not paying that wage.'

The temptation to knock that calm rider from the saddle with a .44 slug was very strong. But it occurred to Drago that it would be interesting to come closer to the man; to discuss various range affairs—and Taunton Basin affairs—with him. The horses were walking or trotting, as the rocky cañon floor dictated. Drago withdrew soundlessly and rode along the edge of the cañon for a little way. It was not hard to keep the hoofbeats behind him, on the right, and, after a while, he found a stock-trail leading down into the dry water course.

The thief had been riding with his Winchester in the scabbard. So Drago scabbarded his own carbine. He pulled in beside a boulder on the cañon floor and waited with thumb hooked in his shell-belt.

The first horse of the band, a long-legged bay, went by. Drago leaned a little. A black and two sorrels passed, then another bay. And now the tall man could be heard. He was singing in a high, whining voice:

'We won't have none of your weevilly

113

wheat,
We won't have none of your barley!
Nothing but the best of wheat
Will make a cake for Charley.
Higher up the cherry tree,
Riper grows the cherries;
More you hug and kiss the girls,
Quicker will they marry!
We won't have none of your weevilly
wheat—'

The song stopped abruptly when Drago rode out from behind the boulder. The lantern-jawed rustler jerked his big black in and stared with deepset gray eyes from under towy brows. He was even taller than he had looked when seen from the cañon rim—at least three inches above Drago's own six feet. Narrow of shoulder, stooping, there was the look of enormous strength and endurance about the lanky body. The enormous freckled hands resting so loosely upon the big horn of his narrow-fork saddle were like nothing so much as a gorilla's paws. He continued to stare when Drago nodded colorlessly to him.

'Your range?' Drago inquired politely.

The other man continued to inspect him, from hat to boots and back again. Then he shrugged:

'It might be,' he said drawlingly in that high, whining voice which for Drago had placed the man instantly as an East Texan. 'Hard to tell, sometimes—in Taunton Basin...'

Then he seemed to wait, as if the words had formed some sort of challenge, which must be answered in a particular way.

'I go by Jack Smith,' Drago told him.

'You can call me Jones,' the tall man answered. 'Some of the boys call me "Gloomy" Jones, but that's just a nickname.'

'Nice horses you're driving,' Drago complimented him. 'I didn't see the brand as they passed me. Anyway, I'm practically a stranger in the Basin.'

With left hand he fished in his shirt pocket for Duke's and papers and—watching those enormous hands that rested so negligently upon the saddle horn—shook tobacco into a brown paper.

'You being a stranger,' Jones grunted, 'likely the brand wouldn't have meant nothing to you if you'd *seen* it.'

'Why, there's a lot to that!' Drago admitted. 'But I reckon a man wouldn't have to stay a stranger in the Basin? I was down at Bellero on the River when I heard about this little fracas you folks have been having in the Basin. So I rode up and—here I am.'

'I can see you,' Jones agreed dryly. 'I see right good. Here you are and—what about it?'

'Reckon you could use a man about my size and build and all?'

Jones shook his narrow head.

'I just ride for the Circle Dot. I ain't got a

115

thing to do with the hiring and firing. Tell you—whyn't you come along with me and meet Hellin, our ramrod? Strike him for a job?'

He grinned and Drago grinned in return.

'Far?' he inquired carelessly.

'Oh—depends on what you figure,' this amazingly calm horse-thief answered.

Then ensued a brief interval of hesitation. Drago gathered up his reins. Jones did the same. But neither pushed his horse forward.

'You'd think—that is, you *could* think,' Drago remarked with small, bland smile, 'that we didn't *trust* each other. And that's foolish. For we can't ride stirrup-to-stirrup *all* the way. Not along a cañon as narrow as this one. What'll we do? You ought to know that I could have shot you from behind this rock, with less trouble than I took to ride out and hail you.'

'That's right,' Jones admitted. 'Excuse me. We kind of get into the habit of not backing up to folks, in Taunton Basin. Show your back to few of your friends, and to no strangers at all, and you live lots longer. You might call that "basinology," I reckon. I'll go ahead.'

He touched his horse with the rowel and rode on after the vanished 56 horse-band. Drago followed and his smile was grim.

'He could have been in Taunton during the late unpleasantness,' he speculated. 'Maybe he owns a draggy gun and wants a sure shot. But, cool as he is—and a hog on ice isn't in the deal with him—he didn't show enough interest in

116

me when I popped into the trail before him. *"Hellin"* ... I'll bet! Drop the "-in" and *that's* the word he meant. I'll meet *hell*, just as quickly as he can manage it. Ah, well, he may lead me to something he's not intending.'

Then Jones turned and waved. Drago rode up beside him. Here, for a mile or so, was room to side each other. And the lantern jaw wagged and Drago listened. 'Gloomy' Jones was both a gifted and a fluent liar. He invented a dozen brands besides those which Tonto Peel had listed as being in the Basin. He spoke of those imaginary spreads' imaginary owners and foremen and cowboys, sketching their portraits with a wealth of detail. His pictures of them were almost like photographs, Drago thought amusedly.

Finally, it came to him that 'Jones'—and Drago was quite sure that, whatever the tall rustler's name might be, it was not Jones— talked in order to keep from answering questions. Nor did it escape Drago that the gray eyes were intently watching the cañon—as if 'Jones' looked for something.

'Or—somebody?' Drago asked himself.

The trail led through fallen boulders, washed down by storms from the cañon walls. 'Jones' seemed to feel no hesitation, now, about turning his back upon his companion. He took the lead and kept it, flinging back his comment on the Basin.

'Now, just what does he expect to do, or see?'

117

Drago wondered.

Instantly, the question was answered. For 'Jones' with savage drive of rowel into his black, lunged around a turn of the cañon. Instantly, shots sounded. Drago was perhaps fifty feet in his rear. He pulled in short and jerked the carbine from its scabbard. Those shots *could* be nothing but a signal, for no lead came back his way. He looked flashingly about him. Across the narrow width of the cañon a water-washed arroyo showed, slanting down from the rim. At a glance, it seemed to offer a way out of the cañon, other than the turning back.

'Jones' evidently had stopped just around the crook of the cañon. Now, it seemed to Drago, he heard hoofbeats, a distant clattering that would hardly be made by the 56 horses. The little band had not been within hearing since he and 'Jones' had started this way together.

He pushed Button forward, going straight across the cañon toward that gash in the wall. He watched for sign of his tall rustler. Now, there was no doubt that men—at least three of them—were riding fast along the cañon toward him.

He had one glimpse of 'Jones' sitting the black beside the wall. They raised their Winchesters together. Viciously—he was irritated because 'Jones' had so neatly taken him in with that jump around the corner—

Drago fired three fast shots at the tall man. 'Jones' answered. Lead whined past Drago before Button reached the water-channel in the wall. Drago spurred him into it and, masked somewhat by a clump of *ocatillo* which clung to a rocky ledge, he turned and lifted the carbine, prepared to shoot. But 'Jones,' dead or alive, was no longer in sight.

Drago listened intently. The clatter of those galloping horses was louder, closer. He looked upward. The arroyo was narrow and very deep. But it seemed passable. He got down, reins in hand, to lead Button upward. For ten feet, twenty feet, then thirty, horse and man struggled toward the top. Drago looked back and down. Still there was no sign of this tall, lantern-jawed thief. But three riders were coming in single file between the boulders. They held rifles or carbines up like so many Indians as their heads shuttled from right to left. Drago opened fire upon them.

With his first shot a horse went down, hurling the rider forward. The remaining men jumped their mounts to the side while Drago, preferring the bird in hand, pounded the rocks about the fallen one with slugs. As soon as the reinforcements of 'Jones' had disappeared, hugging the wall of the cañon, Drago continued to work upward.

It was hard going. Button slipped time after time, and Drago must lean against a rock, or cling to some tough root, holding the reins desperately until the big gelding regained his footing.

At last they came out upon a little mesa. Drago looked down into the cañon. He could see neither horse nor man moving, so he swung into the saddle. He rode forward in the direction from which those three had come—the direction in which the 56 horses had gone.

Despite the odds against him, he was grimly determined that those horses would not be taken from 56 range. His talk with Jones had not produced the results he had hoped for. But that error made—holding the slug which would have killed Jones far up the cañon—would not end in the loss of the 56 geldings if he could prevent their going.

The little mesa upon which he had emerged ended abruptly. He was riding slowly down the slope at its end when a distant rifle set echoes rolling in the cañons. Drago swore underbreath. He was exposed, halfway down that rugged, trackless slant. He could not turn back. There was nothing to do but take his chances and let Button pick his way down to cover.

It was not the first—nor tenth—time he had been forced to ride helplessly under fire. His face set grimly. He watched the puffs of smoke blossom by a clump of mesquite far across the broken land ahead; watched the tiny geysers of dust jumping up to right and left of him. If he were going to be hit, he would be hit. When after a furious volley the firing stopped, he guessed it was merely for reloading. He ventured, now, to touch Button gently with a star rowel, and send him plunging down the final yards of less-steep slope.

'And now, Friends of Mr Jones!' he said aloud, 'the meeting is just about to begin to commence. We'll see who knows the most about this old and always interesting game of bushwhacking.'

He turned left through a shallow arroyo, bending low in the saddle and going fast. When he came to a cross-arroyo, he went up it, straight toward the spot where the shooting had been done. He got off Button occasionally and, from the top of some boulder scrambled upon, hunted expertly and patiently for that rifleman.

Apparently the other was about the same campaign. For now and then Drago could hear the faint sliding of small rocks released by a man's foot. But it was a long hour later that a shabby hat appeared over a boulder twenty yards to the right. Drago waited and a pair of jetty eyes appeared, then the whole of a chocolate-brown face. Delicately Drago squeezed the trigger and sent his bullets at the target. He *saw* one strike the face before the head disappeared.

Then a rifle *whanged*! The shot came from the left of him.

CHAPTER ELEVEN

'TWO MEN ARE ON 56 RANGE'

Even as he turned, the other rifleman corrected his aim. A slug tore through Drago's hat. Another glanced across his back from shoulder-point to shoulder-point, almost. When he hugged the ground the accurate hail of lead knocked splinters of rock from the boulders about him, to sting through his shirt, and flick him upon the face.

Inch by inch he worked backward, feet first. The firing ceased, but he relaxed none of his caution until he gained the arroyo where Button waited with trailing reins. Then, flinching against the touch of flannel shirt upon the whiplash sear across his back, he mounted and set grimly out to find that second bushwhacker.

Time after time during the remaining hours of daylight he thought he heard the man. And since for all his care he could not move among the rocks without making a certain amount of noise, he thought that he was heard, too. The sun dropped toward the western peaks. He came to the rim of a cañon that looked like the one which 'Jones' had chosen for trailing the stolen horses off the 56.

Here the walls were steeper and the cañon

122

narrower. But there were stock-trails following ledges down. He sent Button onto such a trail and rode slowly, with carbine always ready, along the stony trail that wound between boulders. Within a mile he heard horses ahead of him.

He got down and went noiselessly forward afoot. And when he saw lariats stretched from wall to wall, with bits of rag flapping upon them in the small breeze, he stopped short, nodding. It was the temporary holding ground for those 56 geldings. For the horses browsed just beyond the flimsy barrier.

When he was sure that none of the rustlers watched there, he went back to Button and mounted. He jerked the lariat end loose and rode up to the stolen horses. They were not hard to drive; when he started them back along the cañon, they moved at a walk. He could turn them toward the ascending trail without trouble. Before the sun was out of sight beyond the peaks, they were moving steadily back toward the Needle Pasture.

Jogging behind them, Drago grinned slowly at last. After all, it had not been a bad day for the 56. The calm rustlers, who seemed to have been used to riding across the 56 range and quietly gathering what stock they wanted, had been jolted out of that habit. Four of them had not been able to run off this little band when one 56 hand had objected.

'They'll have to remodel their ideas,' he

123

thought humorously. 'Change their methods and come down in more force. But I do wish I knew which side "Jones" was working for ... Maybe Tonto will place him. He's not a usual man.'

He let the horses go on alone, when thick darkness came. He made camp by a *tinaja*, a rock tank of seeping water, and ate the remainder of his lunch. There was no alarm during the night and he was up before the light, to kill a rabbit and cook it. He did not stay long over breakfast. He was too much interested in this section of the 56 range.

By noon he had ridden the width of Needle Pasture. The recovered horses, he thought, were down on the flats by now. He tallied more than eighty head of cattle, yearlings for the most part, and renewed his resolution to come back here and brand mavericks. But the most interesting find was the trail of two men appearing, vanishing, reappearing. They had ridden this range within a day, he was confident.

He was looking at their fresh tracks, where they skirted a stony ridge, when he heard a horse coming up the other side of that little rise of the land. He stepped behind Button and put his carbine across the saddle. Marjorie Littell appeared on the crest and, seeing him, instantly reined in.

Drago walked out, to touch the rim of his bullet-pierced hat. His shirt ballooned in the back, where that rustler's slug had cut a long gash in the flannel. His face and hands and leggings were dust-smeared. She frowned at him.

'You—seem to have had an accident,' she said awkwardly. 'Have you had—trouble today?'

'Nothing to speak of,' he told her carefully. 'Just a little course in "basinology." The word's not mine, by the way. I had it yesterday from the tallest Son of Ananias it's ever been my lot to meet.'

'Suppose you try plain English!' she said shortly. 'I gather that you met someone yesterday. You might go on from there. You had trouble with this man?'

She rode down the slope toward him. He made a cigarette when he had rammed the carbine back into its scabbard. He lighted it and drew in smoke, watching sardonically the disapproving face so stonily turned toward him.

'Tonto sent me out to check the cattle in this pasture. I ran into this tall, gray-eyed, very self-possessed stranger—he says he goes by "Gloomy" Jones, but I'm inclined to be doubtful about that. He was very blithely annexing a half-dozen head of very good 56 geldings. We talked about this and that and the other in quite a friendly way. But now that I look back upon the incident'—he waved the cigarette airily—'I doubt if I really trusted him.

I suppose it was the fact that he was engaged in grand larceny when I met him that made me suspicious...'

'If you don't mind, will you tell me exactly and directly what happened?' she prompted him in a tone so vicious that he stared in real surprise. 'Just the bare facts!'

'Since you ask so courteously, how can I refuse?' he sighed. 'Well, I was trying to pose as a newcomer to Taunton Basin; trying to act as—well, as I was on the hotel porch when you were practically clubbed into hiring me. As a wandering killer, hunting scalp money by the job or by the month. But Mr Jones didn't fool easily. He played his part and we rode along in the dust of your horses until he had me where he wanted me. And that was all but up against the muzzles of some friends of his, who seemed to be waiting for him.'

He shrugged and regarded her pleasantly.

'More by luck than brains, I got away from the four of them. We played hide-and-seek for the rest of the afternoon. *I* was *It*! I got a hole in my hat; a snag in my shirt; and a very painful raking-over from me, myself. You see, when I first sighted this rustler, Jones, I could have killed him with no trouble whatever. And then the horses could have been turned back to 56 range. Everybody would have been happy except Mr Jones. And he wouldn't have been in condition to complain.'

'You mean, the horses were stolen? The six

geldings? I had a sale for them—I'm sure it's the same band—at seven hundred and fifty dollars for the lot.'

He watched her steadily. She had turned white and he saw that she hardly considered him now. She was staring blankly straight ahead.

'I thought a half-dozen times during the afternoon,' he said thoughtfully, 'that I should have killed Jones and recovered the horses. But, knowing how you feel about killing, even in Taunton Basin—'

She looked at him and flushed.

'Because I don't encourage murder; because the 56 has never hired killers—'

'All right! I won't hurrah you. I did recover the horses. I killed one rustler and pretty certainly shot another so badly that he's not likely to show on this range for some time to come. Perhaps I got in a lick at Jones. I don't know.'

Her eyes widened as she watched him.

'You—killed one thief, wounded another— and perhaps another; you recovered the horses from four men; and make nothing of it! I—I really don't know what to make of you, Mr Hoolihan. But I am grateful about the horses. We've lost so much during this so-called "war" that we simply can't afford to lose any more. I counted on that sale to pay expenses.'

'*De nada!* It's nothing,' he told her quickly. 'As Tonto remarked, the 56 occupies the rôle of that famous innocent bystander at a fight; the one who always gets hurt. But and yet, there are ways of changing that. It may be, even, that you'll look back and not be too sorry that Tonto talked you into hiring me. We'll see. Meanwhile—'

'Meanwhile, you haven't had anything to eat for quite a while, have you? You left after breakfast yesterday.'

'I finished the lunch Chin gave me, last night. But I knocked over a cottontail for breakfast. I was just debating something when you came up; wondering whether to turn back to the house, or go on exploring the 56 edges.'

'There's a lunch in my saddle pocket; plenty for three or four. You won't have to go back, unless you're ready.'

'There's a spring yonder, in that ledge of rocks. Suppose we ride over to it. I want to get out from under some of this dust I acquired yesterday, when the Society of the Friends of Jones was chasing me up and down.'

She kept her *palomina* at his stirrup for the five hundred yards to the yellow cliff he indicated. He swung down and put out a palm for her foot, to let her dismount. Then he went down the narrow stream away from the spring, and splashed in a basin of rock.

When he came back she had spread sandwiches and half a pie upon a napkin. She waved her cigarette at him.

'From your tobacco. Nita taught me to roll

them last year. That, and riding tolerably, are about my only Texas accomplishments. Sometimes I think I'm terribly miscast, trying to manage a ranch. But there wasn't any choice, when I took the job. And we managed fairly well until this fighting began.'

As he ate, back comfortably against a flat, worn slab of rock, he found himself thinking of Sara Belk. Odd, he told himself, how far away and unimportant that seemed now. He wondered how it had ever bulked so large. Memory of Sara inevitably brought memory of the Leandro courtroom and jail and he stared grimly down the slope. More than at any other time since he had left Sarkey and Ferg Ingram senseless in Ancho, he felt his outlawry.

'That is my sort of girl,' he told himself, staring covertly at Marjorie's clear face. 'There was a time when I could meet her on an equality. Now, she suffers me because she hardly knows what else to do. But that's all! I'm a killer, in her eyes. And so—'

He was jerked back from moody recollections by her voice. He looked directly, inquiringly at her.

'I said: You're from the Border, aren't you? Mexico?'

'I rode into the Basin from the Rio Grande country, yes,' he answered carefully. 'I really didn't intend to stop here. I was heading for the Camel Flat range, job-hunting.'

'Then, why did you stop?' she demanded

flatly. By her tone, the answer was important. 'Why didn't you ride on?'

'Because—oh, it may be because of the way the Basin folk rose up and set their private affairs down on my lap. That Wyoming Dees, for instance. Dees is the sort of killer I can't stomach. I've seen quite a few of his stripe, here and there. He walked on my toes when I came to Taunton, a perfect stranger; he and his friend Olin Oge the saloonkeeper. So I hit back. Then, seeing no difference at all between the two sides of this war, I held up my end in a fight with some of Wade and Rust's hired killers. Tonto Peel helped me in that deal. And when I found that he was bucking both sides, I let myself be talked into tying down my holsters instead of going on to Camel Flat.'

'Tonto is—utterly loyal. But he has violent prejudices—'

'Tonto has forgot more about men than you'll ever know,' Drago said calmly. 'One of the most amusing things that's ever been rammed down the world's neck is the idea that women understand men. That must have been published originally by some lady novelist. Actually, not one woman in ten thousand knows more about men than that they're whiskery animals wearing pants. Beyond that—'

'And I suppose men understand women?' she interrupted him mockingly. 'Men being so superior.'

130

'Not at all,' he admitted placidly. 'That doesn't follow. But I do think that when men come to understand women, your lot is going to be harder. What I started to say is, Tonto's summing-up of Lige McGinsey is neat and accurate. You haven't met many McGinseys in your day. Tonto has seen plenty of them.'

'And you agree with him?'

'If I told you what I really think of him,' Drago said smilingly, 'you'd have to rise up and paw the air. In self-defense. So I won't tell you. *No es importe*, anyway.'

She studied his calm face, wiping her fingers on the grass. He made a cigarette and handed her tobacco and papers. She frowned down at them.

'I like him!' she burst out presently. 'Nobody else seems to—Tonto, Clint, Nita, now you! But I like him and I don't believe, just for instance, that he'd shoot at Tonto from ambush. Tonto is enough to make any man feel murderous—'

Drago got up, shaking his head. He went over to the *palomina* and busied himself with her saddle girths. She followed him, and now her face was hard, unfriendly, once more.

'Very well! I can't change your opinion, but I can say this: You're not to imitate Tonto while you're on the 56. You're not to annoy Mr McGinsey when he visits me.'

Drago said nothing as he picked up the *palomina's* reins and passed them up. He held

131

his palm for her foot again. She swung into the saddle and took the reins from him.

'Now,' she said briskly, 'I want you to bring those geldings in. I won't take chances with them again. I'll tell the buyer I accept his price and we'll get rid of them. Can you find them today?'

'I don't know. I'm not going to look for them. What *I* am going to do is escort you back to the house. And for a little while to come, I wish you wouldn't ride out so far.'

A slow wave of color came up in her neck and face as she met his inscrutable eyes. Her mouth tightened.

'I don't need any escort to the house. And I want those horses in the corral tonight, if possible. Tomorrow forenoon, anyway. So, *if* you don't mind—'

Drago mounted and turned Button. He rode back toward the ridge where he had been when she found him. She followed and stared at the ground when he swept his hand toward the hoofprints that marked a soft place between stones.

'Well?' she demanded irritably. 'I've seen hoofprints before. Is this the trail of the horses?'

'No. That's the reason I'm riding back to the house with you. Two men are on 56 range— unless they've got off it very recently. A big man and a small man, to guess boldly. I've found their trail several times this morning.

132

This is the freshest specimen. It might have been made today. Anyway, I am riding back with you. The ordinary breed of horse-thief wouldn't bother a woman. He might even be a family man when home. But you seem to have unusual kinds of men in the Basin. I'll not take a chance.'

'I *order* you to bring in those horses. I'll take care of myself,' she said flatly. 'Either that or—'

'Don't be silly,' he advised her flatly. 'I'm not an ordinary hand on the 56. You know it as well as I do. So don't try to treat me as if I were some twenty-year-old cowboy to gape wonderingly at the gorgeously beautiful owner of the outfit. I'm here to help Tonto Peel pull your chestnuts out of a pretty hot fire. More or less because that amuses me for the time being. If the wages interested me, do you think I'd be on the 56 at all? Come on!'

'None the less,' she cried furiously, 'I happen to be the owner of the 56—'

'Yes?' he drawled. Then, indiscreetly, because she had ability to infuriate him: 'I've managed an outfit that would use the 56 for a feeding pasture! And every minute of the time I managed it, I knew *exactly* what I was doing. In brief, Miss Littell, I know the cow business. Right now, I know something else: You're going to the house where you'll be safely out of the way until it's safe for you to ride this range.'

He made a small, remorseless gesture

toward her reins.

'Either you come back to the house with me, holding those, or I lead the *palomina* by them.'

'Very well!' she agreed. Her voice shook and there were blazing patches of color on her cheeks. 'Naturally, I can't keep you from dragging my horse back to the house. But as soon as you get there, you will leave. I don't doubt'—she had spurred the *palomina* forward, and now she turned in the saddle to face him again—'that you're the superlative warrior you admit being.'

Drago came after her, face blank.

'If you want to talk, the trot's no gait for it,' he said. 'You lose all the effect. The words are jolted out and they sound just alike. Try a lope—and talk in between jumps.'

She stiffened, then instantly relaxed and pushed her horse into the gentle, suggested gait.

Drago came to her stirrup and nodded approvingly.

'That's more like it. Now, you can express yourself with feeling. Odd ... The general run of women want to talk, but so often they don't get in position to do it. Now, what was it you were complimenting me about?'

'I said,' she told him smilingly, 'that after you're gone the 56 will doubtless never be the same. I don't doubt even that you're telling part of the truth about managing a big ranch. In spite of the fact that women don't

134

understand men, I can understand that you would be thoroughly efficient at most things. I suppose it's the way you sit a horse; the way you walk—as if the ground belonged to you and you were daring anyone to contest your title...'

He smiled at Button's ears. This ride promised to be amusing. Then, abruptly, he sobered. With recollection of what he was, there was no amusement left in the situation. He saw her, suddenly, trying to fill a place which would have been difficult for an experienced and battle-scarred man.

'She doesn't have a real idea of what she's bucking,' he thought, with something like pity. 'But she's shouldered the load and she's trying to keep the outfit going. And that useless Clint is just another pound on her back. Tonto is a good foreman and a fighting fool, but he's just one man.'

She met his quick shift to gravity with a small frown.

'Probably,' he said indifferently, 'you're right about me. So far as you know. The Basin has drawn gun-fighters from up and down. Both sides to this war have imported them. You don't want killers riding for the 56. But you're in between the lines; and the lawlessness that the war naturally breeds sends down onto your range all the petty thieves that flourish in such times. So you're forced to fight back in self-defense. And that explains me...'

They were riding down a grassy slope toward a narrow creek. Mechanically, he looked at the ground, as mechanically he had been watching the rimming hills around them.

'You think'—there was uncertainty in her tone—'that the 56 needs you; needs your guns...'

'I think,' he said almost absently, 'that you can go on alone now. I've got to turn off here.'

CHAPTER TWELVE

'WHO ARE YOU TRAILING?'

Marjorie stared at him, then looked all around at the quiet land. Last, she looked at the ground.

'But—' she began, then stopped.

'You'll be all right, riding by yourself,' Drago assured her. 'So go on. But please go straight to the house.'

'I don't understand you,' she confessed. 'A little while ago it wasn't safe. You would drag Dulce by his bits, if necessary—Now, you tell me I'm safe—'

'Things change! Did it ever occur to you that it only takes seven minutes or thereabouts to hang a man? But if you have to know, back yonder all I was sure of was that two men are on 56 range. I couldn't tell where they were or which way they were heading. Now, at least I know that they're not going toward the house. You are, so—*Hasta la vista!*'

And without waiting for her reply, he spun Button to the left and rode, with those fresh hoofprints to guide him, along the bank of this little creek. He looked back once, to be sure that the girl obeyed. She still sat the *palomina* at the edge of the water, looking after him. But when he turned in the saddle, she lifted a hand to him and sent Dulce into the creek.

'By God!' Drago grunted when she waved. 'She doesn't seem able to make up her mind about me—not that it matters!'

The lure of the trail gripped him again. He forgot Marjorie and her attractiveness. Those two sets of hoofprints, that represented two predatory animals ahead, were the most interesting things in the world.

'It's not "Jones," unless he's riding another horse,' he said aloud. 'For I know the tracks of that black he was on. He called up three friends to meet me ... I certainly finished one, and I can't believe that man I pounded in the cañon was less than seriously drilled. That would make this seem like "Jones" and the fellow I played around the cañons with.'

But, he must remind himself, in the Basin there were plenty of men with whom either 'Jones' or that efficient bushwhacker who had torn his shirt might ride.

He tensed a little, mile by mile, as the tracks
137

showed fresher. Now he topped no rise without dismounting and looking over it from the shelter of bush or rock. But always the pair were out of sight ahead of him.

The trail twisted toward the hills and on rocky slopes became harder to follow. In mid-afternoon it vanished in the stony bottom of an arroyo, and, while he sat frowning from left to right, looking for the sign, horsemen came around a butte and clattered toward the dry water course in which he sat.

They saw him as soon as he saw them. They were barely fifty yards from where he had halted. Theirs was the advantage of momentum, if he ran. He must come out of this shallow arroyo and send Button plunging into a gallop, with the half-dozen of them shooting at him. So he did not run. Instead, he lifted his right hand and watched them spread fanwise to come toward him.

A wispy man, hard-featured, graying, was in the center of the crescent-shaped line. He pulled in his gray horse and looked curiously at Drago, with an intent stare that seemed to absorb and file every detail of him. Then:

'I'm Sheriff Azle, of Parlin,' he said grimly.

'Glad to meet you,' Drago told him calmly. 'My name's Hoolihan and I ride for the 56. I'm more or less strange to the Basin. Am I over your line?'

'Do 'no',' the little sheriff grunted. 'How long you been riding for the Littells?'

'Just a few days. But time's a funny thing. Yesterday was full as lots of months could be on other ranges.'

Very briefly, he told of meeting 'Jones' and the other rustlers. Azle listened with unwinking dark eyes boring into Drago's face. The other men—a rather usual mixture of cowboys and adventure-hunting townsmen such as posses often draw—seemed as interested. A tall and thin blond man looked at Azle when Drago had brought the report up to the vanished trail here in the arroyo.

'Could them two be our two?' he inquired doubtfully.

'Could be,' Azle said tonelessly. 'They could have cut over the Caballos by a half-dozen trails and got over toward the Needle, after they lost us.'

'If it's not a secret,' Drago broke in upon the sheriff's moody staring at the ground, 'who are you trailing?'

'Couple train-robbers,' Azle told him curtly. 'Was three. They stuck up the combination on the edge of Parlin County—five of 'em. They split up and the V Up and Down boys corraled two of 'em when they tried to steal fresh horses. Shot 'em into dollrags. Found sixteen hundred dollars in their saddle pockets. One of the V boys cut across and told me about it. This posse was trailing the other three. Three nights ago one of our three sneaked away. Since then we've been after the two that's left. We lost the

139

trail yesterday afternoon.'

'I was hoping,' Drago said wolfishly, 'that these two I've been trailing would turn out my two left-over rustlers. But I don't see how those thieves could be your train-robbers.'

'Me, neither,' the little sheriff agreed shortly. 'Let's back up to where you lost their tracks, last.'

Drago turned Button. With Azle and the tall blond man to right and left of him, just behind, he led the posse up the arroyo and out of it. When he sent Button lunging up, Azle's gray grunted and almost jumped the low bank, so that the sheriff was at Drago's stirrup at the top.

'There! As good a set as I've seen since leaving the soft ground along a little creek where I picked them up. And'—he looked at Azle with a slow smile of perfect understanding—'over there is *my* trail, coming this way. I rode to the side, of course. Those prints are bigger than my horse's...'

'So they are. And I'd know those other prints by the feel!'

'Your men?' Drago asked him.

Azle nodded slowly, very grimly, staring down at those hoofprints.

'Our men! And, *por dios*, we'll snag 'em, now...'

Then, abruptly, he showed his leadership. He turned quickly upon the men of his posse and jerked his hand in a sweeping gesture.

'All right! We'll start out and pick up this trail. They're certainly ahead of us—and that's more'n we've known for sure since yesterday. Whitey, you go to the left, account you're the best trailer among us unless'—he looked thoughtfully at Drago—'Hoolihan here can match you. Anyway, in spite of the fact that you're not in my county exactly, I'm going to borrow you from the 56 awhile. That all right?'

Drago shrugged, smiling faintly.

'I'd feel pretty much hurt to be left out, now.'

'All right, then,' Azle barked. 'Let's hightail!'

When the posse had spread over a hundred yards or so of range, Drago and Azle rode stirrup-to-stirrup down the arroyo where the trail had vanished.

Presently Drago grunted and pointed stabbingly at a scarred place on the arroyo wall.

'That's where they topped out,' he said, rather unnecessarily.

Azle complimented him with a long stare.

'You got the kind of eyes Indians are supposed to have, and Rangers in my day used to really have,' he drawled. 'Done a lot of trailing, have you?'

Drago shrugged. But that word 'Ranger' started a train of thought. There was no doubting the sheriff's original suspicion of him, and he was by no means certain that, even now, Azle took him for face value, as an

141

ordinary hand. And life in Taunton Basin was very likely to become complicated if, to the hostility of both factions in the war, were added any official activity. This was a grim and efficient little rooster, the Sheriff of Parlin! No Berry Nicks occupied the next county's shrieval chair. So he considered what might be most profitable...

'Yes, I've done considerable trailing, one way and another,' he admitted—rather as if speaking without thinking about it. 'Indians are pretty good trailers, sometimes. We had a couple of Tonks one time. Sometimes they were pretty good.'

'We used 'em in my day, too,' Azle nodded. His voice was very soft. 'They hated rain. Come wet weather, or cold weather, they always wanted to curl up around a fire. Wasteful sons, too! Let the camp starve while they killed a deer or beefed a steer inside two hundred yards. Never bring in a bite of meat for us.'

'That's the way they are,' Drago agreed, still watching the ground and still seeming to speak absently; without the degree of caution proper in a Ranger sent *incognito* into a hostile land.

Then, as if conscious of a slip, he jerked his head about and looked at Azle.

'And where was this you was trailing with Tonka-was?' Azle inquired blandly.

'Oh, a long time ago, 'way over in the Panhandle,' Drago told him quickly.

They had followed the trail of the robber pair out of the arroyo.

'There they go again! Mister, if they get behind one of those rocks up in the mountains, yonder, they're going to deal us plenty misery.'

'Well, that's supposed to be a sheriff's life—or a Ranger's,' Azle answered calmly. 'When did you come into the Basin, ah—*Hoolihan*?'

'Just a few days ago. Rode up from Bellero. Did these fellows get anything much in their stick-up?'

'Four thousand, altogether, out of the express safe. But what roused me up was the way they shot the messenger when there wasn't any need for it. He died next day. You know, I've been kind of *looking* for somebody to drift into the Basin. Both sides of that damn' war have stayed pretty well out of my bailiwick, or I would have sat down on 'em long since. But Berry Nicks is no part of an officer. And it's no secret to him that I feel that way. I certainly told him, three-four times.'

'I had to drop one of their warriors in Taunton,' Drago said slowly. 'During the proceedings I got a pretty good look at Mr Nicks. I didn't say anything to him, but I wouldn't be surprised if he's got a rough idea of what I think of him. I—looked at him pretty hard.'

'Who'd you get?' Azle demanded fiercely. 'Not that Wyoming Dees?'

143

'No; this was a dark cowboy they called "The Breed," on the other side; Rust and Wade's side. That Judge Bell in Taunton seems quite a man.'

'It'll take a company, and a good company, of Rangers to settle that fool business,' Azle grunted irritably. 'What makes us so hot, in Parlin County, is the way every two-bit rustler and killer is riding loose now. Of course, the fighting covers them up. Nobody knows who did what. But a company will *just* about handle the deal.'

And he looked inquiringly at Drago.

'You don't *have* to tell me a thing if you don't want to,' he went on, when Drago said nothing.

'Thanks,' Drago told him—his tone grateful. 'If I have to do any talking, or if I happen to need any help, I'm frank to say I don't know anybody I'd rather turn to than the Sheriff of Parlin. Well, right up that cañon went our train-robbers.'

The trail was easily followed now. It was as if the two fugitives felt themselves safe, so far from the scene of their crime. The cañon into which they had gone opened like a great bay between rounded buttes. At the mouth of it, the posse came together again. Azle jerked a thumb grimly.

'Something tells *me* there's a fight in the pot,' he informed the possemen. 'Maybe not tonight, but, unless they do some good, fast riding, we'll hem 'em in by tomorrow.'

Part of that prediction was borne out when, with dark, the posse gave over the trail. They made camp in a hollow of the butte and ate a cold supper from their saddle bags. Azle permitted no fire, and during the night he was up constantly, and prowling about, as Drago, also restless, knew. Near dawn he walked out to where Azle squatted, smoking one cornhusk cigarette after another in the shelter of a pile of boulders.

'I've been wondering about something,' Azle told him. 'Look up yonder. Can you make out something—a kind of twinkle—on the side of the butte, that looks like it might be a pinpoint of fire?'

Drago stared at the place indicated, a spot halfway up the butte on their left. He nodded.

'It certainly *is* a fire! The damn' fools! Men with no more sense than to make a fire for breakfast oughtn't to be *in* the train-robbing business! I guess that's our signal to move, Sheriff? They're likely boiling their coffee by now. And they won't stay there long.'

'That's my idea. We'll rouse the boys and, if you don't mind, you and me can lead off and see if we can't get on the other side of that coffee of theirs.'

Within minutes the posse was mounted and going as quietly as possible up this wide cañon between the buttes. When they came to a cross-cañon, Azle sent the tall, thin 'Whitey' straight

145

ahead with three men. He, with Drago and a cowboy, turned left, and the horses picked their way between the rocks and cactus and mesquite of this narrower, rougher, gash in the mountains. The cowboy yawned continuously and loudly.

'For God's sake, Tim!' Azle addressed him at last. '*Can't* you cut that out? Them fellows could hear you two miles away.'

'Can't help it, Sheriff,' Tim apologized. 'You yanked me out of Parlin at the end of a three-day session, and I ain't had a bit of sleep since I been on the trail with you. Hell with this night-fighting, anyway. I don't mind staying up late to get a crack at somebody, but I'm damned if I like to get up in the middle of the night to shoot 'em. Why'n't you officers hold your battles in the daytime?'

'Those *gunies* up ahead'll like night-fighting a sight less than you do,' Azle said dryly. 'They must think they're in the clear, by now. And we'll land on 'em like a brick smokehouse falling.'

Going almost wholly by instinct through the darkness, Drago and the sheriff presently found a shelving place in the cañon wall, by which they gained the top of that butte on which the firelight had twinkled. It was not so rough up here as it had been in the cañon. They went forward steadily, pretty quietly, at a walk. Drago and the sheriff were sniffing, hunting for the odor of that fire.

Then, a shot sounded far below and to their right. Instantly, it seemed that a hundred rifles had taken up the battle. The echoes crashing in the cañons doubled and redoubled the sound.

'I'll bet somebody shot off his gun by accident,' Azle grunted disgustedly. 'Some half-asleep cowboy like Tim here. There ought to be a law against a cowboy carrying a gun. All he can use it for, anyway, is to hammer steeples into a fence post.'

Tim yawned again.

'Now, Sheriff,' he said soothingly, 'trouble with you is you need your breakfast. And I bet you're homesick for that red plush sofa of yours in your office. *I* ain't dropped my gun, have I?'

Then he leaned in the saddle, sniffing audibly:

'I think I smell coffee!'

'I'll bet Tim'll fight, too,' Azle told Drago, 'if somebody gets between him and that coffee. Let's try it a little faster.'

They pushed the horses forward, then, at a trot. The firing, a ragged rattle, sounded nearer. Then the three of them pulled in short. They were on the very edge of a cliff, the end of the butte here. The firing was below and beyond them.

'Yonder they are,' Drago grunted. 'On that little *cerro*. We can hammer their camp from here.'

'There goes the fire,' Tim observed, with

147

disappearance of the red glow on the little hill they watched. 'Hope they never used the coffee to put her out with ... Well, what's the powders, Sheriff?'

'Whitey and his bunch can work around,' Azle meditated. 'One man up here is good as ten. Tell you, Tim, you're a tolerable shot with a rifle. You stay here and Hoolihan and me'll work down to join edges with Whitey's men. Then nobody'll get off that *cerro*—not with all his teeth and his health and everything. Wait till we're down the butte so's they won't notice us. Then start whanging away at 'em. You got the location of that fire spotted?'

'Yeh,' Tim assured him—and yawned. 'I'll dust 'em.'

Azle and Drago rode to the left, hunting for a way down. The sheriff turned abruptly and called to Tim, who had yawned again.

'If you go to sleep up here, I swear I'll have the whole damn' posse wake you—dusting *you* from down below.'

'They couldn't hit me,' Tim told him placidly. 'I'll be behind a rock. I'll stay awake. I want to get this over and get to that coffee. I *hope* they never spilled it...'

Drago found a long, eroded break in the butte's edge. Button went carefully down, forelegs outthrust, sliding rather than walking. The sheriff let him get well ahead, then followed. They came out on the rocky floor of the cross-cañon. The shooting was steady, if

148

irregular, to the right of them and, apparently, beyond the dome-like hill on which the train-robbers had made their camp.

'Looks like they don't suspicion trouble from this side,' Azle grunted, staring upward through the graying dark. 'If we could sneak up on 'em—'

'Tim has come to the ball!' Drago said suddenly, for from the butte they had left a rifle began to sound with deliberate regularity, rather as if Tim were counting ten between shots. 'They'll be watching this side now!'

And as if in answer to his speculation, someone on the hill began to shoot over their heads. The lead made metallic sound on rocks in Tim's neighborhood.

'Let's try it afoot,' Drago suggested. 'Maybe they'll be too busy watching Tim—or dodging his slugs—to notice us.'

They left the horses in shelter of some rocks and went inching up the hill. Light came before they had covered more than a few yards of the steep slope. Azle grunted in satisfied tone. Drago understood him to say that the advantage was now all with the attackers.

Still the shots came from above, in answer to Tim's fire and to the shooting of other possemen. They made the shelving crest of the hill and waited, flat on their bellies, listening, watching.

Drago shifted a little to whisper to Azle:

'Only one man shooting up there now. He's

shooting fast, to make it sound like two. Either one's been dropped, or he's gone to get their horses while the other holds us off.'

There was a quick thudding of hoofs from somewhere beyond them. Drago lifted himself with carbine ready. And now, in the growing light, he could see a man squatting behind a wall-like ledge of stone. There were the wet, black remnants of a fire behind this man. Drago lifted the carbine a trifle and sent a .44 bullet whining past his ear.

'Drop it!' he called. 'You're covered all around.'

The man whirled, putting a hand to the ground as if to support himself. Drago, with Azle to the side of him, walked up, and the man hoisted his hands slowly as he stood erect.

He was a square-bodied, square-faced towhead, with grim blue eyes and a mouth that was no more than a crayon-white gash in the stubble of mustache and beard. Almost unwinkingly he faced them.

'Where's your partner?' Azle demanded. 'Come away from that Winchester, though, before you start talking.'

He let his carbine down and drew a Colt.

'I'll frisk him,' Azle grunted. 'You might yell down to the boys that we've got one.'

Drago called to Whitey and the other possemen; and the shooting stopped. Up the hill from some concealed attacker came an inquiry about the sheriff.

'He's here!' Drago answered.

'Hell! Then it must have been the other scoun'el that rode off!' the posseman yelled furiously. 'I thought 'twas Azle. He was forking a gray hawse just like the sher'f's!'

Drago turned back to where Azle was questioning the prisoner. The man had his hands down.

'I called him 'Pache, because he looked like one,' he was telling the sheriff. 'Met him a couple of weeks back at Spoon's store in Taunton County. Him and some friends of his. We planned the train-job and we pulled it off. That's all there is to it. He went to saddle our hawses a minute ago and I reckon the dirty son run out on me. So—'

He shrugged and scratched his side. And his hand went on behind him, to reappear with a Colt that, evidently, had been in the waistband of his overalls behind. It flashed up, cocked. Azle whipped up his own gun flashingly, but it was Drago, drawing from the thigh, who fired first. The towhead coughed, leaned forward, and shot once into the ground. Azle swore furiously and caught his left ear between finger and thumb of his left hand. Drago waited grimly with pistol cocked, but there was no need of a second shot. Azle took his hand away and looked at the blood on it.

'The tricky scoun'el!' he said, in a tone almost of admiration. 'He certainly fooled me! I would've *swore* he was naked after I looked him over. Well, we live and learn ... Thanks, Ranger. He would've got me while I was getting him. Let's go see what we can find.'

They crossed to the depression on the other side of the hill, where a saddle lay upon the ground and a bay horse branded Double Slash stood hobbled. The saddle pockets gave up almost eight hundred dollars in bills and gold, wrapped in a dirty shirt. There were other odds and ends, but nothing to show where the towhead had worked. The saddle was a form-fitter with twisted fork and dished cantle.

'Buster's saddle...' Azle said thoughtfully. 'Good hull, too. One of Sam Myres's trees ... And that's a damn' good horse. The Double Slash raises as good horses as the 56, if they don't raise so many of 'em. You know, I bet you when we come to check up, we'll find that part of that *gunie's* tale was straight: he may not have met up with the other four two weeks back, but I wouldn't be surprised a-tall if he really met 'em at Alonzo Spoon's store. And I bet he stole this bay off the Double Slash because he was fast and a stayer. Old Man Tower owns the Slashes and runs it with his two boys to help. If he'd sold this horse, the brand'd be vented. Well—let's see about that trail!'

CHAPTER THIRTEEN

'I'M A PECOS MAN'

When they went down the hill upon the trail of the gray horse, the rest of the posse were gathered about Whitey. He was mounted and staring at the ground where between stones deep hoofprints had scarred softer earth.

That posseman who had mistaken the fugitive for Azle was being examined by the cowboy Tim, who had come down from the butte and gathered Button and Azle's gray on his way.

'You say he was fourteen foot high and when he turned his head he kind of snorted and long flames shot out of his mouth?' Tim was inquiring solemnly. 'Well, then, no wonder you figured it was the sheriff. He's always like that, when he ain't had his breakfast. My notion is—'

'Let him alone, Tim!' Azle commanded. 'You never got any kind of look at him, I take it?'

'I never,' the posseman said sullenly. 'He was about your size and he was riding that gray hawse like a bat and a half out of hell. I just got the one look and I lined the sights on him, then the hawse looked like yours and I figured you was maybe after something. Then you-all

153

yelled from the hill—'

They mounted, overruling Tim's suggestions that coffee would 'go down like as if it was greased.' Whitey and Drago led the way, and for a time the trail was not hard to follow. But they lost it in stony ground, in a welter of shallow arroyos.

Azle stared longingly around, then shrugged:

'My guess is he's heading straight into Taunton County. That would line up with what his pardner said about Alonzo Spoon's ... Line up with that Double Slash bay, too. I certainly would like to hang and rattle with him until we fixed him up with a nice new pine overcoat, like the others—most of the others—already got.'

'Not a bad record, at that,' Drago consoled him. 'Three out of five wiped out. About twenty-four hundred of the four thousand they lifted recovered. And three men for folk to look over, for identification. Hard to believe that none of the three will be recognized, either in Parlin or Taunton.'

'Yeh, that's right. Ought to make out to recognize one out of the three. We'll ride back past the V Up and Down and pick up those bodies. Might be a lead to show who the ones that got away really are. Well! Let's go back to the hill. Tim won't be happy till he finds out if they spilled the coffee.'

When the towhead had been moved, the

posse rebuilt the robbers' fire and ate breakfast, drinking the coffee which, Tim announced triumphantly, had *not* been spilled. During the meal, Azle and Drago and Whitey held a council of war. One of the possemen would ride to the Double Slash and learn if the bay had been stolen. Drago would notify Berry Nicks that the escaped robber had probably headed into his bailiwick.

'Not that he'll do a damn' thing about it,' Azle prophesied sourly. 'But I have got to notify him, just the same.'

'It's been a tolerable sort of day, just the same,' Drago said as he got up. 'Three out of five!'

'And the gang's the same as smashed, too,' Whitey reminded the sheriff. 'Ought to be some reward coming to us.'

'I reckon,' Azle admitted. 'Well, Hoolihan, so long! And before we split up for the time being, I want to tell you I don't know as I've ever met a man I'd like better to side me in an armload of trouble and fighting.'

'Why, same to you!' Drago told him smilingly. 'My notion is, if the taxpayers in Taunton would break down the fence and throw the two counties together, with you for sheriff, there wouldn't be any war between Rust and Wade, and Gotcher and McGinsey. There wouldn't be any need for—my kind.'

'Well, likely I'll be seeing you again before your job is finished. I'm bodaciously glad it's you on the 56, not me. Marjorie Littell is enough to keep an old bachelor worried, and with that breed girl Nita popping in all the time—Uh-uh! Not for Alf' Azle. You ain't careful, you'll find yourself wearing hobbles. 'Course, there's *some* don't mind it...'

Drago patted the brown stock of his carbine and grinned:

'Here's my Old Lady,' he said. 'Well—be seeing you!'

He waved generally to the posse and rode down the cañon. Tim and Whitey, standing together with tin cups of coffee, grinned pleasantly, fraternally, at him. And as he went past, Whitey's murmur carried to him:

'A Ranger! And an old-timer! You can't fool me, son...'

It was good dark when Drago pulled in at the 56 corral. He came up quietly, but Tonto appeared from the shadows near the bunkhouse, called softly to him, then came to stand beside him while he unsaddled Button and rubbed him down.

'Marje said you rode off and left her, going som'r's on a trail you'd cut. She hired a new man today; goes by Hurd. She says she fired you out on the range for not taking orders. That the way it was?'

'Something like that,' Drago admitted indifferently. 'I cut a trail several times in the Parlin side of Needle Pasture. I thought it was the frazzled end of our rustlers, looking for

156

whatever they could pick up. Now, I think it was a couple of strangers who were off their trail, wandering around. A couple of the Parlin sheriff's train-robbers...'

He told of meeting Azle and the Parlin men and of the fight in the hills.

Tonto swore angrily.

'And me out of it! I would have give a month's pay to round them up. Who was with Azle? He's a fighting fool and I bet you when you and him got together that made it *three*!'

'I didn't have much of a look at his posse. But there was a tall, thin man, Whitey—'

'Whitey Stull! He used to be a bullwhacker in the Brushy Country. A good man! Who else?'

'Yawning cowboy named Tim—'

'Tim Loney! That's a fool Irishman that don't have an idee about what ought to scare him. Pretends to be the laziest white man in Texas. But he ain't. And he's surprised plenty of hard cases. I punched cows with Tim, once, over on the Hashknife. We had a tough horse-wrangler and, one day, all of us chipped in and bought a keg of whisky. We had a yaller nigger for cook; freckledest thing *you* ever saw on two legs. We called him Spotted Tom. That night when we was drinking up the whisky, Tom fell off a case of air-tights into the fire. This tough horse-wrangler yanked him out. Tim got up and he yawned and he said, like he was about asleep:

'"Hey, you!" and he belted the wrangler

157

over the head with his gun-barrel. "If that spotted nigger wants to warm hisself, you let him alone!" And you had him . . .'

'Any notions about any of these men?' Drago asked him. 'My tall rustler—"Jones"—for instance? This towheaded robber that said he met the gang at Alonzo Spoon's?'

'I think I sighted that tall fella once, in Taunton. He was talking to a bunch of Gano Gotcher's LL cowboys. But that wouldn't have to mean anything. The towhead I don't place, account there's so many of the breed. Texas—and hell, I reckon—owns plenty cottontops . . . Well, you ready to eat?'

'Maybe I'd better see the Boss first,' Drago suggested. 'Give her a chance to fire me again so it'll be official.'

'Hell!' Tonto grunted. 'I told her that when you rolled your bed I rolled mine. And somehow, even with Clint and this new hand she's took unto herself, she didn't seem to want to do without me. You ain't fired! Come on up and eat.'

Chin was still in the kitchen. He put out a steak and two fried eggs and an array of canned vegetables that made Drago lift his brows.

Chin looked at him and shook his head:

'Hoolihan! Ahhh! Hoolihan not a name. But new cowboy come today. Now I call you Hoolihan.'

'No jump like glasshoppeh, me?' Drago inquired gravely. 'Somebody say *pssssh*! Gun bang yesterday. Gun bang again. New cowboy still on 56. Maybe-so I last, huh?'

'Maybe-so,' Chin admitted. 'I feed you fine. You get killed, you like big steer—plenty fat.'

Marjorie Littell came into the kitchen. She stood, a little stiff and very obviously uncomfortable, while Drago got up and faced her. Tonto, leaning on the door frame, continued to smoke and merely watched her with a small frown.

'Did you—find anything on that trail you followed?' she asked.

'A little,' Drago admitted colorlessly. 'You have cause to put in a bill to Parlin County for my day's work. I rode with Sheriff Azle yesterday afternoon and part of this morning. The tracks I found in Needle Pasture weren't made by rustlers. You heard about the train-robbery?'

She shook her head, watching him stiffly.

'It was like this,' Drago said, then stopped. For Clint had come into the kitchen behind Marjorie and at the words 'train-robbery' he looked interested. 'The combination was held up in Parlin County and the messenger murdered—'

'You couldn't do anything but ride with the sheriff,' she said, when he was finished.

'You say one of 'em got away and headed into our range?' Clint grunted frowningly. 'The towhead said *he* called the other man "Apache" because he looked like one. That

159

would mean he's dark, wide-shouldered, and pretty thick, if the towhead knew Apaches very well ... And they were strangers to our country, going by the way you found their trail circling around.'

Drago made a cigarette and mechanically Marjorie watched the evolution. He was putting the sack away when he noticed her eyes upon it. He looked at her, with a faint smile almost covered by his mustache. But she saw and a slow wave of color came into her face. She straightened and looked past him.

'If you're finished with your supper, I want to talk to you,' she said quickly. 'I'll be on the veranda. Good night, Tonto.'

She turned, passing Clint to go back into the living quarters of the family.

Clint looked at Tonto, then at Drago. He grinned and shook his head.

'The Boss has something on her mind, Tonto,' he said. 'I take it that we're not included in these conferences. That dark train-robber is interesting. I wonder if there's a reward?'

'There's been a reward ever since the other robbery at Mesquite Hill,' Tonto reminded him. 'I reckon it would have to be proved this gang was the same one that done the first job. You got back some of the money, off your towhead, you say, Hoolihan. And there was more on the two killed at the V Up and Down ... Reckon that leaves sixteen hundred or so divided between the two that got clear. There's men in the Basin would crack down on them two for half that much. And the express company never would see a nickel of it, either!'

Drago said nothing. He wondered what Marjorie had to say to him. He guessed that she wanted to explain that he was not discharged. She was the sort who naturally saw a great gulf extending between herself and those she employed. In spite of what he had said to her on the range, she would be thinking, now, that he was no more than a cowboy to be hired and fired, if a rather tougher cowboy than most. So—

He nodded to Tonto and went out of the kitchen. Rounding the house, he found her sitting in a great porch chair and mounted the veranda steps at his catlike, almost noiseless step. He leaned against one of the veranda posts and waited. And when she spoke, he was surprised that she said nothing of what he had expected.

'Those six geldings,' she almost whispered. 'Do you think you could find them easily? There's no chance that the thieves came after you and stole them again?'

'I think they're all right,' he assured her, and told her why. 'If you want 'em rounded up—'

'I do. But not tomorrow. I would like to have you ride into Taunton after breakfast and try to find a stock-buyer named Bates. He is the man who offered me seven-fifty for the bunch.

161

Tonto thinks that's not enough...'

'So do I! If I know anything about horses, they ought to bring you a hundred and fifty a head. You don't want Tonto and Clint to know you're selling the bunch...'

'Not until the deal is completed. You see, I *have* to sell them. And the man Bates is the only buyer who'll take them quickly, for cash. Tonto doesn't understand—'

'You can't blame him, exactly. You tell him he's the ramrod of the 56, but you don't let him rod it. He thinks you get robbed every time you make a buy or a sale. Maybe you do. This deal with Bates looks like that. There's always a bunch of sharpshooters buying; Bates sounds like one of the breed. But you haven't deputized me to do anything but find Bates and—I gather—tell him that you'll sell the geldings. Right?'

'I want you to ride into town without saying why you're going. Find Bates and tell him if he still wants the horses—'

'Will you do a little more than that? Will you let me find Bates and, if I can lift that seven-fifty price a trifle, authorize me to get more for the geldings than he offered?'

'You don't know Bates! He's exactly what you said—a sharpshooter. And I can't jeopardize the sale because I have got to have the money for operating expenses.'

'I won't throw a single extra wheel into your wagon. But there are ways and ways to handle

162

the Bateses of the world. I have met 'em by the drove, the pack and the herd.'

'Very well, then. If you can persuade him to pay more for the geldings—and do nothing to force me to accept less than the price he offered—I don't see how I could object to it. But, to be perfectly frank with you, I don't see why you're interested in 56 troubles; why you've taken so much trouble to help—'

'And I'm not going to try explaining,' he said amusedly. 'I'm not sure that I know. Say that I was born to drop into particular situations and, landing in them, act as if they belonged to me. You've no reason to object! All you have to do is take advantage of somebody's willingness to help.'

He fished the Duke's and papers from a shirt pocket and began the inevitable cigarette. He held out tobacco and papers to her and she accepted them.

'Won't you—sit down?' she asked him hesitantly, as if he had been a guest on the 56, not one of the hands.

He moved to half-lean, half-sit, upon the arm of the chair beyond hers. He flicked a match into flame upon his thumbnail and leaned to her.

'There's one thing you *could* do,' he said slowly, choosing his words very carefully. 'If it's not too much trouble; if it doesn't necessitate too much revising of your ideas; you might think that, however it came about,

163

I'm here and, while I stay here, whatever I see fit to do will be for the best interests of the outfit.'

'But why *did* this come about?' she demanded sharply.

'Telling you that is not in the bargain,' he objected. 'You will just have to bear knowing that the hard-case gunfighter from down on the River is working for you. And now, I'll turn in. After breakfast, I'll ride to Taunton and find Bates.'

'Thank you,' she told him hesitantly. And again, it seemed to Drago, it was as if she spoke to an equal who was offering her a favor. 'And whatever you can do with him, to make him pay a fair price, I—I'll very much appreciate.'

He nodded and turned away. There was a light in the bunkhouse when he approached it. Tonto and Clint and a stocky man of sun-reddened, immobile face, were playing stud. The new hand of the 56 turned his dark head a trifle with the clump of Drago's heels in the doorway. Smallish hazel eyes came impassively to Drago, studied him without expression, then shifted back to his cards.

'I'll up that two dollars,' he said to Clint, pushing in eight matches. 'Account if I got a king in the hole my pair will kick hell out of your jacks.'

Drago sat down on the edge of a bunk when he had unbuckled his leggings.

Tonto turned his hand over and jerked

bristly head toward the new man.

'This is Hurd, Hoolihan,' he said.

Hurd nodded slightly.

Drago looked him over with intentness masked by his careless expression.

'Hurd...' he said. 'You wouldn't belong to the Tarrant County Hurds? I knew the family well, years back.'

'I'm a Pecos man!' the stocky cowboy said grimly. 'No kin in the State I know anything about. I'm a Pecos man and proud of it. They raise 'em big and tough in that country—'

'And wide in the mouth,' Drago put in softly. 'I've known a man or twelve from the Pecos. But, I suppose, if you take 'em by and large, they average up to some other parts of Texas.'

Hurd stared at him, but said nothing. Clint had the deal. He looked inquiringly at Drago, who nodded. The table was shoved over so that Drago could play, sitting on the bunk. Thereafter, for an hour or so, the game seesawed between Clint, Hurd, and Drago. But once he had learned Hurd's method, Drago began to win. Clint he thought a poor player; he simply caught the cards tonight and won on unbeatable hands.

When Drago was nearly twenty dollars ahead, Hurd slammed his cards viciously on the table and announced himself ready for bed. Clint, too, with a rueful glance at Drago's pile of matches, nodded. They cashed in.

'Looks like Hurd and me—with a little help from Clint—kind of put on this *baile*,' Tonto said humorously. 'Lucky as you generally are, Clint, if you'd take a lesson or two from Hoolihan, you'd own the country in a month.'

They undressed and Tonto asked Clint what he planned to do the next day.

'Catch up those mavericks around the Needle,' Clint said thoughtfully. 'And you and Hurd will be free to round up the horses, Tonto. That bunch Hoolihan rescued from the thieves ought to come down closer to the house for the time being.'

'My idee,' Tonto agreed. 'We'll run every head of hawses down out of the hills.'

'I'm going to town,' Drago said generally to the group. 'I promised Azle I'd tell Berry Nicks about that robber breaking into Taunton County. Miss Marjorie knows that I'm going.'

' '*Sta buena!*' Tonto said. 'But don't shoot up the battlers if you can help it. Save 'em till I can come along and help put in the licks where they'll hurt worst.'

When the light was out and the bunkhouse was silent, Drago grinned faintly with recollection of Clint's assumption of work in Needle Pasture.

'He's got that train-robber on his mind,' he thought. 'I hope—for Marjorie's sake—that he can't find him. 'Pache is proved cold-blooded enough, and quick-thinking, to make Clint pretty limber competition for him. But I suppose it's the reward that's riding him.'

And as if his thoughts carried, from the next bunk Tonto's grave voice carried:

'Oh, Clint! If you should happen to run onto that feller 'Pache that Hoolihan told us about, will you kindly remember that cowboys branding mavericks draw their pay at the end of the month—but cowboys that go out shaking a big loop for wild train-robbers, they mostly collect misery right in a wide place where it hurts most? You think about that, tomorrow, up in Needle Pasture, huh?'

'Will you kindly go to hell?' Clint grunted.

CHAPTER FOURTEEN

'GRAND BUSINESS AT SPOON'S'

He had covered more than half the distance to town, and had passed the corner of the 56, when he saw a rider on his left. He watched mechanically for a time before getting out his glasses. Then, recognizing Nita Fourponies, he pulled in and waited. She came down a slope, through a short arroyo, and so to the road. She held her hand high in the ancient greeting of the plains.

'So the warrior's back,' she addressed him.

'Is *that* your road home?' Drago inquired, jerking his head at the gash in the hills out of which she had come.

Her olive face settled in a mask. She shrugged.

'Injun gal live every place. White man like to buy nice bead?'

Drago grinned at her.

'In other words, it's none of my business what you were doing up there.'

She shook her head and the mobile features expressed the ultimate in amazement.

'The man's bright! Just one small hint and he understands everything! Whither away? Town? If you are, and it won't hurt your social position to have me siding you—'

'I'll risk it,' Drago assured her. 'Do you know, I've been thinking about you a good deal.'

'*You* have been thinking about *me*? Shades of my Bronze Forefathers! And why, pray, have you deigned to look down from the heights of the palefaces to the—'

'I was wondering,' Drago told her gravely, 'if you could afford to marry me. I haven't had a chance to talk to anybody about your position, but the general opinion seems to be that your horse-ranch does pretty well. Of course, I'd have to have references before I could consider this seriously.'

'I don't know,' she said. 'You might turn out to be an expensive luxury, and, too, there's the possibility that, even if you didn't cost much to support, you still wouldn't be worth it.'

'Oh, no! There's not a chance of any such opinion as that. Satisfaction is guaranteed. All of my marriages have turned out very well—so long as the lady could afford me.'

She looked at him critically and shook her dark, sleek head.

'You do almost tempt me. Big and dark and rather good-looking—in a crude way, of course ... But still and yet, I think I'll have to stick to Clint Littell.'

Drago looked ahead at the hill over which the road dropped out of sight.

'And will Clint stick to you?' he asked her softly.

'Brother, you're damn' well right he will, if I take him on!' she said, with the utmost conviction. 'He will or I'll come as near breaking his neck—'

'And breaking your heart,' Drago interrupted her.

'Nothing of the sort! Any time I break my heart over any two-legged critter in pants—'

'Words!' Drago scoffed at her. 'Words, and nothing but words.'

He shifted in the saddle and quite openly studied her.

'Well?' she demanded after a long half-minute of the survey. 'What about it? Now that you've looked me over—'

'I don't believe you're going to marry Clint. I—have an idea that you've got bravely over that particular infatuation.'

'A mind-reader, too,' she cried. 'The sum-total of your talents is rather amazing, Mr—ah—Hoolihan. So I've decided against Clint, have I?'

He nodded quietly.

'You have! And for your sake I'm glad. Clint today is exactly what he'll be twenty years from now—except that a lot of his pleasant attractiveness won't be there.'

'Well, now that *that's* settled, what do you think of the new hand—Hurd, isn't it?' she inquired blandly.

'I don't know. He tells us he's a man from the Pecos country and down there they raise some pretty salty customers. I suppose you've heard the old phrase, to "Pecos" a man?'

She shook her head, watching him steadily.

'Well, it means to rub out his mark—I suppose it came of the cheerful little habit they used to have, of dropping a dead man in the Pecos River. Up there the verb is not only in the language, it's in the practice!'

'And still you haven't told me what you think of the new man...'

'Why, I did! I told you the truth. I don't know anything about him. Just why do you think I ought to be worrying about him?'

'I move around a good deal, from here to there. Sometimes I'm there before people know about it,' she said, shrugging. 'It was like that yesterday, when Hurd and Clint were discussing you. Of course, it might just be his

170

natural interest in the man he's supposed to ride with on the spread. But Hurd certainly was interested in you.'

Drago nodded and they rode without words for a mile or two.

'*He* came from the River, too,' Nita said suddenly. 'Did you by any chance marry and leave a gal who had a brother about Hurd's size and general shape?'

'I always married orphans,' Drago told her lightly. 'Rich orphans, of course. That was what attracted me to you. Many a man is fooled by a pretty face, but not the—'

'Hoolihans,' she supplied for him.

'Hoolihans, yes. I always pass up beauty in preference to other qualities—orphan condition, just for instance. No, if Hurd's interested in me, I don't know exactly why that is. Of course, it might be about that orphan asylum I burned down, that time in Montana.'

He shook his head and sighed.

'Of course,' he went on thoughtfully, 'I could ask Hurd—but he might not tell me, and even if he did tell me, he might not tell the truth. You've no idea, Nita, how deceitful the human race is. Well, yonder's town. What are you in for? A spree, or just to get salt and sugar?'

'Oh, I just ride in occasionally to admire the white man's civilization. But today it's to get the mail. I ought to have a couple of new French novels in from New York. Then there's a red silk shirt that's supposed to be on the way

171

from El Paso. They sent me one *they* called red. The damn' thing was really nothing but an anemic tomato. I shot it back to them and informed them that when Nita Fourponies says "red" she means "scarlet"!'

They rode up the street of Taunton, past Dennis Crow's restaurant and the Cattlemen's Bar of Olin Oge. Nita looked at the saloon, then at Drago.

'They seem to remember you there,' she said amusedly. 'Wyoming Dees, in particular ... You know, I've wondered a time or six whether Lige McGinsey isn't a little bit sorry he ever hired that rascal killer. If *I* were The McGinsey, I think I'd wonder how I'd get rid of Wyoming. And if I were Wyoming, I believe I'd watch my trail plumb cat-eyed, for fear Lige the Young Rifleman might decorate the landscape behind a bush or a boulder.'

'"Who sups with the Devil needs a long spoon," they say,' Drago agreed. 'If they managed to kill each other off, that would be the perfect solution. My lovely employer is likely to marry McGinsey if he lives, I take it?'

'And what'—she looked at him blankly—'is that to you? If I read your brand aright, you'll not be long in Taunton Basin. Why should you worry because a girl makes an idiot of herself?'

'Do'no' ... Except I'm the kind of nitwit who seems to stumble under the other fellow's troubles. Of course, a girl ought to be entitled to one or two mistakes. The trouble is, one

172

mistake in the marrying line is about all the average girl can bear. Maybe I'm old-fashioned. Maybe it all depends on the girl. But I have seen a few who married in haste and repented in the traditional way. The experience always marked them, it seemed to me. Well—there's Berry Nicks on the sidewalk. I have a message to deliver. From Sheriff Azle of Parlin.'

'What about?' she demanded curiously. 'Those rustlers?'

He told her briefly, sitting in the middle of the street with the lank sheriff staring curiously at them, of the towheaded robber killed, and the dark 'Pache who had escaped. She did not take her eyes from his face until he was finished.

'No use telling Berry!' she said contemptuously at the end. '*He* couldn't find a charcoal elephant in a snowdrift. He wouldn't go up to it if he found it, if there was the faint sound of *boo*! Rust and Wade put him in just to have a sheriff they could handle. Do you think this man you killed told the truth about his partner?'

'It's a question, of course. He might have lied. Even though the other man did hightail it when he was supposed to be saddling both their horses for the getaway. We found the towhead's saddle by his horse; this 'Pache just threw the hull on his own gray and pulled out to save his own skin. I don't know—but it's

173

Nicks's job to do something.'

'This 'Pache—he was heading into Taunton County when you lost his trail? Heading into the 56 range?'

Drago nodded and lifted his reins. She sat staring intently at him, then pushed her paint horse into a trot and crossed the street. Drago went on to Nicks and stopped Button. He sat with hands folded on the saddle horn, looking at the sheriff.

'Sheriff Azle asked me to bring you a word,' he drawled.

'Azle?' Nicks grunted. For an instant his roving stare met Drago's eyes; then it shifted again. 'Oh. Well, what'd he want? Yelling about Taunton folks doing all the crime in Parlin County again, I reckon!'

Drago told him of the train-robbers, pretty much as he had just told the story to Nita. Nicks shrugged.

'Sounds like a hurrah to me,' he said. 'I been out at Spoon's store. There was a lot of shooting out there. Spoon and some others was killed. Do'no' who killed 'em. And some more men was killed on the road between here and the store. I got a lot of trouble on my mind, without hunting for no train-robbers that Parlin County can't keep up with. But if I run onto the man, 'course I'll arrest him for Azle.'

He seemed thoroughly uninterested in further conversation. He twisted about and slouched off toward the Longhorn. Drago watched him briefly, then turned and rode over to Crow's restaurant. He swung down, hitched Button, and went in. The peg-legged man grinned at sight of him.

There were two or three customers, cowboys and townsfolk. Drago went down the counter until they were isolated from the others.

Crow leaned to him:

'Grand business at Spoon's,' he said in a low voice. 'I was kind of wondering if you and Tonto Peel didn't maybe get mixed up into the edges of that. Way we piece it out, Wyoming and Olin Oge heard Silent Wade and some more of the Lazy R and Half Circle W crew was at Spoon's. So they took out a bunch of gunfighters and cleaned up.'

Drago looked around the room and, finding nobody who seemed interested in their conversation, leaned in his turn.

'Tonto and I happened to know that Wyoming and Olin Oge planned that. So we sent out a kid to the store with word. Wade was ready for Wyoming, and *that* accounted for the men of Gotcher and McGinsey who got wiped out. After the smoke blew away, Tonto and I walked in on Wade's party. They tried to wipe us out, naturally, but they couldn't *quite* get there.'

Dennis Crow stared at Drago very much as Tonto Peel had stared on the night when Drago had outlined this plan. He shook his head at last.

175

'Well, sir, I never would have thought of that one. Fixed it up so they'd have a good chance to kill each other off and soften 'em for you two! What brings you to town today?'

Drago told him, and Dennis Crow nodded.

'Won't be no trouble to find Bates. He eats in here when he's in Taunton. I ain't seen him today, but I reckon he's in town. Wait a minute.'

He walked down the counter and spoke to one of the cowboys. When he came thumping back, he said:

'Bates is getting a skinful down at the Longhorn. That cowboy will tell him you want to see him down here. Now, what else have you been up to?'

Drago told him of the encounter with that tall rustler 'Jones' and his fellows, in Needle Pasture.

Dennis Crow screwed up his face thoughtfully.

'I seen that fellow—ungodly tall with big freckled hands. He et in here two-three times. Let's see—Yeh, he come in with McGinsey and Gotcher once or twice, and by hisself the other times. I never did hear his name. Oh—I got a letter for you. Somebody sent it up from Bellero and I happened onto it in the postoffice. They was holding it for you. So I brought it along.'

He clumped out of the room and came back with a soiled and creased envelope. Drago

176

opened it with more interest than he had expected to feel. There was neither salutation nor signature. Old Keats Tucker had written:

'Attley says tell you he is on somethin lookes like a reel line tyed to thatt cutter you no about ande soon hopes we have somethin goode to writte you nothin else nu butt they are *hott* outt for you son be cairfull the cuppel you no of are now stepping dubble since after you left all friendes sende the best to you.'

Drago read it three times frowningly. So, Sam and Sara were married. They had been married immediately after his escape, it would seem. For this letter had been some time getting to Taunton. And Judge Attley was patiently and faithfully working on some clue connected with that gun of Nevil Jacklin which had vanished in the alley, the absence of which had put him facing a murder charge and the hangman's rope.

'But he can't find anything about that now,' Drago told himself, irritated because of the thrill the thought gave him. 'Somebody friendly to the Jacklins picked up that Colt and hid it just to try hanging me. It would be necessary for the Judge to not only locate that Jacklin man, but make him admit that he had taken the gun—for that reason. And the man who so hated me that he would pick up Nevil's gun and hide it would hardly confess doing it. He'd know what would happen to him the first time a Jacklin got him out in the brush. I'm just a damn' fool!'

He ate his midday meal at Crow's, and, after he had written a brief note of thanks to Keats Tucker, he went out on the street.

Bates, the stock-buyer, he met on the street with the cowboy who had been eating in Crow's.

'Well, now,' Bates said, with a shrewd glance at Drago, 'I don't know about them horses, after all. Time I made Miss Marjorie the offer horse-business was better—'

'That's perfectly all right, Mr Bates,' Drago checked him briskly. 'Times change with all of us and it's as I told Miss Marjorie; she felt obligated, but I wasn't sure at all after the Parlin buyer said what he did about you—'

'Huh?' Bates cried, gaping. 'Schultz said what about me? Why—'

'It's perfectly all right,' Drago told him again. 'I was coming to town, anyway, and Miss Marjorie thought that you were entitled to meet the price—'

'Wait a minute!' the harried Bates yelled. 'What's all this, anyhow? I offered her a fair price—'

'Mr Bates!' Drago said reprovingly. 'A fair price for geldings like those ... *You* wouldn't want me to think you're *serious*! If it costs the 56 a hundred and fifty to drive six head of horses to Parlin, something's wrong with this county besides the weather. And—'

'Did that damn' fool offer nine hundred for

them horses?' Bates cried—face and voice both agonized. 'He couldn't *git* nine hundred for 'em!'

'Then what's he doing? Running some sort of charity?'

'Damn' if I know! But I offered seven-fifty and I'll pay seven-fifty here in Taunton at the livery corral—'

'Then why did you get redheaded about what Schultz said?' Drago asked curiously. 'It's nothing to me; Schultz will serve my turn for all the stock that's to be sold off the 56. But I don't see what kick you've got coming, when he outbids you.'

'I *might* raise that price to seven and three-quarters,' Bates said thoughtfully. 'Delivered here. I wouldn't send a man out for the price. Damn' if I believe I'd make four dollars to pay him, at that price.'

'Well, you can always bid on the next bunch,' Drago drawled. 'Glad to've met you, Mr Bates. And if ever I want to *buy* a horse, I know you'll have something cheap to show me.'

Again he turned; again he was checked by the buyer. And now the real debate began— conducted bitterly on the part of Bates, calmly, if remorselessly, on Drago's part. Eight hundred and ninety dollars was the price they shook hands upon. And Bates agreed to accept delivery at the 56 home corral.

'By God!' the buyer cried admiringly. 'Now,

you ought to buy me a drink, after hanging my hide to the fence like you done. Times certainly look different on the 56. Miss Marjorie got herself a trader when she took you on.'

'I'm no trader,' Drago said modestly. 'I just know what good horses are worth—same as you do. Now that I think it over, eight hundred and ninety dollars—'

'Wait a minute! Don't you go thinking about it, now. I'll buy the drinks and the eight-ninety price stands like we said. I deal with you, huh?'

'You already have! Miss Marjorie didn't have the faintest idea about the price I intended to make you for those geldings. All you have got to do is hand her your draft or the cash and take the horses. All you need to say to her is: "Good morning, here's your money!" And I tell you that they're in better shape, ranging where they've been, than they could have been when you first looked at them.'

They turned into a small saloon behind them for the formal drink that sealed the bargain. Bates said that he would go out to the 56 with a man that afternoon. Drago nodded.

He saw the townsman 'Sam,' whom he had first encountered upon the night of his arrival in Taunton. Sam crowded up to the bar as Bates left. He grinned admiringly at Drago:

'Well, sir, you kind of been making history,' he said.

CHAPTER FIFTEEN

'I'LL CERTAINLY GUT-SHOOT YOU!'

Drago stared blankly at him. He pushed the bottle Sam's way and the little man poured himself a drink, still grinning:

'Yes, sir, you certainly have been making history—ever since you hit Taunton Basin. But I do'no' as you ever done anything harder than put your loop over that Fourponies looker! Ain't many she'd ride into town with—just to be a-riding with 'em. Uh-uh! She's hard to dab a loop on, Nita is.'

'And when,' Drago inquired, 'did Miss Fourponies *do* this? She came to town for the mail.'

'Yeah?' Sam grunted. 'Maybe she came to town for the mail, but she sure as hell never got it. *I* seen you two ride in, and set there in the street talking. Then she rode right across, and in between some buildings, and she more'n fogged it out, going back home.'

Drago stared at him. Casting back to what they had discussed, he could recall nothing which would have sent her out of town, without stopping for the French novels and the red silk shirt she had expected.

'I told her about the train-robbers,' he thought. 'And she wondered if they had turned

181

back into Taunton County; back onto 56. She might have been worried about 'Pache being loose on Marjorie's range ... But—I don't know.'

In this small bar where they stood drinking, the train-robbery was under discussion. Some of the V Up and Down men who had killed the two robbers were well known here. And word of the fight with the towhead and 'Pache had already reached Taunton. So far, Drago gathered, none of the dead men had been recognized.

'Out-of-the-country men,' the bar-tender said wisely. 'Else somebody would have placed 'em before now. Old Hard Hat Worrell of the V Up and Down, I bet you he knows every puncher from Camel Flat to Bellero and crossways.'

Drago drank and kept silent. It seemed that Taunton had not heard of his presence at the battle and he was as well content not to be noticed. He was standing with back to the door, hunched upon the bar with glass between his hands, when instinct—he was sure there was no sound—impelled him to shift his gun-hand slightly and rest it upon the butt of the Colt under his arm. Then he turned his head quickly—in time to see a man disappearing from the street door. It might have been some cowboy looking in, but he pushed back his glass. The wolfish instinct that comes to the man on the dodge, as it comes to the hunted animal, moved him now.

'It may not be a thing,' he told himself. 'But in Taunton I don't *think* I want to take any chances. So—'

He moved quietly, without change of expression, down past the half-dozen men who were still discussing the train-robbery. He stopped well down the bar, near the back door of the place and, with hand near the open front of his shirt, waited for what might come.

He watched both doors, the front and the back. But the rear door had most of his attention. Something told him that if an attack upon him was intended, it would logically come from the alley-entrance of the saloon. That man who had looked in would believe his victim would be more watchful in the other direction.

His guess was borne out when, with the slightest rasp of feet upon hard dirt, Wyoming Dees slid into the rear door. His hand was down along his thigh. In the gloom of the place Drago could not see whether that right hand held a gun. He drew his own swiftly; so smoothly, easily, that the men at his elbow did not observe the motion. And then, while Wyoming stared up the room, toward the spot where he had been, Drago began to polish his cocked weapon with the end of his neckerchief. The muzzle was pointed directly at Wyoming Dees.

Seconds passed while the bat-eared gunman

frowned intently, his head moving from right to left as he studied each back along the bar. Drago coughed softly and with the small sound Dees tensed. His narrow, dark eyes shifted flashingly. Drago smiled at him, a small, utterly humorless lip-stretching. With sight of that leveled Colt, Dees's thin mouth sagged a little. But he was not one to be thrown off-balance easily. Drago had not thought him nervous. Dees would quickly 'size' any danger that faced him, and move quickly in the direction and the fashion best for him.

Now, caught at a disadvantage, he moved that half-concealed right hand; moved it back a trifle, so that it was completely hidden from the view of any in the bar-room.

Drago understood and his thin smile widened:

'Hello, Dees,' he said evenly. 'Didn't you expect to see me—down here?'

Dees said nothing; merely continued to stare with murky, murderous eyes.

Drago's grin was unchanging.

'Come on in, man!' he cried. 'Don't stand there like a bashful kid. Come in. I'll buy the drinks.'

Dees's hand—that concealed hand— twitched. But it was not, Drago thought, because all along the bar men had turned at sound of his name and sound of the tone which Drago used. He was ramming that Colt of his into his waistband, in back. And when he stepped forward his huge hands were swinging loosely at his sides. With sight of them both, Drago did flashing magic with his own Colt. His hand lifted—Dees watching steadily with those reptilian eyes—and the pistol vanished with only the faint creak of the holster-spring to tell of its settling under his arm.

'All right,' Dees said, with a kind of harsh good-humor. 'All right, you can buy me a drink. Maybe I'll even buy you one. Just because I'm going to rub out your mark is no reason I won't drink with you.'

'No reason in the world,' Drago agreed. 'Especially when you'd have to catch me asleep, or standing with my back to a door, to do that rubbing out. Step up, man. Don't let my fierce face scare you off. I've been out killing horse-thieves and the like; when I'm cleaned up you wouldn't know me from a preacher! What'll it be—*Four Roses*? I always did believe that was just the right amount of roses. But I told you that, the first day I saw you. Remember? It was in the Cattlemen's. And that reminds me—how's your friend and fellow-thug, Olin Oge? Not so well, I trust? Was he one of the gang that got shot up when you boys tried to bushwhack Silent Wade at Spoon's?'

Only the satanic grin he turned upon Dees bore even the semblance of good humor. His tone was drawlingly contemptuous—the sort of tone a grown man might use, addressing a windy youth.

Dees's dark face was darker than normal, with congested blood. Thickly, he said:

'I think I'll gut-shoot you. Let you put in a half day at the dying; yelling your God-damn' head off for somebody to put a slug through your head and let you out. Yeh, I'll certainly gut-shoot you.'

Drago laughed. Left-handed, he drew the bottle toward them and held it over a glass. He looked inquiringly at Dees:

'Say the word, Single-Barrel. A hard-tie man wouldn't know what you can stand. Do I fill her clear up? Make this a kind of special occasion? Say the word...'

'You are—almost a funny hairpin,' Dees said very slowly, his voice even thicker, shakier, than before. 'Yeh, *almost* funny. I damn' well know I'll gut-shoot you!'

They had the attention of every man in that little bar-room now. For those who had not seen or heard the first of this meeting had been jogged to notice of it, by those who had seen or heard. They stood together, then, each with his glass in left hand, each watching the other with hawk-like intentness.

Suddenly, Drago's grin widened, became thinner:

'That trick of yours—ramming a gun into the back waistband—reminds me of a towhead I met the other day. I met him yesterday, if you want to get the dates exactly straight. He was a

186

two-bit train-robber and, along with the sheriff of Parlin County, I ran into him on the edge of the 56 range, Wyoming. He put his hands up and stood search, when we took him. Then he saw his chance to get a cutter out of his back waistband and he pulled—pretty fast, too, for Taunton Basin.'

'Yeh?' Wyoming Dees snarled. 'He pulled and—what?'

'Nothing—to speak of,' Drago said in a careless tone. 'I slammed one in his face, he keeled over, and the funeral will be soon. It's nothing to talk about, as I said. I just thought I'd mention it to you. From the way you're packing that second gun of yours, I thought you might be kin to him.'

He lifted his glass formally, said '*salud y pesetas*!' and tossed the whisky down. Nothing he had done since arrival in the Basin had given him the juvenile pleasure that he knew now, as he stood like a man before a dangerous animal, poking it with one hand, holding it in check with another. Wyoming was on the ragged edge of murder. Drago knew it and that knowledge amused him enormously; gave far more lift to him than the stinging corn whisky. He spilled silver on the bar and waved the bottle invitingly. Wyoming snarled—like that savage animal to which Drago had compared him.

'I'll buy this one. That evens us. Rake that money in.'

'How about moving over to the table yonder, and finishing the bottle?' Drago inquired politely. 'That is, if a dally-man can stand the half of a quart, all in the same week...'

'Yeh? Yeh?' Dees yelled. 'Here—you take this drink I'm buying. Then we'll see about the quart business. Nosey! Bring us two full quarts. We'll find out about this fella's insides. You better watch yourself'—he glowered at Drago now—'else when you get into the bottom of the first pint, you'll probably fall over and some sick Mexican'll roll you for them funny-looking chaps you got. I said a Mexican, because nobody else'd wear the damn' things.'

A highly nervous bar-tender brought the bottles and opened them, while the two drank formally. Drago surveyed the quarts critically and shook his head. The bullet-pierced black hat was shoved well back on his dark head.

He looked genially at the bar-tender.

'I take it you're Nosey ... Mister Nosey, it may even be? Well, sir, be that as it may and possibly is, my advice to you is to collect the price of one quart from him, now, before he begins to pour that liquor down his neck. For when a rimfire man like Wyoming begins to match drinks with a Texas *vaquero*, he's likely to end up his fourth drink by not recalling that he ordered the whisky...'

Wyoming snarled again and threw a gold

188

piece on the bar. Drago matched it smilingly. Then each picked up his bottle and glass. While the bar-room watched breathlessly, they crossed to the rickety pine table that stood against the far wall. They sat down at the same time, rather like figures moving in a drill.

Drago smiled at Wyoming:

'Want to take that hogleg out of your waistband and put it back in the holster? Not that *I* mind hideouts—when I happen to know where they are...'

'I'll wear my cutters to suit me, not you!' Wyoming informed him flatly. 'Pay you to mind your own...'

Drago nodded and looked for Sam, who had been standing far up the bar when he moved to the back of the room. But Sam was not in sight. So he picked out a solemn cowboy who stared at them with the roundest of china-blue eyes. He beckoned and the cowboy came reluctantly toward the table, moving with soft *clink-clump* of spur rowels and high heels, and with the manner of one who approaches a deathbed.

Drago regarded him benignly, but the cowboy waited stiffly.

'Young man,' said Drago, 'do you know a short, fat, red-faced stock-buyer using, in this part of Texas, the go-by of Bates?'

'Yes, sir, I certainly do,' the cowboy answered. His tone, like his manner, was that proper at a funeral. 'And I seen him just a spell back, too. Yes, sir!'

'Do you mind going out and finding him for me? I'd like to have you tell him that Mr Hoolihan, stock-seller-in-chief of the great 56 ranch, intended to ride out with him. But a small matter'—he looked thoughtfully at Wyoming, then back at the cowboy—'occupies me at the present moment. It may take ten minutes; it may require as much as a half-hour, though I doubt that last figure. But, the point is, I'll not be riding out to the 56 with Mr Bates. Tell him for me that he can take his man and go out. And say that I trust he'll remember the exact terms of the bargain we made, and hold to them. The alternative being—'

'I can tell him about whut you mean,' the cowboy interrupted. 'But I wouldn't make out to tell him the way you're saying it.'

'That's of no importance. You give him the gist of the message and say that, if he doesn't follow the arrangement we made, to the letter, it will be my not unpleasant next chore to shoot him in the exact geographical center of those checked pants he was wearing when last I saw him.'

'Yes, sir!' the cowboy breathed. 'I—I certainly will tell him. Leastways, I certainly will try.'

'Thank you. Have a drink on me at the bar—unless you'd like to sit down with us, here?'

'*No, sir!*' the cowboy said emphatically. 'I—

I'll have one at the bar and thank you.'

Drago's hand twitched and a silver dollar flashed through the air, to be caught mechanically by the drink-dispenser, who was staring, like the rest of the room, at this impending duel.

'And, now, Mr Dees,' Drago addressed his enemy courteously, 'about that drink . . . May I pour you one?'

He filled their glasses and they emptied them. Wyoming put out a huge hand to the bottle and lifted it. He faced Drago with contemptuous jerk of mouth and poured the second drink. Thereafter, each pouring in turn, they drank until the first quart was gone. Drago drew the loosened cork from the second bottle and grinned at Wyoming.

There was the slightest haze between him and the McGinsey gunman. So much the whisky had done, but no more. He studied Wyoming shrewdly, noting the laxing mouth, the glassiness of the murky eyes.

When they finished their first drink from this second bottle, he sighed:

'I forgot to warn you—my people came to Texas from North Carolina. Up in those hills a ten-year-old who couldn't pass for a two-bottle man was dropped into the French Broad River, with a jug of sarsaparilla tied around his neck to make sure he'd never come up again and disgrace his family. I'm sorry I didn't tell you about that before. But if you want to back out, now—'

'You got a long tongue!' Wyoming said thickly. 'Pour the drink or le' me pour it. Any Texas man can out-drink me—'

The second quart went down in jerks. They had an audience, now, that seemed to include most of Taunton. Drago saw peg-legged Dennis Crow in the group at the bar. Crow's face was grim, a trifle anxious. Drago caught the restaurant man's eyes and smiled faintly.

Then Wyoming leaned suddenly across the table and banged his big fist so that the bottle jumped.

'I never liked you when I first set eyes on you!' he said blurrily. 'I took one look at your damn' face and—'

'Of course you didn't!' Drago agreed. His own voice was liquor-thickened. 'No rattler ever liked the man who'd smash his head. If you hadn't felt that way, I'd have been ashamed of myself. Nobody but your breed of snake could put up with you. Take a drink!'

He poured Wyoming's glass brimful and the squat gunman scooped it from the table, splashing whisky. Drago watched, to be sure that this was drunkenness, not pretense. Certain that it was, he leaned back and surveyed Dees critically.

'He can't shoot; he's not fast on the draw; he won't take a chance with a man who's in front of him,' he said—in tone to be heard the bar-room over. 'Finally, he can't handle his liquor.

And yet'—he paused, to be sure that those Gotcher-McGinsey factionists certain to be among the crowd could hear—'they tell me he's the best man in Taunton Basin!'

'Who's best man—Taunton Basin?' Wyoming grunted, tilting his head to look up squintingly at Drago. '*I'm* best man—Taunton Basin! Think Gotcher's somebody? Think McGinsey's somebody? Ahhh! Two nitwits! Wyoming Dees, by God! Wyoming Dees's best man—'

Drago stood. He looked around at the faces which ringed the table half-about. He saw a mixture of expressions. Men were in that group who eyed him coldly; others were merely curious; perhaps half-grinned at him in friendly fashion. He turned to Wyoming and found him getting the gun from his waistband. He watched the sleepwalker's motions with which Wyoming put the Colt on the table, then leaned.

His hand pushed the cocked gun down flat, while his thumb slipped between hammer and frame.

Wyoming swore in a monotone and tried to free his hand.

'Goin' kill that son!' he said slowly. 'Goin' kill him.'

Drago twisted the Colt away from him and let the hammer down. He shoved it into his own waistband and moved to get the second gun out of Wyoming's holster. He caught the gunman, then, by his waistband, and drew him up. Wyoming's knees were without stiffness. Drago held him by sheer force upright. He slipped behind him, using both hands to grip him. The crowd opened as he carried Dees up the bar-room and outside. Wyoming only mumbled over and over that he would kill him.

There was a watering-trough before a store, two or three buildings down-street from the saloon. Drago carried the muttering Dees down to it and dropped him into the water. When he turned, he found the sidewalk before the saloon crowded with men who had followed him out. These came slowly down to look at the splashing gunman, who had hooked a hand over the trough and was trying clumsily, unsuccessfully, to sit up on the slippery bottom of the great, hollow log.

'Eventually, I'll kill him, of course,' Drago told the watching men. His tone was thoughtful. 'But taking advantage of him now would be too much like the regular Taunton Basin style of murder.'

He moved slowly off and had gone a half-dozen steps when he saw Lige McGinsey, appearing on the street as from some saloon or store. McGinsey looked blankly at him, then seemed to observe the crowd beyond and, last, Wyoming Dees splashing feebly in the trough. He stared; scowled; began to move more quickly that way. Drago turned to watch. When McGinsey came up to the trough, he looked at his chief killer, then at the silent watchers.

One of these moved officiously toward the Walking M owner. He said:

'He done it, McGinsey! *Him!*'

McGinsey put out his hand to catch Wyoming's. But Drago, coming silently and quickly up behind him, tapped his arm.

'Let him alone,' Drago commanded. 'If he wants to break the habits of years and take a bath—you let him do it.'

CHAPTER SIXTEEN

'HOOLIHAN'S GOT TO GO!'

McGinsey stared as on that other night, in the 56 stable, with dark, handsome face near-demoniac. But he caught himself quickly. His tone was almost even when he inquired:

'*You* are telling me what to do?'

'You know I'm telling you what *not* to do; just as you know you're stalling until you can decide what to do about it. It's hard for you—naturally! Because I'm not out on the range somewhere, with my back to you. Don't you ask questions, McGinsey. Not when we both know the answers to them. Tell me, if you want to, that in your opinion you and Gano Gotcher are loud noises in Taunton Basin. Tell me how you will have me ganged or bushwhacked, for getting in your road. Tell me that and—'

He laughed suddenly, with a note of genuine amusement, like a man who had suddenly recalled something:

'Tell me that and I'll almost worry. A threat like that might have scared me out of the Basin, if Wyoming hadn't got just drunk enough to tell everybody in Taunton that you and your friend Gotcher are just two—what did he say? Oh, yes! Two nitwits. And that he's the best man in Taunton Basin. You can understand that, thinking as I do of Wyoming's caliber, it'll be a trifle hard for you to worry me. For *I* think Wyoming was telling the truth: he *is* a better man.'

McGinsey regarded him blankly—but not without first bestowing upon Wyoming a quick stare. Wyoming, now, had got both hands up to the edge of the trough. He had managed to find a hold for his high heels upon the trough bottom. He was squatting. With some trouble, he stood erect, swaying. Instinctively, he lurched with hand out and touched McGinsey's sleeve.

McGinsey stepped back and Wyoming, missing his grasp, fell forward. His chin struck the edge of the hollowed log. He fell face-downward in the water again. McGinsey turned and the watching men opened a path for him. Drago looked at Wyoming, who was grunting and splashing in the trough again. He nodded—Drago—and went on down the street. He crossed over to Crow's restaurant. He was sitting on the first stool at the counter, ordering coffee from Sam, when Crow came in.

'Well!' the peg-legged man said explosively, stopping before him. 'You just about stood the town on its ear today and kept it there a-staring, now, didn't you?'

Drago grinned and lifted the thick cup which the gaping Sam had shoved across to him. He drank half the scalding black coffee and let the cup down.

'It's like this,' he said slowly. 'The two sides to this war have come to think that they're all that counts in the Basin. And they've managed to make everybody else believe that. They're tougher than anybody else. Average good men have been pretty slow to tackle even a poor man, if he wore the brand of one side or the other. I've seen that happen before in feud neighborhoods. It's one of the reasons for a feud lasting. Usually, more or less by accident, somebody shows up the feudists. Then the outsiders gang up on both sides and clean 'em out. All I was doing, today, was showing up Wyoming Dees and his boss, McGinsey. Maybe it will have an effect. Maybe some man who's been wondering if he wouldn't have a short chance with these imported gunmen will be encouraged to crack down on one of 'em. Anyway, it didn't do any harm.'

He finished his coffee and signaled Sam to

197

bring more.

Dennis Crow sat down on a stool and openly regarded Drago as if he were a strange and interesting animal. At last, he shook his head resignedly:

'Well, you beat me. I never run onto a man that took so much trouble over other folks' affairs. How do you feel about the 56, anyhow? Going to—stay on there?'

He was not looking at Drago, now. His bland face was turned toward the back of the restaurant.

'No. Not any longer than necessary. I'm a saddle-tramp. My kind's not likely to settle down. I like Tonto and he's bucking more than any one man ought to buck. So I'll stick until the 56 looks happy, then—'

He shrugged and lifted the coffee.

Dennis Crow turned his head slowly. His belligerent eyes were narrowed:

'Even a saddle-tramp could find a worse place to settle down on. If he was your kind. Marjorie—'

Drago got up and fished for silver in his pocket. He was in no mood to discuss Marjorie Littell and her attractiveness.

'Marjorie is a fine girl,' he said heartily. 'Don't know that I ever met a finer. I reckon I'd best be getting back to the ranch. Bates has gone out to buy some horses. Berry Nicks will arrest any train-robber who comes into Taunton jail and surrenders—with the understanding, of course, that the man has to lock himself in a cell without any Nicks help. So my errands in town are done—'

'The two quarts and ducking Wyoming and calling McGinsey you just count for amusement, I take it?'

'Just a sort of *pelón* for the day,' Drago assured him smilingly. 'A little extra like the pair of galluses we used to get when we bought a pair of breeches.'

Sam was down the counter, waiting on a cowboy.

Dennis Crow propped himself on the stool and regarded Drago owlishly over the arm on which he leaned:

'*Like* I was about to say, Marjorie is entirely too fine a girl for the like of Lige McGinsey. Everybody, seems like, can see that but Marjorie. I have kind of hinted something to that effect. Tonto has come right out in the open and told her he aims to kill McGinsey. Even Clint has said his piece. But to my notion that's not the way to handle it. Trouble is, she's got nobody to take his place—big and good-looking and smooth-talking like he is. Now, a man like you—'

He stopped short when Drago faced him tight-mouthed and grim of eyes.

'Listen to me, Dennis Crow,' Drago told him slowly, with bitter emphasis. 'Listen well, for it's the last word I'll be saying on the subject. I know what you think of her. You wanted me to stay in the Basin and take on with the 56, not for any particular friendliness you felt at sight of me. You figured me for a sort of human wolf who might be persuaded to do some killing for the 56's benefit. I know that!'

'Ah, now—' Crow began awkwardly.

'I know that—and I don't blame you. A gunman to fight gunmen is the regular thing. And the 56 was in sore need of a few loose-holstered hairpins. You thought that, even if I got myself rubbed out, I'd take along a few of these hard cases and that would be so much to the good. Maybe you hoped I'd tangle with McGinsey and kill him. What happened to me wasn't important—so long as I fought awhile for the 56. All because you think the sun rises and sets in Marjorie Littell! Well—'

He grinned openly, if without humor, at the red-faced, squirming restaurant man.

'I understand how you feel because—because I feel very much the same about her. Nothing personal! Don't get that notion. It's just that I think she's about the finest woman I've ever seen, and working like the devil at a man's job that's far and away too heavy for her. It makes me want to slide in and take as much of the load off her as I can. As I said, it is *not* any foolish feeling of—of—It's not in any sense the kind of feeling that—I don't know how to express this, exactly . . . I feel like—well, as if I were an old friend of her father's, say. Anxious to help and—'

200

'I know exactly how you feel,' Dennis Crow assured him gravely. Embarrassment was gone from his face now. He nodded. 'I know ex-act-ly. You're sticking on the 56—'

'Because it's too big a load for a girl to pack,' Drago said, eyeing Crow suspiciously. 'No other reason. What other reason *could* I have? A man like me; with the kind of back-trail I've got. Any other feeling would be pure nonsense. I know it and you know it. As soon as the 56 is rocking along quietly, I'll be on my way to the top of the next hill. And I don't want to have to discuss this again!'

'You won't have to. You have made it absolutely clear. I know just how you feel and—and I'm glad you feel that way, and—and maybe you'll believe I got quite a friendly feeling for you, now. No matter what I might have been figuring at the beginning, when I didn't know so much about you.'

Again Drago studied him with suspicion, but there was no reading the blank face.

'She ain't sure about McGinsey,' Crow told him thoughtfully. 'Seems to me like sometimes she thinks she'll take him, and again she thinks she won't. Nita Fourponies keeps her undecided, *I* believe. Nita hates McGinsey like poison; he was one of the damn' fools that figured a breed girl was fair game—and easy—for any white man. He packed a quirt-stripe across his face considerable time, account of that mistake. Nita talks to Marjorie and Lige's

201

price kind of goes down for a spell. But he's smooth! And I'm afraid he'll make the grade with her, one of these days...'

'If we catch him on the 56 like the fellow in *Chisholm Trail*, with a rope in his hand and a cow by the tail'—Drago's tone was very grim—'I promise you he'll be the damnedest looking bridegroom ever *you* saw. And if that lanky rustler I met was using around Taunton with McGinsey and Gotcher—'

He stopped short. That round-eyed cowboy who had carried his message from the saloon to Bates the buyer walked into the restaurant and came straight toward Drago. His grave face held something like worry, now; his round eyes were like marbles. Drago grinned at him, but the cowboy remained solemn.

'Howdy, Mr Crow,' he said to Dennis. Then, to Drago: 'Mister, I heard something a spell back that I reckon's got to do with you. And after the way you showed up that killer Dees—'

When he hesitated, Drago looked at Crow. The restaurant man nodded slightly.

'You can trust Prim the whole road,' he said. 'This is Prim Tower. He rides for his pa on the Double Slash. Prim's a good boy and the Slashes has had about as much trouble as the 56, with the LL and Walking M chewing 'em on one side, the Lazy R and Half Circle W biting down hard on the other flank. What's on your mind, Prim? You can talk straight and plain here, to me and Hoolihan.'

'I was down at the livery-corral,' Prim Tower said, all in a breath. ''Twas after I'd found Bates. After you called Lige McGinsey, for that matter. And I was hunting through my saddle bag for a list of stuff I got to send out when I heard somebody talking in a stall down the line. Never figured it for anything until somebody said right loud:

'"Hoolihan's got to go!"'

'Somebody else said:

'"Shut up, you damn' fool! You aiming to tell the world about it, maybe?"'

Drago grinned and waited for the solemn Prim to go on. Prim, too, seemed to be waiting—perhaps for indication of concern on the threatened man's part. A little irritably, he said that he had sneaked down the line of stalls until he could hear plainly the lowered voices of several men.

'Way they talked, they aim to bushwhack you on the way out to the 56. And they're waiting for Norris—you know him?—to come into town. I couldn't see who it was a-talking, but Norris always has hung out with McGinsey and Gotcher, when he was in Taunton. He's et in here with 'em, Mr Crow—'

'Wait a minute!' Drago grunted. 'Is Norris a god-awful tall man with little gray eyes and—'

'And the damnedest pair of big, freckly hands ever I see!' Prim finished the description. 'He was a sheriff back over in East Texas som'r's, years ago. He helped stick up the county seat bank, Pa says, and got suspicioned. But him and the others shot loose from that loop and got off—but not taking the money. Since then he's been a hired killer. Pa run into him down in Mexico one time when he was buying cows. Somebody give Pa Norris's pedigree, down there.'

'Norris . . . Norris . . .' Drago said absently. 'I place him! He was in the *List of Fugitives from Justice* for years. Bank-robbery and double murder from Westham. I wonder that I didn't place him the other day, when I ran into him. So that's Mr "Gloomy Jones"! Why was this gang waiting for him? Or could you hear?'

'It's him that's to do the bushwhacking. He's got a grudge against you, they said. You kind of branded him some with .44s and he put your name down in a book. They went on talking, but I figured I ought to get to you in case you started to ride out of town without knowing the plan. Way they talked, they expected Norris in right quick. Maybe he's already down there.'

'You haven't got an idea about the men who did this talking?' Drago asked the boy. 'If you have, but would rather not spill it—'

'I got an idee, yeh! It was the LL and Walking M; maybe Gotcher and McGinsey the'selves. It wouldn't be anybody else, seems to me—not talking about Norris and the horses you got back from him and the others and the way you killed two of the thieves. I

204

couldn't swear it was Lige McGinsey talking, but I know it was. I know damn' well it must have been.'

'So do I,' Drago agreed. He was staring blankly at the door. 'And I don't know of anything that pleases me more than this news of yours ... For it gives me a crack at McGinsey and his pets which won't be like the playing around with Wyoming Dees! Can I get into that corral from the back?'

'You ain't aiming to try it alone?' Crow snapped. 'Man, that bunch'd just love to see you light on that 'dobe wall. They'd have you down off it, shot to doll-rags, before you had more'n lit! There's, anyhow, four-five of 'em up there. Maybe more that can get into a fight. Tell you, I got a old double-barreled ten-gauge. It's kind of old. I ain't shot it off since I shook out the loads at Two-Card Frio couple years back, when Frio got sore over a stud-game we'd staged in the Cattlemen's. But I bet you it'll hold down on one of them Gotcher and McGinsey men as neat as it done when I peppered Frio.'

'I'd like to have you,' Drago said, not altogether truthfully. 'I'm not intending to gather Norris's tail-feathers—I mean, that's not all I'm after. I want to find out what is bringing him to town. What that gang is planning to do on the 56—if the 56 is their next bull's-eye. And if I can catch him with Lige McGinsey, fine!'

'I'll meet you out back, with the shotgun,' Dennis Crow said curtly. 'Drift through the kitchen.'

'Thanks a lot for bringing me the word,' Drago told Prim Tower. 'Maybe it'll turn out to be a tolerable job of work on the Slashes' account, too. See you!'

'I'll go along if you want me,' Prim volunteered.

'No, Dennis Crow and I will be plenty. More would be hard to cover on the way to the corral. But thanks, just the same.'

He went through the kitchen and found Dennis Crow standing impatiently behind the restaurant. Crow slapped his loose pants-leg.

'My gun's sawed-off,' he explained briefly. 'Let's go.'

He led the way along the backs of buildings until they stopped at the edge of an open stretch that was walled on the far side by a fort-like structure of 'dobe, blank on this face. He gestured briefly:

'We can hoist up over the wall and drop into the yard. We can pick us a place where nobody's apt to see us drop.'

Drago looked to right and left and, seeing nobody moving, stepped into the open. They made the wall and went around it quickly, listening. When they were opposite a line of covered stalls, Dennis Crow gave him a hand up. Drago caught the top of the wall and looked over.

To his left was the straw-littered yard. Except for a Mexican asleep in the shade of a building near the street, the yard was empty. Just below he could see the line of rent-stalls. He drew himself up and put a hand down to Crow. The restaurant man made harder work of getting up, with his peg and shotgun-stiffened other leg. But when Drago slid over into the yard Crow came down quickly and easily.

Now Drago could hear the mutter of voices up the stalls. He and Crow began to move that way. A harsh command sent them into the nearest stall. For that rasping voice said:

'Look out and see if you can see him coming. Take a look at the back. He won't ride up the street.'

A short, sandy man came out into the yard and walked limpingly toward the wide front entrance of the corral.

The rasping voice continued irritably:

'Didn't he give you a notion about what he found out? I swear! He gets mysteriouser every day. Old age, maybe. Funny that four of 'em couldn't rub out that Hoolihan's mark, between 'em, when they had him out where nobody never would've found out what happened to him.'

'What d'you fool with him, for?' a lazy drawl inquired. It carried over the stall-tops quite plainly. 'Like you said, he's getting old. He was a good man, one time—'

207

'He's the best damn' man of the pack of you yet!' the rasping voice stopped him flatly. 'And that goes for Wyoming, too! Wyoming could shade Norris on the draw. Likely, he might out-shoot him cracking at a bottle. But Norris has got something you nor Wyoming nor any of the rest of you ever will have. That's judgment! Yeh, he's slow, but he's the old pacing horse that *gets* there in the end. Wyoming's a lightning gunslinger—and what happens to him? This Hoolihan takes his damn' cutter away from him and chunks him into the stove at the Cattlemen's. Today, he catches him trying to do a dry-gulching and makes a fool out of him at drinking. Chunks him in the watering-trough!'

'And then calls McGinsey,' the drawling one added, with a surprisingly pleasant laugh. 'He certainly done that!'

Footsteps in the yard drew Drago's eyes. He looked cautiously out past the edge of the wall. The limping man came toward him, but looking up sidelong at the tall, calm rustler whom he had known as 'Jones,' and now knew as Norris.

The pair went into the stall where—Drago guessed—Gano Gotcher of the LL waited with one of his killers. Drago was about to beckon the moveless Crow, who stood now with shotgun across his arm. But the rasping voice—which he took for Gotcher's—sounded in another command to the limping one,

208

ordering him to sit outside the door and keep watch.

The voices dropped. Norris's whining drawl was audible, but not the words he said. Gotcher, too, spoke more softly. His questions carried, though:

'How do you know? There's talk of the Slashes and Circle Bar, even the V Up and Down, siding in?'

Again Norris talked, and at the end Gotcher said:

'All right! But if we run into a jam, it's your tail-feathers, fellow! It sounds all right, but—'

'It's a clean-up!' Norris cried. 'I'm too old a hand at this not to know what I'm about.'

'All right! All right!' Gotcher grumbled. 'I'll get the boys off the mesa. You pick up the main bunch on your way out. Now, I got another job for you—kind of side-line you ought to be tickled to take a crack at: this *gunie* Hoolihan. He's in town and he got Wyoming drunk and chunked him in a watering-trough. Whole town's laughing at it. We got to get Hoolihan before we start out on this scheme of yours. Dark'll be soon—'

'All right!' Norris agreed calmly. 'Find out what saloon he's in. Have somebody go in and tell him the sheriff wants to see him outside. I'll get him when he steps out—'

'Uh-uh! None of that. I don't want him got in town. That was Wyoming's notion. He seen Hoolihan at a bar and he sneaked around to the back and found himself looking square into Hoolihan's gun. You couldn't toll him out like that. Besides, I ain't sure about him. I about half-think he's a Ranger working under cover. Either he's that, or he's a lightning gunfighter from som'r's. If he's a Ranger and he's killed in the town, we'll have a company of them sons down on our necks. We don't need any Ranger in our business.'

'Bushwhack him on the trail, huh?'

'That's the idee! He'll be riding out soon. You waylay him from that big rock the trail crosses the arroyo by. Tie him on his horse and lead him off to the *malpais*. Shoot the horse and dump both of 'em into some crack with rocks over 'em, and the Adjutant General can wait till he's grizzle-gray for this fellow to report how things are in Taunton Basin.'

'All right. I'll slide out soon as you stock me up with grub. Chunk in a few quarts. The boys'll be thirsty. When I get done with this Hoolihan, I'll ride on and get the bunch together. Bring up all of 'em to the old place.'

'That's the idee. You can't miss, this time.'

CHAPTER SEVENTEEN

'GOOD-BYE, MR HOOLIHAN!'

Norris was left alone. Looking out of the thickening shadows of the stall, Drago saw a thick-bodied, dark man in wide, white hat walking between the limping cowboy and a lanky, dudish man. Dennis Crow peered at the trio.

'Gotcher in the middle,' he whispered. 'Going down to augur with Norris? The murdering sons! You could think they was figuring how to fix a fence! Gotcher and McGinsey'll be plumb surprised to find their pet rustler-killer down.'

Drago, spinning his Colt by forefinger in the trigger guard, shook his head.

'Let's get out of here! I don't want Norris, right now. Seems to be a habit of mine—passing up chances to kill him. But I've snagged a better notion, I do believe. Let's go.'

Cautiously, watching for sign of Norris, they went back to the wall. Once more they scaled it and moved back toward the restaurant. Crow looked curiously sidelong at Drago.

'The thing we want here is to bring this business to a head,' Drago said slowly, as if thinking aloud. 'A bunch of one-man fights can go on for years without settling anything.

Now, the LL and Walking M—and possibly a half-dozen or so of independent thieves—are planning some sort of lick. I want to know what it is. When I do know, there's the chance of putting a good, big spoke in that wheel. And the way to find out is to trail Norris. So that's what I'm going to do.'

'You think you can trail that wolf, maybe for two-three days?' Crow demanded incredulously.

'I think so. At least, I'm going to try it. He'll wait for me at that rock—I remember it; it sits on the far side of an arroyo about six miles out of town. But when I don't show up, he'll think I've taken a shortcut or ridden off to the side of the trail. He'll be too busy with this other chore of his to spend any time looking for me. So he'll ride on and *I* will be on his heels. I'll ride out after a while with all of Taunton to see me. Then I'll round over to wait for Norris.'

He ate supper in Crow's, and the customers there looked at him curiously. Crow brought Button around to the back and fed the gelding. Also, he packed Drago's saddle bags with food and slipped a quart of whisky in, 'for snake-bite,' he said grimly.

'Only,' he prophesied gloomily, 'the kind of snakes you likely'll meet will bite where whisky can't help.'

The night promised to be dark, Drago remarked with satisfaction. When he saw the lanky, silk-shirted cowboy who had

212

accompanied Gotcher out of the livery-corral, watching him from the door of the restaurant, he grinned slightly.

The dudish cowboy vanished. Drago paid Crow and went out to get Button. He mounted and rode around to the street. The silk-shirted one was loafing at a corner. Drago nodded to him and the lanky man returned the greeting solemnly.

'See you some more, Dennis Crow!' Drago called into the restaurant. 'I'll be riding in from the ranch pretty often, for the next little while. *Hasta la vista!*'

He rode for a mile along the road. But he did not count altogether upon Norris's ambush being at the rock indicated by Gano Gotcher. Norris, he thought, was entirely too expert at this form of murder to be reliable. He might be lying behind any of the boulders which bordered the trail. So, once out of sight of any who might watch him from Taunton, Drago carried his carbine across his lap and held himself ready to sway right or left as conditions dictated.

But he had no sight of the tall killer within the mile. He turned off the road and began to ride a great half-circle in the darkness until he judged that he had come back to the road at about the location of that arroyo indicated by Gotcher. The last few hundred yards he covered at a walk, Button making little sound on the greasewood flat. He reached an arroyo and judged it to be the same that went on to cross the road. Now, he dismounted.

It occurred to him, as on many other similar occasions, that nothing else he had ever known offered the thrill of man-hunting. No other animal could match in suspicion, in alertness, in sheer, calculated savagery, that long, calm man ahead of him. Nor could any of the great cats match the weapons Norris owned.

'I would like,' he thought, 'to have nothing to consider but getting him. I would like to toss a rock down the arroyo to warn him, then get him for all he could do.'

He recalled the day he had made some such offer to Nevil Jacklin; an offer to meet him in the brush of the D Bar pastures for a duel that would prove very completely which was the better man. Jacklin had refused shortly. And if he were to yell, now, to Norris, the lank killer would doubtless jump on his horse and gallop off, to wait for a sure shot at an unsuspecting victim.

He worked noiselessly along the arroyo until the great rock by the trail loomed ahead, a little darker than the surrounding darkness. He sprawled on his belly, then, waiting. A horse stamped softly. It stood in the shadow of the rock. And that sound was followed by a rasping cough.

Drago made himself comfortable. It seemed to him that he could outline Norris's body on the rock. It amused him to consider how hard

214

the killer's perch must seem, now; and how much harder it would be two or three hours from now, if Norris owned patience enough for so long a wait.

Time dragged, but it was not uninteresting to Drago. Every time Norris shifted position, with tiny dragging, scratching noises, he grinned. At last, Norris could endure the rock no longer. He slid down with a soft oath and seemed to be working his stiff body about. He stayed there at the base of his rock for minutes, then there was the creak of his saddle.

'*Hell with it*!' his grim resignation carried plainly to Drago, as the horse moved off.

Drago trotted back to Button and mounted. It was not hard to follow Norris; he was riding quite openly at a trot and it was necessary only to be sure that the hoofbeats continued in the lead; that Norris did not halt warily somewhere, to shred a pursuer with lead.

But he seemed to have no idea that he was followed. With short halts, he pushed into the night. Sometimes he was well ahead; again he pulled in to a walk and Drago matched that pace hardly a hundred yards behind.

With dawn, Drago sprawled upon a hill and watched Norris eat. He drew upon the food Dennis Crow had put in his *alforjas*, and when Norris remounted, after more than an hour of rest, he took up the pursuit again.

It was slower, more dangerous, now. He crossed no ridge without first bringing the glasses into play from its crest. Once the lenses picked up Norris looking over his back-trail, but without the help of binoculars. He stood beside a rock for minutes, his head moving to left and right. Drago could see the movement of Norris's jaw-muscles as the tall man chewed upon his tobacco.

At noon Norris rode down a long slope to a dugout. Before he reached it a cowboy came out with a rifle, then, seeming to recognize the tall man, let it slide down to rest butt on the ground. He and Norris talked awhile. Then the cowboy got a horse from somewhere beyond the rude dwelling and rode off. Norris sprawled comfortably on the ground, after unsaddling the chunky black he had ridden.

'Ah!' Drago said to himself. 'Remounts all along the line. Old-timer'—he slacked the *cinchas* on Button—'you're just going to have to prove that you can outrun and outstay anything Taunton Basin gives that sidewinder.'

The cowboy came back within an hour, leading a tall and snorty roan. There was trouble about the saddling. The roan's grunts and squeals carried faintly to where Drago smoked behind a boulder. And when the saddle was on, Norris would not mount. So the cowboy, with scornful jerk of the head, threw himself into the narrow-forked hull and rammed in his heels.

'Good boy!' Drago complimented him. 'I

don't know that I blame Norris for not choosing that one, before he's softened!'

He watched critically the exhibition of bucking—and of riding—before the dugout. The roan, with head down all but between scooping forehoofs bucketed in a short circle. Those shod hoofs dug earth with each jump and the roan grunted each time he landed— that retching, explosive belly-grunt which the buster translates: *'I—WANT—you! I— WANT—you!'*

But he began to buck less vigorously after two minutes or so; began to run in circles.

Drago nodded, like a paid spectator in a *rodeo* grandstand:

'To a frazzle-dazzle, yes, sir. You rode him to the well-known fare-thee-well, my son.'

The cowboy swung down and let himself slump. Drago grinned. Very well he knew that shakiness the buster indicated, upon dismounting from a big bucker like the roan. The powerful glasses showed the cowboy's hand shaking, as he held out the reins to Norris. He was a slender, good-looking youngster, no more than twenty-two or-three. When he faced Drago's concealment momentarily, his dark, reckless face was clear. He and Norris talked at some length, before the towering killer accepted the reins.

Norris gesticulated; waved his long arm and jerked his stooping head to the east. The cowboy nodded. As plainly as if his voice were

217

audible, he said:

'All right. I'll go.'

He went into the dugout while Norris waited. When he came outside, he was buckling on a pistol-belt. He took the Winchester from where it leaned against the dugout and got his horse. Norris turned to the roan and eyed it for an instant. He mounted quickly and there was relief in every inch of his long body when the roan only fidgeted under his weight.

He and the cowboy lifted their hands in brief salute and rode, the cowboy to the east, Norris vaguely north. Drago saw them over ridges before he tightened his *cinchas* and rode boldly down to the line-camp. Only one thing might be found in the dugout, he thought—something to show the outfit for which that salty young buster rode.

Pistol in hand, he went into the dugout after he had listened for a moment at the door. And, for all his caution, he was almost trapped. The Winchester that came thrusting up out of the gloom to the left of the door all but jabbed his thigh.

Automatically, he went backward—so that the shot did no more than scorch his leg. Automatically, too, he slapped downward with his left hand and, when the carbine muzzle touched the dirt of the dugout floor, he stepped upon it. His pistol came around then. And his eyes, becoming used to the gloom, made out

218

the man lying on the floor.

'Take it easy!' Drago warned the other. 'Every dog's allowed one bite and I suppose every man's allowed one shot. But after that— What are you so nervous about?'

'That, now, you might call a question of the asinine variety, in Taunton Basin,' the sprawling one replied scornfully. He made no move to rise. 'The Basin is the place where that ancient adage about "threatened men" is proved false. All the Walking M hands have been threatened. And threatened men do *not* live long; not in the Basin. Who the hell are you?'

'Well, anyway, I'm not a Rust-Wade gladiator,' Drago informed him. 'I go by Jack Smith and I'll tell you the same thing I've told some others of the Basin: I'm not wearing the brand of either side in this dog-fight that's called a war. I belong to the genus Saddle-Tramp. What's the matter with you? Sick?'

'Compound fracture of the left humerus; simple fracture of the left femur. In other words—'

'In other words,' Drago nodded, looking at the thin face stubbled with black beard, 'a pilgrim from some peculiar section encountered that variety of *eohippus* known as the Texas horse. Doubtless, the acquaintance was brief, if painful. And—don't bother to throw any more of that college education at a stranger than you feel is absolutely essential.

219

Your brand isn't hard to read. I've seen fifty like you. Usually, they die young.'

'There's something to anticipate!' the man said, with a sort of bitter sincerity. 'All right, Jack Smith. You are, by virtue of superior armament and physical condition, the majority opinion here. Make yourself quite thoroughly at home. If you're hungry, there's the remnant of a pot of *frijoles* yonder, with some very durable Dutch oven biscuit, the product of my partner, Mr Utt. He isn't here; if he had been here, the sum of our equation would doubtless have been rather different. You would be far removed from such temporal pangs as hunger, while Bronco—'

'Bronco Utt would be emulating the grave-diggers out of *Hamlet*.' Drago nodded. He had placed the cripple accurately. A 'lunger' was no unusual thing to find on the range. This one was merely possessor of more education than most. And the black eyes, which were the only live feature of his face, showed some sort of sardonic contempt—for himself and his condition, Drago thought, as much as for the world about him. 'I see! You've a good deal of confidence in Bronco Utt.'

'Implicit confidence. But you won't try our beans and biscuit? We're out of beef for the moment. Bronco has been threatening to beef one of our own steers, if necessary. Sorry!'

'I ate on the road. I take it, then, that this is a Walking M line-camp. I didn't know whose range I was crossing. So, when I saw the dugout, I came down to have a look. And, having encountered one or two of your feudists before, I took the precaution of coming in ready for anything. At that, you nearly got me. Taunton Basin seems to have a toughening effect, even upon the humble pilgrim.'

'Too bad I didn't...' the cripple said thoughtfully. 'I have often wondered about the sensation attached to killing a man. But, as you intimate, a Connecticut man like myself, sedentary product of a long line of sedentates—to coin a needed word—is rather a fish out of water in this environment. I have learned to ride and rope after a fashion. They tell me that within a natural lifetime I might make a hand. But setting myself against the like of—Bronco Utt, for example, would result, naturally and inevitably, in my shuffling off this mortal coil. Not that such a conclusion would deter me from the attempt if there were reason.'

Drago nodded, still studying this odd representative of the fighting McGinsey outfit.

'Well, I'm rather pleased that you didn't learn about killing on me,' he said drawlingly. 'How do all these fractures leave you? Able to take a drink?'

'A drink? You don't mean you're offering me a drink? Man! Bring it in. Bronco brought out a quart last week and we finished it at a session. If you know as much about TB as you say, you ought to know that hooch is about the only dissipation a lunger can indulge in.'

'There's a fresh quart in my saddle pocket. And'—Drago shrugged; smiled—'since you're a Walking M man, there's no use wearing the mask any longer. I came out looking for Mr Norris, of the gloomy expression. I'm supposed to catch up with him and, after that, my movements depend on Norris. I don't know what McGinsey thinks of him, but unless Gano Gotcher for some mysterious reason was hurrahing me, *he* thinks Norris is the top of the Basin. Including, he says, Wyoming Dees.'

'I think Lige is of much the same opinion. Norris was here, just a little while ago. He and Bronco were talking outside, about something or other. Bronco caught Norris a horse and, if you'd got here a half-hour sooner, you could have gone on with him. But he won't be hard to follow.'

'Time to kill the quart,' Drago agreed smilingly.

He went out to Button and took the quart from the *alforja*. When he went back, the crippled rider was working up to a sitting position. He was little more than a skeleton, to judge from the brown right arm which lay upon his blanket.

'Pull me over a little,' he said. 'I know every hump in the floor there. Other side of the door, if you don't mind. I can manage to sit for a while. I think the bones are knitting well enough. There was certainly plenty of fever for a week or so. Bronco says he spent most of the time sitting on my head.'

Drago pulled his pallet easily across the floor to the spot indicated. Then he sat with back to the side of the door, and held out the opened bottle.

'I had better rectify a small omission,' the man said smilingly. 'My name is Gunn—with two *n*s. I've been with the Walking M almost a year. When the war broke, naturally McGinsey sent me up here. This is his outside line-camp. He wanted his fighting men close to headquarters.'

They drank and talked and Drago slipped questions casually into the conversation. Gunn answered all inquiries without hesitation. Apparently, he accepted Drago for what he claimed to be—a recruit for the Gotcher-McGinsey side. He said that Norris was the first stranger to visit the line-camp in ten days. Bronco Utt had been away only once in that time—on a short trip to the Walking M house for supplies, four days before. He had heard no news of the way the 'war' was progressing.

'Must be a pretty big lick that Gotcher and McGinsey are planning,' Drago told him. 'Norris is gathering the clans.'

'I guessed as much, from the word or two I overheard. Norris didn't even put his head inside to speak to me. I don't know him very well and he's a suspicious brute. Bronco told me he'd be back before dark and I suppose I'll get the story from him.'

'Probably a raid on the 56,' Drago ventured. If he could get, here, the plan which Norris and Bronco Utt rode to further, there would be no necessity for trailing Norris. Much time would be saved. 'Of course, it might be the Slashes...'

Gunn nodded. The whisky had no apparent effect upon him, except to heighten the flushed patches on his cheekbones under the black stubble of beard that covered his thin face. He shifted a little, bore upon his left arm, and grimaced.

'Might be the 56, the Slashes and the Vs,' he said. 'I heard Norris say that it was the biggest yet—and not a chance of a bobble. You still won't try our beans? Then, if you don't mind, I think I will. But not the biscuits! I don't feel up to those so early in the afternoon. There's a tin plate on that box, with a fork and spoon. And some coffee, I think—cold.'

Drago nodded and got up. He saw the iron pot on the fireplace. But a faint creaking of leather shuttled his eyes back to the pallet. Gunn was sitting straight up, with little sign of weakness. And his left arm was in sight, now—without sling or bandage upon it. He was jerking from a saddle bag beside the pallet, between it and the wall, a white-handled pistol.

The black eyes were very bright. Upon the thin mouth was a cold, merciless grin:

'Good-bye, Mr Hoolihan!' he whispered

mockingly. 'Lige passed on the word about you!'

Drago simply let his knees buckle. He came flashingly to the floor, hurling himself at the open door. He was drawing his own pistol, but Gunn's six-shooter roared before his Colt was out of the holster.

CHAPTER EIGHTEEN

'THE GATHERING OF THE CLANS'

He felt Gunn's bullet in the blouse of his shirt, like the twitch of fingers. He was outside when the second shot roared in the dugout. Flat upon the ground, he twisted, and fired twice over the sill. Following those shots, he heard a telltale coughing within, but there was no time to see if his slugs had struck the target.

Behind him was a distant pound of hoofs. Bronco Utt was coming fast down the slope toward the dugout and his Winchester was lifting.

Drago came swiftly to his feet. In three long strides, he was beside Button, jerking his own carbine from the scabbard. He turned, then, and began to shoot at Utt. The Walking M man fired twice at him, then whirled his horse and, low in the saddle, raced back in the direction from which he had come. Drago watched him go, then turned to stare grimly at the door of the dugout. He shrugged, at the last, and turned back to Button.

'After all,' he told himself, 'it doesn't matter a lot, whether Gunn is alive or dead. I don't think I could make myself kill him, just to keep Utt from knowing that "Hoolihan of the 56" was spying here on Norris's trail. I'd much better spend the time hunting Norris.'

He mounted and sent Button at the lope around the line-camp. And, watching for any sign of Utt, he went fast to the north.

When he had made an undisturbed half-mile, he drew in to search the horizon about him with the glasses. He saw no sign of Utt, but off to the east, tall and murky, a column of smoke rose. He stared at that for a while, then nodded.

'That was what the young buster was about,' he thought. 'The question that interests me is how close are the men that signal is intended to call up? And, if Gunn was alive to tell Utt about me and my would-be clever questions, will the bunch of them come after me?'

He shook dark head slowly, with thought of that icy tubercular. Gunn had known him from the very beginning; his first words had been a part of his calm plan to kill the enemy on Walking M range; his every word and movement thereafter had been skillfully intended to further that determination. Until the instant of producing the pistol—which he had so cleverly induced Drago to put within reach of him—Gunn the cripple had been master of the situation.

'Gano Gotcher may put Norris up at the head of the list for cold-blooded efficiency,' Drago said aloud, 'but if I'm any judge, Gunn was the most dangerous of the Gotcher-McGinsey warriors. Anyway, he certainly took me to town!'

It was not difficult to cut the trail of that big roan horse. It was harder to follow at the pace Norris had used beyond the line-camp. Apparently, he had pushed the roan into the north at a racing gallop.

Ride as he might, Drago found himself far behind with dusk. Darkness came, moonless dark like that of the night before. He went on undecidedly. If the tall messenger rode through the night, dawn would find him far ahead—too far to be overtaken.

Then Drago smelled smoke. He went cautiously in that direction, stopping once to scratch a match and be sure that he was still upon the trail of the roan. It was another line-camp; empty, he learned by noiseless exploration. When he had built up the dying fire, he looked about the untidy interior of the dirt-floored cabin. It was very like the dugout on the Walking M, except that here were the signs of several men using the camp. Drago judged that they had left hurriedly—doubtless in obedience to the word that Norris had brought.

When he went out to unsaddle Button, he heard a horse near-by. He rode toward it and in the darkness caught the unmistakable thudding of a hobbled animal clumsily attempting a gallop. Button overtook the horse easily. It was the big roan which Norris had ridden.

He went back to the camp and made himself comfortable. There was food here—a quarter of beef hanging under the cabin eaves; coffee and beans and cold biscuit. He ate, then searched the cabin methodically. In the pocket of a ragged shirt that hung in a dark corner he found a grimy and folded envelope containing a saddle company's price list. The envelope was addressed to one Henry Weaver and it had been forwarded three times between Billings, Montana, and Taunton. The last address was 'LL Ranch, Taunton.'

Drago nodded at sight of that:

'The gathering of the clans, all right! The question is, now, what had I better do? I think a turn-back to the 56 is on the cards. That bunch is getting too far ahead of me. And there wouldn't be anything to gain by just following them up to some lick they intend to make, and finding myself bucking a dozen of them.'

He went out to Button again and resaddled. He rode for a mile or so until he found a sheltered spot upon the top of a ridge. There, with Button grazing at the end of his lariat,

Drago slept until almost dawn.

With daylight he was pushing toward the 56 at a steady trot. He found no trail of the men who had ridden away from that LL line-camp. But, near noon, he saw a rider on the open range ahead of him and, through the glasses, identified him as young Prim Tower. He turned Button into an arroyo and gained the far side of a steep ridge. Prim, he thought, would not be likely to ride up to any stranger on Double Slash range, these days. So, when he heard the hoofbeats of the boy's horse on the opposite side of the ridge, he called to him, giving the name Hoolihan.

Prim stared at him with round, solemn eyes.

Drago grinned at the youngster:

'Something tells me that you really didn't expect to see me. At that, you came very near to being right.'

'Me and Dennis Crow,' Prim admitted, 'we talked about it after you pulled out. And I told Dennis *I* wouldn't bet a nickel I needed that you'd fool Norris. Not that wolf! Dennis 'lowed you'd come as near as ary man he knew. But he wasn't sure that *that'd* be near enough. But it looks like you done it. Find out anything?'

'I'm not a proud man today,' said Drago whimsically. 'In fact, if you bought me on the basis of the way I feel, the price would be way down from what I would have asked yesterday morning. Did you ever happen upon a

229

consumptive Walking M cowboy—'

'Gunn!' Prim Tower interrupted him. 'That killer! Say, that skinny devil would make Wyoming Dees look like a Sunday School scholar. If he's got a kind bone in his body—I seen him kill a Mexican in Taunton just for looking like he aimed to brush him on the sidewalk. And he grinned when he killed him. He's not so fast with his cutters, but—Where did you run into him? Word was, he got shot up in a fight on the edge of the V Up and Down range and was laid up.'

Drago told him of the affair at the Walking M line-camp.

Prim's solemn face was like a mask:

'You was lucky!' he summed it up at the last. 'Mostly, a man don't expect to have the feller he's drinking with cut his throat from behind. That's where Gunn had the advantage: *he* was bothered about nothing but cutting your throat! That naturally give him a big advantage of decent folks. He drunk your whisky and then he yanked a hide-out on you! It certainly sounds like Gunn.'

'He fooled me,' Drago admitted, 'and I don't know that I bear him any hard feeling—if he's still alive. I was trying to hoodle him and he turned it around and hoodled me. Now, I'm headed for the 56. I think it would be a good idea, Prim, for you to hightail home. Tell your father that Gotcher and McGinsey are up to something. Tell him all you haven't already

230

told him about Norris.'

'I'll do that!' Prim said nervously. 'And my road home is the same as yours for a piece.'

After the boy had turned off, Drago met nobody until, near dark and close to the 56 house, he encountered Tonto Peel and that alleged product of the Pecos region, Hurd.

Tonto pulled in with a wolf-howl at sight of Drago. Hurd merely stared blankly at him.

'Well, stranger!' Tonto greeted Drago. 'I thought maybe you had gone along with some of our horses—the ones that nobody ever saw again. Where you been?'

'Here and there; around and about.'

Drago found himself hesitant, before the surly new hand, to speak freely of his trailing.

Tonto seemed to understand this. He did not press the subject. Instead:

'What kind of stunt did you work on that sharpshooter Bates?' he demanded. 'He come out and he had less to say than I ever dreamed Bates could get along with. He looked at them hawses you took off your long-coupled rustler and he handed Marjorie eight hundred and ninety dollars. He did kind of make a moaning noise or two, but he paid her cash. *I* don't know how you worked Bates to pay an average fair price. More than that, I don't know how you ever persuaded Marjorie to let *you* handle that deal. Mostly, you'd think she was hell-set on handling sales herself, so that she could lose money on the deals.'

'How's Clint?' Drago inquired. 'Did he get those mavericks branded?'

Tonto made a disgusted sound deep in his thick chest.

'Ah! That pup!' he snarled. 'You saw him the last time I saw him. He rode off the same time you went to town. And he ain't been back. Nita Fourponies says when he gets back he had better bring along the liniment. For when she gets done with him, he'll need it! I reckon you had him sized: About one day of work and he figured it out he wasn't so done with that girl as he told us.'

They went on to the corral and, after they had unsaddled and Hurd moved ahead of them toward the bunkhouse, Tonto said:

'Something special? I kind of got the idee that you didn't want to spill it before *him*. Don't know as I blame you. He seems to be a hand; works all right enough; still, I don't think I'd ever get too fond of him.'

Drago began with the tale of his meeting with Wyoming Dees in Taunton.

Tonto checked him, laughing:

'Ne' mind telling about that!' he said. 'That boy that come along with Bates to drive the geldings, *he* told us all about it; how you drunk Wyoming under the table and took his guns off him and chunked him into the watering-trough and made Lige back up. I—wouldn't be surprised if Marjorie didn't hear that tale. You see, I kind of forgot myself and I told Nita about it. What happened after that, to keep you out all this time?'

He whistled softly, incredulously, at the end of Drago's account—told with feeling for the dramatic portions of the narrative.

'By God!' he grunted, there at the corner of the corral. 'I swear I oughtn't to let you out of my sight. If you ain't the damnedest feller to nose around until something happens! And me stuck here working! Well, whatever them sidewinders are up to, I would bet it has got something to do with the 56, like you guess. And tomorrow we had better start watching for signs of it. No use telling Marjorie, you reckon?'

'Not a bit,' Drago agreed. 'Was McGinsey here when you left today? I thought I saw a white-faced horse in the corral a minute ago. He was riding a white-faced sorrel, the last time he was out here.'

Tonto, now leading the way to the saddle-shed, swore viciously. He said that McGinsey had not been there that morning. They hung up their saddles and bridles and went on to the kitchen. Hurd was already there.

Chin turned his wizened face upon Drago and shook his head:

'Call you Hoolihan, a' right,' he said. 'Much time *pssssh*! You still on 56. Call this fella Hurd "New Cowboy."'

Hurd ate silently and left the table. Tonto asked Chin if Clint had come back.

233

The little cook made a disgusted sound:

'Catch'm girl, maybe. No come back. Nita hell-mad.'

'McGinsey here again?' Tonto persisted.

'Flont porch with Nita and boss. Eat supper with 'em.'

There was the sound of a light, quick step and Nita Fourponies stood framed in the doorway. She wore a dark blue shirt now, of heavy silk. The fawn-colored breeches and inlaid half-boots were the same as those she had worn when Drago had last seen her, like the beaded belt with wide silver buckle. She was an eye-filling spectacle and—Drago guessed—she knew it...

'Well, so the warrior's back from the fray!' she cried. 'Catch'm scalp? Steal'm horse, maybe? Count'm *coup*, huh?'

'Catch'm big pain in head,' Drago said smilingly. 'I've been off on a quiet hilltop, communing with myself. Trying to decide that problem we were discussing. I can see that you've been worrying about it, too. There's a subtle something about you, try as you do to conceal it, that gives you away. It's hard to say just how I know that, but—'

He shook his head and sighed and drank more coffee.

'Nothing mysterious about it,' she said. 'After the fifteenth or twentieth time, you develop a sort of feel for the business. But that's not what I'm worrying about, now. Did you *really* throw Wyoming Dees in the watering-trough?'

Her voice had risen a little and she had turned, too; her face was pointed toward the dark room behind her.

'It's possible that he slipped,' Drago admitted gravely.

Nita clucked—quite audibly.

'Ah, well,' she said tolerantly. 'They send to the mail-order house and get 'em a Wild West outfit and they come out here to buy cow-ranches and fight Injuns. And they end up in the watering-trough. Nothing we can do about it, I reckon. You didn't happen to run into that young rival of yours, did you? Clint, I mean. He hasn't been seen around the place since the time he rode out to brand some mavericks.'

'No sign of him. Did you get your novels and your scarlet shirt, all right?'

'Oh, sure-lee. I hung around town for a tolerable while after you had your conference with Berry Nicks. But you didn't show any interest in escorting the Red Maiden around the points of interest and eating, so I gave up and chunked another illusion over my shoulder and cried softly all the way home.'

There was no slightest flicker of embarrassment upon her face. Her eyes were wide and innocent.

Drago nodded.

'I wondered if that happened to be your scarlet shirt. Well, I don't think I can bear being exposed to any more of your personality tonight. I'm tired and sort of weak. I might give in to some perfectly outrageous proposition. Come on, Tonto. Take me away from this dangerous woman. If all the tribe had been her sort, the Cherokees would own Washington and she would be issuing us rations, now.'

'Hoolihan,' Marjorie called, from somewhere in the front.

Drago answered levelly and the girl came to stand beside Nita. The breed girl slipped her arm around Marjorie's waist. Standing so, one so dark and vivid, the other so blonde and self-possessed—if vaguely troubled of expression—they made a picture to harden Drago's dusty, stubbled face.

'I only wanted to say that Bates came out and—quite amazingly—paid a hundred and forty dollars more for the geldings than he had offered. He said something about being skinned alive and bodily and painfully. Whatever you did to him, it's thoroughly appreciated.'

'It was a pleasure, really,' Drago told her formally. 'I thought he was a sharpshooter when you mentioned him and, after I had a look at him, I knew he was.'

He bowed slightly to her and said good night. She did not stop him, to ask where he had been. When he and Tonto stepped out of the kitchen and went slowly toward the lighted bunkhouse, Tonto looked curiously up and

236

sidelong at him.

'You and Nita sound kind of like you're trying to make a case out of it,' he said hesitantly. 'Well, if you feel like that, feller, *I* wouldn't be the one to bother about Clint if I was you. She's a great Nita. I have wished—Ah, hell! Tomorrow we got new troubles. Will you take a sashay up to Needle Pasture again? You might get in a lick or two at the mavericks while you're sort of keeping a peeled eye on the skyline.'

They heard a mutter of voices in the bunkhouse before they reached its door.

Tonto grunted in a surprised tone.

'Now, who would that be? Chin was in the kitchen—'

'Clint, at a guess; back and not anxious to see Marjorie tonight. Dollar to a half it's Clint.'

'Uh-uh. You're too lucky and too good with your eyes and your ears. I hope it's Clint, though. I—I sort of got worried about him roaming around in the same United States a tough stick-up sharp is using.'

'Come in! Come in!' Clint called softly when they were at the door. 'But don't yell at me, Tonto. I'm a tired man and I don't feel like another session with Marje and Nita—not so soon after the other.'

Tonto went across to where the boy sprawled on a bunk. He stood like an irate bantam, hands on his hips.

'Damn your trifling, useless soul!' he said in

237

a grim drawl. And for two minutes he expressed his profane opinion of Clint. 'And that's what I think—or part of it!' he ended.

Clint nodded. His face showed sallow, drawn, under the light beard. There were purple shadows under his blue eyes.

'You're right,' he admitted. His weak mouth quivered. 'I am all that and some more. I never did keep a promise I made, did I? So it's no use saying, now, that I'm through with dallying around. That this time I stick and work...'

CHAPTER NINETEEN

'SO HE'S AFTER MY SCALP'

Tonto did not answer. He went on to his own bunk and sat there pulling off his boots. Drago followed his example. Even his tough body had felt the strain of the past three days. He was very tired. But he watched Clint mechanically and, when the boy shifted position on the bunk and his mouth jerked to the side, he nodded slightly.

'Hurt your arm, Clint?' he inquired softly.

'Arm?' Clint said—in a tone that held too much surprise.

'Yeh, arm!' Tonto snarled. 'What the hell foolishness have you been into, this time? You never run into that train-robber, and tried

238

something smart?'

'Oh, if you have to cluck about it, I might as well tell the story,' Clint said irritably. 'I told you, when I came home the last time, that I'd been playing the jack with a girl and that I was done. In ways there's no use going into, I discovered that I wasn't quite done, even though I wanted to be. And so, instead of heading for the Needle the other morning, I burned the ground going—going to her place.'

He looked toward Hurd's bunk, but the new hand was turned away from the room. It was impossible to tell whether he listened or not. Clint went on, rather deliberately:

'I ran into a little trouble, there. There was a big, dark stranger like the ones the fortune-tellers warn you about. He didn't like me any better than I liked him and there was a row before I got away. He cut my arm a little— nothing to matter, really. And I banged him over the head with a gun-barrel. If I hadn't thought about the tale getting all over the country, and back here, I would have put a dog-size hole in him. Now, you've got the yarn. And I need plenty of sleep.'

'It's your scalp they'll comb,' Tonto said, without sympathy. 'Going to be able to ride tomorrow? There's a hell-and-a-half of a lot of things to do.'

'Of course I can ride tomorrow! How do you think I got back today? Turn off the sermon, will you; and blow out the light. You get more

239

like a damn' old hen every day.'

Drago mulled the story for a few minutes. But he saw no way to check its truth, just then. And, too, with the other troubles faced by the 56, what Clint did or did not do seemed to him rather unimportant. He fell asleep.

Again, he was first out and shaved and bathed. Clint went quietly into the house and Drago, Tonto, and Hurd ate breakfast without seeing the boy or Marjorie and Nita. Lige McGinsey, sleeping on the front veranda, did not put in his appearance either.

Drago left Button in the corral and roped a big buckskin that Tonto proclaimed fast and a stayer. The stocky foreman was in better humor this morning.

'We can use even Clint,' he said. 'You take out for Needle Pasture and Hurd'll hit for the west range. Bring in every head of hawses you can see, Hurd. Run 'em down to the little pasture. Open that far gate on your way up. And be damn' sure you shut it on 'em! I got to stick around here and see what Clint's in shape to do. And, Hurd ... If you see anybody on the range today, what you want to do hangs ab-so-lute-ly on who you think they are and how many's of 'em. If they look like the wrong kind and there's more'n you can handle, hightail it back. You'll be back this evening, Hoolihan?'

Drago nodded. But he was looking at the tall black which bore the marks of hard riding; Clint's horse. Where he sat the big buckskin, he

240

could look into the corral and see what he had not noticed when in the corral—a long, bloody weal across the black's withers...

On his way, he made business at the saddle-shed. Clint's saddle was on the rack. And on the inside of the fork was a scar like more than one Drago had seen in his time—the grayish track of the bullet which had gone through the fork to crease the black horse.

'After hitting Clint in the arm,' Drago thought. 'I—wonder ... How was he heading when he came up?'

Tonto and Hurd were now out of sight. There was no sign of activity at the house. So he went back to the corral and picked up the black's trail. But, backtracking, he came quickly to its double. The black horse's hoofprints were distinctive enough to be recognized easily in this soft ground. He sat the buckskin, frowning at the ground. Then he saw the third set of hoofprints. Which made two trails of about the same age, coming toward the 56, and another going away.

'That's not his trail of the other day, either,' Drago thought. 'No, he rode up to the corral, then came straight back; went so far in this direction and turned toward the corral again. Why?'

He was frankly curious about the boy now. Clint had been mixed in something that he didn't care to tell truth about, he thought. He had been in a fight somewhere. The tale of the big, dark man at the girl's house did not explain a bullet-scar on his saddle, his horse, his arm.

'It might be,' Drago conceded, 'that the new lover ran him. He'd naturally be sensitive about admitting that. He may have preferred to explain a bullet-hole as a knife-slash...'

He rode for a mile, and two miles, without finding anything to explain Clint's double-trail to the house. With the surface of his mind, he was alert to everything around him. But his watch ahead and to the sides—and occasionally to the rear—did not keep his thoughts from straying to Marjorie. He saw her, now, as she had been the night before, so blonde, so lovely, beside Nita.

'The kind of girl I used to know,' he told himself, as he had done before. 'The kind I can't know now. She pulls aside from the killer she thinks I am. Nita—Now, there's the kind who wouldn't pull back from a man; not unless there was a damn' good reason. Just as fine in her way as Marjorie is. Pedigree, nil. Personality, hundred per cent. Clint is getting a lot more than he deserves. And poor old Tonto nursing secret hopes he knows he'll never realize...'

This section of 56 range was gashed with the arroyos that brought water down from the hills in the wet weather. There was much low brush. It was hard to see what lay ahead.

A rifle made flat, metallic sound, forty or

fifty yards ahead of him. Out of a patch of greasewood a plume of smoke came. A second shot followed swiftly, while Drago was flinging himself out of the saddle; then a third.

Drago had moved like an automaton. Here was no cover for a man horseback. He dropped flat on the ground, grateful that he had been riding with carbine across his arm; and that he had left Button in the corral. He began to work forward, keeping as well under cover as he could.

The man in the greasewood was no more a novice at this than Drago himself. The time or two when Drago must show a little brought uncomfortably accurate fire to sing about his head. Life was entirely interesting for Drago as he crawled toward the hidden marksman.

But the other man made the mistake of holding his position. When the smoke showed no more than fifteen or twenty yards ahead, Drago found a shallow depression out of which he could send bullets to spray the greasewood while keeping out of range himself. He shot the carbine empty in a rippling volley, then reloaded while the man fairly blasted the air above him with whining lead. He sent a second volley into the brush.

Silence followed. He inched forward, eyes narrowed, intent. Again he had that lift he had known when stalking Norris at the rock. When he saw an arm in ragged blue flannel, he twisted sideways until he could make out the shoulder.

More slowly, he crawled on, keeping his carbine ready for a quick shot. Then he saw the man's streaked dark face turned toward him. The lids were over the eyes; no long gun was in sight.

Drago got carefully to his feet and covered the motionless figure with his .44. He made the last half-dozen short steps ready to fire.

But the man was dead; fairly riddled with bullets. His carbine had slipped over the edge of a shallow arroyo. He was small and dark. His wide shell-belt supported two holsters, but that on the left side was empty. Upon the man's head a bandanna made a bloody bandage.

In the arroyo behind him, some yards away, a roan horse stood at the end of a lariat; a smaller roan than the one Norris had taken from the Walking M line-camp. Beside a rock was a swell-fork saddle. Drago went down and inspected the saddle pockets. But they were empty. The roan wore a Mexican brand that could not be 'read.'

'Well,' Drago said aloud, turning at the horse's side to look again at the dead man, 'so far, you can say it checks with Clint's story— and with what I know of Clint's movements. He said he had a fight and battered the other man with his gun-barrel ... And this dark fellow—he's not big, as Clint described his man, but they always look bigger in a fight— has the bloody bandage on his head ... Supposing that Clint got to the corral, then wondered if the New Lover had followed him, he might very well have turned back to have a look. Say that he rode back this way and found nothing after a while, so rode to the house again, and you explain his triple trail. The man there wasn't so close behind as Clint had feared. But he comes along and camps, waiting for a chance at Clint. Instead, I wander up and he tries to bushwhack me.'

He shrugged, at last. After all, this was Clint's war. The 56 had battle enough without worrying over Clint's private affairs of heart and hand. He loosed the roan horse and went back to his buckskin. When he got back to the house, he thought, he would tell Clint about the business, and let the boy decide what he wanted to do with the body; what story he wanted to tell, if any.

Riding along the arroyo in the direction from which he guessed the dead dark man had come, he found occasional hoofprints. But they were not plain enough, on the rocky floor of the arroyo, to let him say if they had been made by the roan, or by the mount of some wandering rider—Tonto or Hurd or even Clint. He came to the foothills and saw that trail no more.

A pass opened in the hills. The buckskin seemed to know the way. He turned toward the narrow gash and surged easily up the slope of its bottom. On the other side was a great flat, stretching away as far as he could see. With its curling grama grass and mottes of cottonwoods, it was pretty range. He rode across it and, when he came to a fence, stopped to look around. Tonto had said nothing about a line-fence in this direction.

He was down on the ground, loosening staples in order to cross the fence, when he heard the pounding hoofs behind him. He turned, to face two small groups of riders who came at him as if they rode down the arms of a V toward its point. They were four or five hundred yards away and he could not identify them. Not that it mattered, he thought grimly. Either faction in the Taunton Basin was an enemy of his.

He shoved his pliers at the top strand of wire, snipped it and without haste or waste motion cut the second and third strands. Then he leaned to get the trailing reins and lead the buckskin through the gap. He went into the saddle without touching his stirrups. A rattle of shots greeted that maneuver.

Over-eager men in each group were firing at him. Their lead went wild. There was little probability that bullets flung from galloping horses would so much as come near him, even though the range, now, had shortened to some three hundred yards. He looked behind him and, as the two groups spread to become a fan-like line, he saw the huge figure of Hinky Rust appear, towering above all the other riders.

He had the carbine from his scabbard. He turned and, from the buckskin's steady back, began to fire methodically. He got a horse with his second shot; another horse with his fourth or fifth. Before he emptied the carbine, he saw a man go out of a saddle. That left Rust and perhaps a half-dozen.

They wavered with the hail of lead he sent at them. But someone was yelling savagely—Rust, he guessed. They came on and he whirled the buckskin and sent him across the flat at a pounding gallop. The shooting burst out again, and he grinned.

'I wouldn't be a bit surprised if, by now, Rust has figured that Tonto and I had a part in the business at Spoon's store. A little expert trailing would have told him a good deal and, the Basin being what it is, that expert trailing may have been available to the Lazy R. So he's after my scalp.'

He saw that he was keeping his lead. And as he rode the corners of tight mouth and narrowed eyes lifted in the satanic grin he wore in time of war. If, in the broken country ahead, he could not find a place where a lone warrior might halt, to make his pursuers sorry they had followed, he would be surprised. Very surprised, he thought...

Presently, his lead was increased. And the flat ended in low hills where only stock-trails cut through brushy arroyos. He was watching for the kind of place he wanted. A high pile of

247

rocks on the crest of a hill at first offered a fort for him. But it was exposed to fire from the brushy base. He halted in that shelter only long enough to reload his Winchester—and to kill another horse and knock dust from the rider's shirt as the cowboy sprawled upon the ground.

Then, with the harried warriors of the Rust-Wade side a little nearer—but not too anxious to close up—he rode on. And one of the pursuers thought to do what Drago had been expecting from the beginning. This man drew to the side and began to shoot from a motionless horse. One of his bullets bit a nick in Drago's cantle; another struck just under the buckskin's forehoofs. But Drago went on fast, though he anticipated the thudding impact of a slug at any moment.

He made the crest of a ridge and saw cover before him, in broken, water-carved land blanketed with scrubby growth. And a bullet burned across his hip, pierced his legging, and glanced from the saddle housing into the buckskin.

The big horse grunted and went to his knees. Drago caught at the saddle horn and kicked his feet from the stirrups, to twist and come to the ground as the buckskin crashed. He jerked at the belt of his leggings and stepped out of them. Then he began to run.

He vaulted over the rim of a shallow arroyo and whirled back with carbine over the edge. A horse appeared, the rider so low that the animal seemed to run with empty saddle. Two slugs caught that bay in the thick chest and he jackknifed. The man came off like something hurled from a sling, but landed on his feet and got behind a clump of brush untouched.

Dust rose, just over that ridge. Drago knew, as if he could see, that the others were pulling in frantically. He ran along the arroyo, clambered out, found another and still another. But behind him the yells of Rust's men rose. They were clinging doggedly to his trail and, marked by his high heels, it would not be hard to follow at the gallop.

He worked back and forth, going from one clump of brush to another, without seeing the men who yelled to each other in his rear. Then, making another ridge at last, he looked down upon a dozen, fourteen, sixteen men—he could only guess at their actual number. They were coming at a trot behind Wyoming Dees and the gaunt Norris; they were staring intently in his direction.

'Heard the shooting!' he thought. 'Now—if only I could duplicate the performance at Spoon's and let these two sides run into each other...'

He looked quickly right and left. The men with Hinky Rust were making a good deal of noise as they beat the brushy arroyos on his track. But there was not so much yelling now. He decided upon a dense clump of brush on the rim of a little arroyo as his cover. Then, reloading swiftly, he shoved the carbine out and waited.

Norris and Dees were talking. Drago thought that the pair considered their party strong enough to move boldly forward; they came on steadily. So perhaps a hundred yards separated him from Rust's men and the larger body behind Wyoming. He drew a careful bead on Norris.

'You're overdue,' he said grimly, aloud. 'Long overdue!'

He squeezed the trigger delicately, twitched the ejector, and sent a second shot into the tall killer before Norris had more than jerked in the saddle. Then he fired at Wyoming and, indiscriminately, at the mass of them.

But Wyoming had gone down like an Indian, to shelter behind his horse. He was yelling and his hand and arm showed, waving his men forward. Drago emptied his carbine, then ran stoopingly to the cover he had chosen. The men of Rust were coming fast, drawn by his fire. He dropped down into the shallow water course. From the mask of brush he saw them going by, to set their horses back when they saw and heard the other men. They dropped off with Rust's command and trotted on to take cover and shoot at Wyoming's line.

Drago could only guess at what was happening. But when a nervous horse trotted his way, he got up boldly and went out to catch its reins. The brush was smoky with the firing;

men seemed to be everywhere before him. He mounted and moved to the rear. He had made twenty yards when a Winchester sounded on his right, close by, to send a slug whining past his eyes. He drew a Colt as he turned, letting the empty carbine sag into his left hand.

Hinky Rust had risen from behind a bush. He flinched with the bullet Drago sent at him and began to go down. Drago fired twice, Rust once. The tall man dived into cover again, dropping his rifle. Drago emptied his pistol and spurred furiously on. There were quick yells behind, but whether from Rust or some of his men, he had no idea.

He came to the buckskin and stopped to listen. The battle still raged along that ridge. He looked at the saddle he sat and grinned wolfishly.

'About twice as good as mine was, new!' he said. 'So—'

He dropped to the ground, jerked his scabbard and *alforjas* free from his own scarred hull. With face turned toward the firing, he strapped on the scabbard and rammed the carbine into it. Then, with heavy stock-knife, he slashed the discarded saddle thoroughly.

'For an impromptu battle,' he said thoughtfully aloud, 'I don't know what more I could ask. If Tonto and Hurd and Clint were along, we could make ourselves completely unpleasant to both sides.'

But he thought that, without injection of the rest of the 56, the battle on the ridge would be damaging to both sides. The superiority of numbers on Wyoming Dees's side would be balanced by the advantage Rust's men had owned, in position.

'If Wyoming and Rust are wiped out—that is, if I didn't take care of Rust myself,' he told himself—'that will leave just McGinsey and Gotcher to carry on the war. And they'll be needing some recruits before they can do a lot of fighting.'

He rode with grim cheerfulness back to the gap in the fence and over his trail of the morning. When he came, at last, to the dead man in the arroyo, he pulled in to stare dourly. Then an oddity of the dead bushwhacker's posture caught his eye. He was now lying flat upon his back; not upon his side. And certainly his shirt had not been pulled out of his pants when Drago had last seen him.

CHAPTER TWENTY

'YOU'RE PRETTY DAMN' MYSTERIOUS'

On the ground, Drago studied the man. Someone had been here. When he stared about, he could see the hoofprints of a horse

252

which had come from the direction he had come from in the morning—from the 56 house. Had Clint been here? He could not tell from the trail. But someone had found the dead man and got off to search him as Drago had not searched him.

He bent suddenly and touched the cotton pants, poking at the bulge he noticed above the right knee. He pulled up the pants leg and exposed a bandage of bloody, striped canvas, drew that off, and found a bullet hole through the leg.

The man, it would seem, had been lying here with a shot-wound that should have put him under a doctor's care, a wound received before Drago's appearance. And the bandage—

'An express company money sack, with part of the imprint still on it!' Drago muttered. 'And used for a bandage on a new wound—By God! It wouldn't be much more peculiar if it were an altar cloth!'

But though he searched the man inch by inch now, nothing explained the strip of striped canvas. He wished that he had troubled to make the search that morning! He stared at the hoofprints and shook his head:

'I'd give a handful of dimes to know what *you* found on him!' He addressed the unknown rider of the horse responsible for those marks. 'I would that!'

Presently, he got up with a resigned shrug and swung up. He rode toward the 56 house with thoughtful face. If that dark, little man lying back there were not one of the train-robbers hunted by the Sheriff of Parlin; if he were not the escaped 'Pache; then there was a great deal of coincidence abroad in Taunton Basin. Too much!

He followed the old, worn stock-trail that he had ridden over in the morning, the path in which he had found Clint's trail twice. Mechanically, he looked occasionally at the ground. There were too many dim hoofmarks in the hard soil now to do much toward distinguishing one horse's tracks from any other's. But he stopped to stare when a single horse turned off to the left. There was no more than a pair of marks to show. He pulled in and looked that way.

There was no trail to pull a man aside. It seemed that whoever had ridden off to the left had simply decided to go in a different direction, then reined his horse that way. Drago wondered what lay over that swell dotted with mesquite and bunch-grass. He tickled his horse with gentle rowel and rode that way.

Suddenly, within thirty yards, he pulled in short. There were several marks on the softer soil here. They looked like the broad, smoothing prints of a board—or a palm. They were near a rounded boulder that cropped up from the earth for eighteen inches.

He bent from the saddle to stare frowningly.

There was a rock of perhaps thirty or forty pounds' weight lying at the base of the boulder. And on that smaller rock was a dark smear of thin, encrusted dirt. That rock had been lifted from the ground somewhere and brought here and put against the boulder...

Drago jerked it away and saw a small cavity beneath the boulder. Out of it he pulled a striped bag, of the same kind that dead man had used for a bandage; an express money bag with a rawhide thong closing the mouth of it. A bag crammed with bills, none new, ranging in denomination as high as fifties...

Drago counted the money quickly and frowned. It seemed to him that, if this were 'Pache's share of the loot, it had strangely swelled, unless the dark little man were an odd, saving sort of train-robber. For the men of the gang killed had each carried about eight hundred dollars. He could see no reason for 'Pache taking more. And here in this striped sack were bills totaling more than nineteen hundred dollars.

'I'm banking on my dead bushwhacker being 'Pache,' he told himself. 'It's the only reasonable theory, at that. He got away from us and headed into 56 range. Question—but that's the trouble! There are entirely too many questions. How does this match Clint's story of a dark lover able to put up a knife-fight? Who put this money under the rock? The man who searched my bushwhacker? And who was that?

Clint?'

He gave it up. Until he talked to Clint, there seemed little chance of clearing any of these points. So he replaced the rock against the boulder, smoothing away with his palm all traces of his hands and feet, then straightened. He put the striped sack in a saddle bag and mounted.

He made the 56 house at a slinging trot and swung down at the corral. Tonto's horse was missing, and the gray which Hurd had ridden. Drago unsaddled and turned the captured sorrel in. Then he hung his saddle on the rack in the shed and went slowly toward the house.

Nobody was in sight at the back, so he went around. He heard Nita Fourponies' voice—exasperated of tone—before he came to the veranda corner:

'Granted, my young nitwit—granted! If you *could* put a loop over 'em, and collect the reward, it would be lovely. But—*doesn't* it occur to baby that gentlemen who wander about, making a practice of sticking up banks and trains, are probably rather prejudiced against having loops put over them? And that you hardly qualify as *Diamond Dick, the Terror of the Prairies?*'

'Ah, Nita!' Clint began.

'Shut up! I've got the floor. My idea is, if you should come up with these aforesaid gentlemen, you'd be in the same predicament as the sweet little boy who slipped up behind the big, bad bear, and grabbed him by the tail, and shouted triumphantly: "I've got you, now!" Do you see, Clint—*darling?*'

'You're as bad as Marje,' Clint answered sullenly, as Drago leaned against the wall to eavesdrop brazenly. 'To hear you talk, anybody might think I was about ten years old, and didn't want my ears washed. Here's that bunch, hitting lick after lick in our own country. Counting yesterday's deal, we've had three train-robberies within thirty miles. My notion, all the time, has been that the hold-up artists belong to one of the two sides in the war—the LL and Walking M, or the Lazy R and Half Circle W. And I'm not aiming to *capture* 'em. All I want is the certainty that one side or the other is the gang.'

Nita made a scornful sound, wordless but very eloquent. She had the Indian genius for expressive grunts.

'Damn it all, Nita,' Clint cried irritably. 'Cow-punching never did hit me as a way to make a living. I want a little bit of excitement. Marje has always thought I ought to trot along seven days a week, like an old buggy horse, hoping that I'd be turned out to pasture in about twenty years when I got too old and not able to pull any more. That's why I started sliding out and doing a little bit of gambling and—'

'And woman-chasing,' Nita amplified acidly. 'You see, Clint, I was at the door of the
257

bunkhouse last night. I had a notion you were there. So I slipped up, and so I heard about the girl, and the man who put his knife in your arm...'

'Well, if you heard, you heard what I said about seeing her just to finish that business. But what I didn't tell Tonto was that seeing her was only half of what I was after. It was at a hangout of the bunch I suspect, that she is. Now—'

Drago walked quietly back around the house to the back. Nita was showing shrewdness, force of personality, that he had rather expected of her. More and more he liked the clear-headed, thoroughly competent breed girl of the caustic tongue.

He was leaning moodily against the corral when Clint came up behind him. Slowly, Drago turned, to face Clint's grin.

'You ought to've been around today, Hoolihan. Our noble sheriff was here. He brought a posse composed of the boldest pre-battle warriors the Taunton, or any other Basin, ever saw. That was the middle of the morning. There was a second train-robbery before daylight yesterday, within a couple of miles of the first one at Mesquite Crossing. And Berry Nicks is hot on their trail, he is. He came across our range for a short-cut to the place. It must have been a warm affair...'

'The same place as the first robbery,' Drago said frowningly. 'Probably worked on the theory that the railroad wouldn't expect lightning to hit in the same place. What happened?'

'Nick says it was two men, this time. One was recognized as making a hand in the first gang. The other was a stranger to the conductor. They didn't bother the passengers, according to the Noble Nicks. Just popped into the express and mail car and stuck up the messenger. But it wasn't a bad haul; about twenty-five hundred in bills some outfit was shipping for a payroll. They tied up the messenger, but he got loose and whanged away with a rifle he had hidden in the car. He thinks he hit 'em both.'

'If he did,' Drago told him gravely, 'they ought to be sort of softened for you, Clint ... You can do your detecting—'

Involuntarily, Clint's head jerked toward the house. Then he shrugged, and faced Drago defiantly.

'You heard me talking to Nita. All right, now, you know it, too. But you don't look to me the kind that goes around waggling his jaw just to waggle it.'

'How's the arm?' Drago asked, with seeming indirection. 'Better, is it? Say, was the fellow who knifed you hurt, at that time?'

'*Por dios!* If he was, I'd hate to meet him when he was in good shape! What makes you ask, Hoolihan?'

'I wanted to know. What time of day was it

259

that you had your fight with him, anyway?'

'Around noon,' Clint frowned. 'But I don't see—'

'Noon yesterday...' Drago muttered. 'Noon—yesterday...'

'What the hell's on your mind?' Clint snapped.

Drago stared blankly at him for an instant, then shook his head.

'Clint, are you *sure* it wasn't the day before yesterday that you had that affair with him? You don't have to answer, if you don't want to, but—'

'You're damn' right I don't!' Clint snarled. 'You want to remember you're nothing but one of the hands on this spread and you can hightail off it just as fast as you hit it, or faster! You're pretty damn' mysterious, Mr Hoolihan—*if* that's your name. Too mysterious, it's beginning to look to me. I wouldn't be a bit surprised if there was something on your backtrail you don't want catching up with you.'

'All that talk to keep from saying that knife-wound was made day before yesterday and not yesterday,' Drago said softly. 'Listen. You're making a young damn' fool of yourself. You told Tonto and me all about the battle with the big, dark fellow in the yellow pants and the blue flannel shirt. Now, when I ask you if you're sure it was yesterday you battled with him, and not the day before, you get oddly excited . . .'

'There's no excitement at all! I don't like to be put over the hurdles like I was in court. But it *was* yesterday—about noon—if you have to have all the periods and commas in it—and I was stabbed—in the wrist—by a lanky, Mexican-brown, hard-case hairpin—who was wearing a blue flannel shirt—and yellow pants—'

'When you rode up to the corral here, yesterday afternoon, why did you turn around and ride back the way you'd come, then come back here later? You don't have to tell that if you don't want to. But I saw your tracks and—it made me curious.'

Clint stared hard and blankly at him, then shook his head and grinned.

'You talk like a detective. But if you're worried about my twistings and turnings, when I got up here I had a thought. It came to me that this fellow I'd smacked over the head might be a vindictive soul. He looked it! So I back-tracked ve-ry carefully until I was certain he wasn't trailing me. Then I rode home again with—I'll admit—an easier mind!'

Drago nodded.

'All right. Now, I know what I wanted to know. I reckon you owe me a little, Clint. That fellow was lying up along the trail this morning. He whanged away at me and missed. I whanged away at him and—I *didn't* miss. Not any! Your Mexican-brown, hard-case hairpin is lying dead up the trail in a little arroyo. Clint, I'm not going to waggle my jawbone a bit, about your detective-work. So you needn't cover up with me about it. Did you know this fellow was dead? I mean did you back-track again today, and find him?'

Clint stared, then shook his head.

'No. I haven't been off the place today. As a matter of fact, of our bunch here, Hurd went off as soon as you did. He's not back yet. And Tonto went with Berry Nicks and the posse. Lige McGinsey started off with Nicks, but he came back after a while with his horse lame. He said he'd stay the day out, if we didn't mind. But none of the rest of us left the place, until Marje decided she had business in town again. I don't know what she went in for, but she did. In the buckboard. Lige drove her in.'

He shrugged expressively.

Drago turned and looked through the bars at the Walking M horse. He moved away from Clint and went into the corral. McGinsey's white-faced sorrel, standing as if half-asleep in a corner, let him come close; let him pick up the forefoot that he was holding oddly. Closely, Drago examined the leg. Then he held the foot between his knees and got out his knife. He snipped a constricting hair that had been looped about the leg, and looked at the knot in it.

'So, Mr McGinsey wanted an excuse for staying—or coming back,' he told himself.

'Old, but always good. That is, almost always.'

But he wondered why Clint insisted on lying to him, about having a fight with that dead man; about the day of the fight. Manifestly, if that dead man were at once Clint's opponent *and* a train-robber, he had been shot by the messenger long before noon of the day before. And with that bullet-hole in his leg, to say nothing of the wound on his head, he would not have been able to make the desperate hand-to-hand fight which Clint described.

'You mean,' Clint said angrily, 'that Lige McGinsey lamed his horse, so he could come back here?'

'It certainly looks that way. I don't know what his idea was, but he looped that horsehair around his sorrel's leg. It may be, of course, that Mr McGinsey didn't want to be tied up with a posse; he and Gotcher had various important things in view. Today, I seemed to interfere in some of their plans.'

'You—you ran into that gang? In Needle Pasture again?'

'You might have thought the Basin was turning out for my reception! First Hinky Rust and a prize half-dozen of Lazy R and Half Circle W bushwhackers. Then Wyoming Dees and my tall rustler Norris, with nearer twenty men than a dozen. They killed that buckskin I rode out. I had to steal one of their horses to keep from walking home.'

He told the story of the fight.

'You're without doubt the luckiest man in Texas,' Clint said at the end. 'It will be perfectly lovely, if you got Rust. And Rust's gang got Wyoming and most of those killers. Well—'

He stretched elaborately and turned toward the house. But within a step or two he stopped.

'Hurd ought to be back, by now. Want to ride out with me and see if he made the pasture with the horses all right?'

'One should be enough,' Drago said carelessly. 'And it may be a good idea to have one man on the place, with those highbinders loose in the Basin.'

'You're right. Nita being here, and all, you'd better stay. I'll find Hurd. We ought to be back by seven or eight at the outside.'

Drago nodded. He was hardly thinking of what Clint said; or of the horses. Mechanically, he watched the boy go to the saddle-shed and come back with silver-trimmed swell-fork and one-ear bridle of the same fancy trimming.

Clint roped a thick-barreled dun and cursed the horse when it fought against the bit.

'I'll break him of that,' he said irritably, 'if I never break another horse!'

He had more trouble with the saddle. Drago went over to hold the dun while the front cinch was drawn taut. Clint mounted and, once in the saddle, seemed to lose the bad temper he had displayed. He grinned at Drago; that flashing, utterly boyish grin which seemed to soften Marjorie and Nita; even the grim Tonto

Peel.

'Wouldn't be a bad idea to carry a rifle, from what you said,' he grunted. 'Think I will.'

Drago watched him go up to the bunkhouse, get off and go inside. He came back with a long Winchester and belt of shells. He waved and rode away. All the Western horizon was colored red-gold by the sunset. The boy and the dun were creatures on some old tapestry, silhouetted as they were against the unreal loveliness of that sky.

Drago watched briefly, then went moodily toward the bunkhouse. He went inside and sagged upon his bunk, to make a cigarette and light it and sit smoking.

There was a round iron stove in one end of the room. He got up suddenly and went to it. He opened the door and struck a match. There were ends of burned sticks in the firebox. There were crumpled papers and envelopes. There was a striped express bag, the mate to that one in his saddle pocket.

He had no need to open it. A gentle shake produced a metallic rattle and the rustling of bills. He stood for a long while staring at it. He heard no faintest sound, but something hard punched his back.

'Now that you've found it,' a slow voice drawled, 'what do you think you'll do about it, or with it? Don't move. *Don't—move...*'

'You're the doctor,' he said calmly. 'I might have expected you to be around. And, knowing

265

you, I think I would have expected you to arrive without any announcements.'

'Well?' Nita prompted him. 'What do you think you'll do about it? And don't waste time, trying to think of a trick!'

CHAPTER TWENTY-ONE

'FOUR OF THE FIVE ARE DEAD'

Drago raised his hands, to pinch the shoulder-seams of his shirt with thumbs and forefingers. Then he turned his head to look at her. She did not lighten the pressure of the gun.

'Great minds; great minds!' he said. 'They seem to run in the same channel here ... I was asking myself that very question, when you so neatly captured me.'

'I imagine,' she nodded. Her face was set like a mask. 'I can answer it, though. Steve Drago, wanted for murder, is not apt to do *anything* about it! I didn't tell you, for there was no real reason to tell, that, after Judge Bell so kindly identified you that first day in town, I went over to Berry Nicks's office. I found a circular on his wall. Being there in plain sight, Berry would naturally never notice it. How did it run? Oh, yes! "Wanted for Murder of Nevil Jacklin in Leandro County—$2500 Reward—" Yes, I read it very carefully. So—'

'I'm no detective, then. You know that!' he said calmly. 'Perhaps you'll understand something else; that in thinking of this business, I'm not really thinking of Clint except as a side-issue. He's a young fool—wanted for murder in connection with the Parlin County robbery, even though he didn't fire the shot—'

'A young damn' fool, who thinks he's very clever—perhaps is clever, except when bucking one like you. That describes him,' she nodded.

There was a slight lightening of the deadly mask of her face. But she did not take the rock-steady pistol from his back.

'I heard every word you said to him. I saw that you were leading him on, to see if he'd lie about that imaginary knife-wound. Then I followed you in here. Do you believe that I'd calmly put a hole in you, before I'd let you open your mouth?'

'Why, of course! And say that I attacked you,' he told her, and nodded in his turn. 'I don't blame you.'

'Exactly! So—you're another victim of blue eyes and yellow hair, are you? You're thinking of Clint in connection with Marje?'

'Victim?' he said between his teeth, dark face grimmer than her own. 'Hardly. Remember that I've known her only for days. But I've seen enough to make me sorry for her—as she'd be with her brother swinging for the murders his gang committed. Don't you understand that even a killer like—like me can have a decent thought occasionally? She—she's the kind of girl I used to know. She wouldn't touch a man like me with a pole. She has had a hard time of it, trying to handle a job that would crowd a good man. All I want to do is cover her. Now, you can either take that gun out of my back or shoot. For I have said my piece.'

'What are you thinking of doing?' she demanded, stepping back. 'How will you cover her?'

He turned, dark face grim, thoughtful. He stood staring at her, but hardly noticing her. It was another girl he saw. And he could view himself sardonically, knowing that in so brief a time he had come to the place where anything he could do for Marjorie Littell he would do, regardless of the risk, without any hope of reward.

'"Another victim of blue eyes and yellow hair,"' mentally he repeated Nita's scornful phrase. 'Not quite that. In fact, not that at all. She's simply the sort of person to make me feel this way and—'

Angrily, he made himself think of Clint.

'Here's the picture, as I see it,' he told Nita. 'Clint hung around Alonzo Spoon's store and probably got to gambling with hard cases who cleaned him expertly. That towhead I killed mentioned Spoon's as the hangout. This gang must tie to the store. The gang was made up of five men—four, besides Clint. They stuck up

268

the train at Mesquite Hill Crossing. Got a hundred or so apiece. They felt pretty safe. Clint—'

He shrugged and smiled faintly at her. She nodded. The pistol sagged at her side now. She seemed to have forgotten it.

'Clint came home and told a tale of winning the money gambling,' she said. 'And, unusual as that was, we believed him.'

'It was unlucky for Clint that his first try was lucky,' Drago went on. 'If he'd had a good scare on the first robbery, he might have settled down and decided to work for a living. But the other day he went out with the gang again, and they stopped the train in Parlin County. As usual, they split. Two men went one way, three the other. Clint was one of the three, my towhead and 'Pache were the others. Clint—fortunately for him—decided to go it alone. The towhead was killed and 'Pache headed into the 56 where he could depend on Clint for help.'

'And you came back from riding with the posse, and told him that 'Pache was somewhere on the 56!'

'Exactly. So he rode out to find him and did find him. And the two of them for some insane reason decided to constitute themselves a two-man reign of terror. They went back to Mesquite Hill and robbed the express car, all right, but they were hit when the messenger opened fire as they rode away. 'Pache was creased and struck in the leg. A slug went across Clint's lap and through the saddle and gashed his horse.'

He looked narrowly at her: 'How long have you suspected Clint?' he demanded.

'Ever since the first Mesquite Hill robbery, I suppose. But it was suspicion, more than anything else. You see—those three robberies aren't the tally. Not by a long shot. We've been hearing of ranchers held up and robbed of their payrolls; of little banks being taken, two hundred miles away, sometimes; and stages stopped here and there. Always Clint was "off gambling" at the time. When you told me, in town, that the lone train-robber had headed into 56 range, I came straight here to see what Clint was doing. But, about Clint, now—'

'Four of the five are dead. Alf Azle was going to have everybody in Parlin look at the three bodies he's got. By this time it's fairly certain that somebody has identified one or two of the men. And Azle is a good officer; he'd naturally try to tie them to—to Clint, if possible. If he does find someone to say that they hung out with Clint, Azle and the detectives for the railway company and the express company, to say nothing of Rangers and United States Marshals, are going to be looking for him. So—Clint has got to leave. South America will be the best place for him. He'd better be on his way—fast!'

She nodded. Her expression was merely
270

interested. She met his eyes steadily.

'I'm not going with him, if that's what you mean!' she said calmly. 'I will stake him for his run—more for Marje's sake, though, than for his. Five hundred won't dent me. Take it out of the sack, there—he must have that much in it. I'll replace it in town. I suppose that's juggling evidence, but a little thing like that won't keep me from sleeping. When will he be back, do you think?'

'We won't wait for him to get back. I don't see any use in letting Hurd know any more than he has to know. I'm not sure of him. I'll ride after Clint. That dun he took is not so good. I'll take him a better horse, and the five hundred—'

'But he went to find Hurd,' she objected. 'They'll be together—and *I* think Hurd is a Ranger, on your trail!'

'Oh, no, he didn't go looking for Hurd,' Drago assured her. 'He didn't ride west for five hundred yards. Just got himself out of sight. Then he burned the ground getting to 'Pache. He tried to pump out of me whether or not I'd found 'Pache's share of the loot on him. He decided that I hadn't looked for it. So *he* went tearing that way to get it. I'll find him around there. And I'd better be moving.'

'I'm going with you!' she said quickly. 'He'll listen to me when nobody else can influence him. Rope that bay in the corral. Next to your horse, he's probably the best on the place. And

271

Clint's going to need that—the best horse!'

She put the pistol back into its holster. Drago counted out five hundred dollars and put the bag in his shirt. Then for an instant they faced each other. Drago reached impulsively to take the slim, strong, shapely hands and hold them.

'You're a grand girl, Nita,' he told her softly.

She smiled up at him twistedly and her fingers closed upon his. She leaned a little toward him:

'The same to you! Don't think I don't know how hard this must be for you. Clint doesn't mean anything to you. And you have to forget the days when you were a Ranger; when your job was to put handcuffs on criminals. You're not a criminal, now. That charge of murder—'

Suddenly, her face settled into composure almost stony. She drew away from him; pulled her hands free.

'We'd better be going!' she said tonelessly.

At the corral, Drago got her horse and whistled for Button. When he had led both to the saddle-shed and saddled them, he looked with a shrug at Nita, then tossed the bag of loot into a dark corner where he had put the money got from 'Pache. They mounted and rode back to the corral. There, Drago roped the tall bay she indicated and they went toward the arroyo where 'Pache should still sprawl. The bay led easily.

They had covered a mile silently when the

sound of distant shots checked them.

Nita jumped her horse up beside Drago:

'Could he have run into officers already?'

'I don't know. He *could* have met just anybody. I've got to see. Will you stay here with the bay?'

'Tie him!' she snapped. 'I'm going with you.'

And for all his arguments, she went. They left the bay tied to a mesquite and rode fast through the dusk that was beginning to be darkness, with a pale moon showing above the hills. The firing was a ragged sound; several rifles rattling over a narrow front, Drago thought.

'At a guess,' he told Nita, 'five or six industrious bushwackers have got someone holed up. It might be three to a side, of course. But, with Clint in this neighborhood, the other theory is more probable. Well, we'll have moonlight before we work up and really see.'

'I wish I had a Winchester!' she said grimly. 'This popgun is all right for short range. But I can drive nails with my .38-40. You don't think it could be officers? If it is—'

'If it is,' he drawled, 'you leave things to me. I'll do my best to draw 'em off. But—I don't see how it could be! Azle wouldn't be over in Taunton County. And Nicks wouldn't know what we know about Clint. Besides, Tonto's with him...'

They came closer, moving quietly. Drago swung down and grunted to Nita. This time she nodded obediently. He went on afoot and presently saw, dim in the pale light of the rising moon, a low rise from which flashes of gunfire came. And all around that little hill were men shooting up at the single rifleman. Coming closer still, Drago made out a still figure sprawling on the slope—then another.

'If that's Clint up there,' he thought, 'he's putting up a lone-wolf battle! Now, if I could get up there to him—'

He worked nearer the spot where a man fired steadily uphill. He was within five yards of the man when a round rock turned under his foot and he stumbled. He put out both hands automatically, to catch himself, and made a good deal of noise. From behind a clump of mesquite a man lifted, facing his way, carbine pointed straight at him. It was Gano Gotcher. He gaped incredulously for perhaps two seconds. Drago propped himself up with left hand and began to twist his own carbine toward the LL owner. But Gotcher's Winchester twitched as he jerked down the lever.

Then from the hilltop a shot came and Gotcher crashed upon his face almost at Drago's feet. He did not move again. And Drago, sliding to that clump of brush which had sheltered the LL man, yelled furiously:

'All right, Clint! We're coming! We downed Gotcher!'

Men yelled and the firing about the hill

274

stopped short. Drago yelled again and again, loudest voice of any. And the brush crackled as men scrambled away from Drago. Quickly, the pound of hoofs carried to him, where he was climbing the hill. The LL men were leaving!

He found Clint upon his face, cheek against the stock of the long. 45-70 he had carried out of the bunkhouse. He did not move. Then Drago saw the spreading patch of blood beneath him. He knelt beside Clint and touched his shoulder. Without moving more than his lips, Clint said gaspingly:

'They jumped me—while I was by Jap's saddle. Gotcher and—half a dozen. I got three I know about. Gotcher last. Almost—couldn't hold down—on Gotcher. Wish I could—have got McGinsey! He—He—'

Words ended in a bubbling sound. Drago was feeling for his pulse when Nita bent beside him. He touched the sticky breast of Clint's shirt and shook his head.

'Shot to pieces,' he told her grimly. 'But he went out like a curly wolf. Gotcher and two other killers—yes, he piled up a score...'

She said nothing, but eased the still body over until it was face up. She shook her head and stared down at the boy.

'He never grew up,' she said huskily. 'I guess that was what made us all feel as we did toward him. Just a little boy who hadn't found out that life's no Christmas stocking with whatever you want in it. We kept watching him, waiting for

275

him to learn what everybody else knew—'

'I think Gotcher's outfit is gone,' Drago told her softly. 'I'll get the horses. We'll take him back.'

He brought Clint's dun up. It had run a little way when Gotcher's men had surrounded the boy. He lifted Clint across the saddle and led the dun downhill. Nita rode ahead, carrying Clint's rifle. She led the bay back to the house, while Drago followed with the dun at the end of Clint's rope.

When Clint had been put upon a bed in the *casa grande*, Drago and Nita faced each other.

'I'll ride in to get Marjorie,' he said. 'I wonder what took her into town, anyway ... And what made Lige McGinsey so anxious to dodge riding with the posse ... Well! I'll take a look in the bunkhouse, for Hurd.'

CHAPTER TWENTY-TWO

'THIS—IS IT!'

But, before he went to the bunkhouse, he led Button to the shed to put the striped express company sacks into his *alforjas*, with the five hundred dollars replaced.

He rode to the bunkhouse and called Hurd. Groaning answered him and he swung off quickly, to step inside, into darkness. A pistol rammed into his side and Hurd said grimly:

'Grab those ears, Drago! Leandro folks'll pay the reward for you dead or alive! They—'

Drago twisted abruptly and jerked up a knee. Powder-flame scorched his side; set his shirt afire. He struck out at Hurd and the other's pistol rapped on the floor. But he had no chance to draw his own. Hurd's thick arms went around him and held his elbows to his sides. They staggered across the floor, crashed into the bunks and wrestled away.

Then Nita called Drago:

'I can't tell you apart! Hold him still a minute and I'll settle him!'

Hurd snarled furiously at her:

'Keep out of this! I want this man for murder. I'm a deputy sheriff, Sime Sarkey, from Leandro. This is Steve Drago.'

'Can't hear you!' she said calmly. 'Hold him—Hoolihan!'

But Drago had taken advantage of Sarkey's relaxation. He burst loose from those thick arms and jerked both guns.

'Stand still!' he snarled. 'You don't take me anywhere.'

He walked in on Sarkey. Over his shoulder he said:

'Let's have a light, Nita.'

'You can't get away with this, Drago!' Sime Sarkey told him furiously. 'I spotted you almost from the beginning. I picked up your trail at Bellero and trailed you straight to

Taunton, and then out here. And I got more lines on you than just here. Now—'

'That's fine, Nita,' Drago told the girl, as if he had not heard Sarkey. 'Now, young fellow, I suppose you're packing a set of cuffs. Even a thickhead deputy trying to arrest the wrong man should have bracelets.'

In the light of the oil lamp he studied Sime Sarkey. There was nothing about him to suggest the brutal-faced Vic Sarkey of Leandro. That fact rather relieved Drago; he had thought that Vic's ugly features were so impressed upon his memory he could never forget them.

He backed Sarkey to his bunk, and returned right-hand gun to holster. Under the bunk was the deputy's war-bag. Drago raked it out, and shook its contents upon the floor. As he had expected, a pair of handcuffs jangled among the clothing. Sarkey submitted sullenly to being cuffed to the rail of his bunk. But his eyes followed Drago grimly to the door. Drago picked up Sarkey's Colt and removed the cylinder. He tossed the frame back into the room.

'All right, Nita,' he said drawlingly. 'Blow out that light and we'll be going.'

Outside, Nita looked at him tensely.

'Sime Sarkey,' Drago said. 'I wonder if he is brother, or cousin, to Vic Sarkey ... I left Vic handcuffed to another deputy in a restaurant, I recall ...'

278

'What are you going to do now? You can't come back here. You ought to be leaving the Basin. I'll ride in—'

'No. It's not that close a thing. I'll go on; finish the thing I started to do. After that—can I come to your place on the Perdida? Just to hear from you what's happened?'

'Of course! You know you can come there—any time you want to—and stay as long as you like. You—you know that!'

Her eyes were narrowed; a corner of her scarlet underlip was caught between her teeth.

'She's a peculiar sort. She—I think she'll appreciate your help here, even though she can't openly associate with your sort. She's a kind of—oh, idiot, I suppose I mean. Like most women. You ride into town, then. And don't stay there long. Come to the Perdida and ride up it to the cottonwoods above the house. I'll meet you there as soon as I can.'

'Lige McGinsey is the angle I don't understand,' Drago said frowningly. 'Why he was here—'

'I don't know what he was after. But when he turned up with that conveniently lame horse of his, they talked for a good while. Then she came out of the house, with few words and short for anybody. She was going to town. In the buckboard. Lige would drive her in. She wouldn't have Clint. She didn't want me. So—she went.'

Drago shrugged again and turned to Button.

He mounted and touched his hatrim. Nita was standing there, a vivid figure in the moonlight, when he looked back. He waved again and she lifted her hand in answer.

All the way to town, Button's hoofs drummed out a sort of irritating accompaniment to his thoughts. Clint was dead—and dead as a warrior. It would be a blow to Marjorie, of course. But it was a better solution—even if she could not believe it—than having him dodging the law for the rest of his life. She would grow used to thought of his death.

'And when they come to look at that battleground of his,' Drago summed it up, 'even 'Pache—Jap, as Clint called him—may pass as an LL man. And when he's identified as one of the runaway train-robbers, people will look toward the LL and Walking M, rather than toward the 56, for the missing robber.'

He could not be troubled by thought of Sime Sarkey, handcuffed to the bunk. Sarkey would hardly be free in time to interfere with him. He would tell Marjorie of Clint's death, give her an evasive answer about what he intended to do, then leave a trail pointing in the direction opposite the Perdida. And, when he had spoken again to Nita, he would ride.

'Back to Bellero, this time,' he decided. 'And over the River. Texas is too warm for my clothes.'

It was after midnight when he pulled in

behind Dennis Crow's restaurant. But there was light in the building. He let the reins trail and went up to the back door. From somewhere along the street a tinny piano sent the tune of *Old Joe Clark*. Taunton, he recalled, was an 'all-night' town, a 'hurrah' town. He went into a sort of storeroom and through it to the kitchen end of the eating-house.

Dennis Crow and his sometime helper Sam were at the counter on the customers' side. Crow sat with elbows behind him on the counter-top, his peg thrust out comfortably. Otherwise, the place was empty.

Crow turned with sound of Drago's heels. He stared, then his red face twisted in a grin:

'The man hisself!' he grunted. 'I was just saying that you have done some things—or got 'em done—in Taunton Basin! Who's left, of the two sides? Nobody but Lige McGinsey and Gano Gotcher—'

'McGinsey only,' Drago corrected him. 'I'll take some coffee, Crow. Clint wiped out Gano Gotcher tonight, on the 56. Along with a couple of other LL hands. You're telling me that Rust is out?'

'You or Wyoming's crowd fixed him not to float!'

Crow got up and stumped behind the counter, to come back with the coffee.

Drago lifted the cup.

'Clint was killed, though,' he said grimly. 'I

came in to find his sister and tell her.'

He ate doughnuts and drank the coffee. Sam and Dennis Crow gave him the details—as these had arrived in town—of the battle between Wyoming's men and those led by Hinky Rust.

'This kind of leaves McGinsey the top dog,' Sam summed it up. 'Rust and Wade and Gotcher never had kin anybody knows about. He can take up the three outfits, if he wants 'em, pretty cheap. But the Taunton Basin War is plumb finished!'

'And the 56 and the little fellows will be as badly off as ever,' Drago grunted. 'Well, I've got my errand...'

'This is going to jolt her,' Crow said solemnly. 'She's the kind to take responsibility heavy. And she thought the world and all of that fool-kid. Nothing she wouldn't have did for him. She's at the ho-tel now. She was looking for Judge Monroe Bell, but he's been gone all day. Reckon he's not back yet. You seen him, Sam?'

Sam said he hadn't and Drago nodded and went out. He was looking down the street, thinking that Berry Nicks's posse had drained a good many men from the county seat, when Crow called to him. He had a letter for Drago.

'I'll get it after while,' Drago answered. 'I'm leaving my horse in back. Keep an eye on him, will you?'

He crossed the dusky street and moved

toward the Longhorn. There was little danger of finding any of the LL and Walking M warriors in that hangout of the Rust-Wade faction. But mention of Judge Bell had brought thought of those striped sacks in his *alforjas*. He wanted to talk to the old justice.

He stopped and looked over the swing-doors. There was nobody in sight, at bar or tables, who looked hostile. So he went in. The bar-tender stared as at a ghost, then grinned:

'Come in! Come in, feller! By God, you showed some folks around here you could play more'n a piano! You let 'em listen to a couple good tunes of Winchester-music!'

He moved in to the bar. Immediately, he was surrounded by the half-dozen drinkers. They asked questions which he parried with shrugs or nods. When they gave him up and scattered again, he asked the bar-tender about Judge Bell.

'He ain't been in town all day. You been to his house? It's at the end of the street. He might be there, but I hear he was left a message to see Marjorie Littell.'

'I reckon I'll try his house,' Drago said slowly.

He turned from the bar and made two steps when the swing-doors flapped violently and Wyoming Dees lunged through. Dees had a pistol in each hand, leveled waist-high. His battered head was shoved forward. His thin mouth was open over snarling teeth.

'*This*—is *it*!' he said raspingly.

Drago was hardly conscious of what he did. Instinctively, with the smooth movements of long practice, he jerked the Colt from his belt-holster, lifted it and let the hammer drop. He knew that Dees had fired but he felt no slugs tearing into him. He thumbed back the hammer and let it fall again—and a third time. Wyoming Dees swayed forward, his hands sagging as if the Colts were too heavy to hold up. Drago continued to fire at him until the hammer dropped upon the empty chamber. His last bullet struck Dees just before the stocky gunman's bending knees touched the floor.

Drago drew his second Colt and put the empty gun in its place under his arm. Stark amazement was in every face he saw at the bar. Slowly, his own dirty stubbled face twisted, and he grinned mirthlessly.

'I'm not leaving town,' he informed the bar-tender.

He went out. A man was running toward him. Gaspingly, he asked what the shooting had meant.

'Man was shot in the saloon. Wyoming Dees. By Hoolihan.'

'But—but *you're* Hoolihan!' the man said bewilderedly.

'That's right,' Drago admitted, brushing past.

He found Judge Bell's house, but a Mexican

woman said the judge had not come back. He came back and stood staring across at lighted windows in the two-story building that was Taunton's hotel. It seemed so long ago that he had followed Tonto Peel around that veranda, to find Marjorie Littell. Now, he was going there again, to find her. But this would be the last time. The last time he would ever see her . . .

He went across the street, moving neither slow nor fast. He stepped upon the veranda and stopped there, looking through the door into the hallway. A little Mexican with bare, gray head was moving in the hall. Drago went in and asked in Spanish which room Miss Littell had.

'Above, and on the right at the hall end,' the man told him indifferently.

He climbed the stairs quietly and went down the gloomy hall. At her door he hesitated, then knocked.

'Come in!' she said, and he turned the knob.

She was sitting in a big rocker by the window. The light on the table made her pale face seem ghostly. She stared at him, then stood quickly.

'I thought it was—I thought you were on the ranch.'

He closed the door behind him and stood, hat in hand, then moved slowly toward her.

'There's been a fight—at the ranch, this time,' he told her quietly. 'Gano Gotcher and some of the LL and Walking M killers jumped

285

Clint. He killed Gotcher, but—he was killed.'

She was rigid, staring at him. Suddenly, she sat down again. But her wide eyes never wavered from his face.

'It—it doesn't seem possible,' she said dully. 'Clint—dead. He was always so—'

'I know. Nita said that, when we found him. But, I think you know certain things. I think McGinsey told you, when he came back to the house today. Didn't he?'

She shook her head violently.

'Please! Please go away now. Let me alone. I deeply appreciate all you've done, since you—adopted us. But I can't talk about anything now. Clint's dead—killed in this horrible fighting. All we've known for months has been killing. I can't talk now. Please go away.'

'I'm afraid you have to talk—a little more. McGinsey told you about Clint, didn't he? He found Clint's partner, dead on 56 range. He recognized him; found express company money on him. He told you that Clint was one of the gang—'

'How did you know?' she gasped. 'Does everybody know?'

'McGinsey, Nita, you, and I. No more. Nobody will need know. Anyway, Clint is beyond their fingers. He would have had to run. Nita and I were going to start him for South America. But Gotcher caught him there beside the dead man—'

She turned away from him, with a hand over

her eyes. He could hear her crying. He moved closer, to look down on her. He touched her shoulder gently.

'Nobody needs to know,' he said again. 'All you have to do is—'

'I—I—There are limits to what I can do, even to keep it quiet,' she told him gaspingly. 'I promised to marry Lige McGinsey, to buy his help. Now, I'll have to go on with that, or he'll tell that Clint was really a thief. I can't do more than beg you—'

'You don't have to beg me to do anything!' he told her angrily. 'This, any more than whatever else I've done on the 56. And you don't have to marry McGinsey, now, if you don't want to; if you wouldn't have married him before. Let him talk! Clint and you are different persons. Nobody can hold you responsible for what a wild boy did. He—'

'No, I have to go on with it. I couldn't bear everyone knowing about Clint. I have to marry him, no matter what I think of him—now! I have to do it. But I thank you—'

CHAPTER TWENTY-THREE

'WHAT'S FUNNY ABOUT SARKEY?'

Drago stared grimly at her. She met his eyes steadily.

287

'I'm trying to tell you not to act the idiot!' he said roughly. 'Isn't your life more important than an attempt to keep folk from saying that Clint was a train-robber?'

'*And* a murderer, or associate of murderers! No! I can't bear that. If I have to buy his silence, I have to marry Lige McGinsey. Clint—Ah, *don't* you see? I was the big sister. I was responsible for him. It was all my fault; really it was!'

'All right! But what if I tell? What if I beat McGinsey to it—stand at the Longhorn bar and tell that Clint was—'

'You wouldn't do it! You're not that sort of man,' she told him. 'I don't know who you are, really. But I know *what* you are. You could no more do that than—than you could shoot a man in the back.'

He stared angrily at her. But she could look him down.

'All right, you win. I couldn't do it. So the top gunman of Taunton Basin will make his bow. I think I have a right to that title, now— the champion killer of the whole Basin. One way or another, the "war" has been ended. We've settled every faction-leader except McGinsey. And his chief killer went down awhile ago in the Longhorn. Wyoming Dees, I mean.'

He showed her his mirthless smile. She frowned at him.

'So, I'll say good-bye. There's no more need

for killer-guns; for the pistol passport. I'll be riding. Tonight. I—'

'You mean you're just going to ride out of the Basin tonight? You're leaving and—you're not coming back?'

He laughed, and managed to make it sound genuine.

'I have to. You see, you've been entertaining *Notoriety*, unawares. Shackled to one of the bunks at the 56 there's a very irritated deputy sheriff from Leandro County. He let twenty-five hundred dollars slip through his hands today. He had a gun against Steve Drago, the most valuable man in the State. They want to hang me, back in Leandro.'

'Drago! I read about your trial. You—They said you shot an unarmed man. But the San Antonio papers spoke as if that were incredible—You didn't murder that man! I know you didn't because—you couldn't have done it.'

'No. He had a pistol. Some of the Jacklin side stole it. But you see why I can't stay in the Basin. You see why—understand the reason for a lot of things. Please give Nita my very respectful respects. I was going to deliver them in person, but there's no point to that now. Tell her how much I appreciated knowing her and—Good-bye!'

He turned quickly to the door. He opened it without turning. He heard her quick, soft word, but went on out and closed the door behind him. And he all but ran downstairs.

When he came to the veranda a small, erect figure was crossing it, entering the hotel. Drago stopped. Judge Bell looked at him.

'Oh,' he said. 'Hoolihan ... I have just come from the Longhorn. If you were troubled about that affair—which I seriously doubt—you may enjoy an easy mind now. My inquiry was brief, but quite comprehensive. You were completely exonerated, despite certain efforts of Mr McGinsey. Nothing but my official position keeps me from offering congratulations—and thanks.'

'You were going up to see Miss Littell. That won't be necessary now. I've talked to her. And you can do something for me. I want to leave with you some of the loot from the Parlin train-robbery and what is probably all that was taken in the last holdup at Mesquite Hill. I found it close to the body of a man called "Jap" or "Apache." He had holed up on the 56 range. He tried to bushwhack me. Will you return it, without drawing me into it?'

'Of course! I hear that Clint, who never knew how to live, managed to prove that he knew how to die. I will take the loot with pleasure—and say nothing of the way it came to me.'

'Then if you'll wait at your house, I'll bring what I've got. I'll be there within five or ten minutes.'

He went between the hotel and the store adjoining and got back to Button. He mounted and rode quietly back to where Judge Bell waited. He handed over the striped bags.

'And now, I'll say *adiós*. Thanks for the favor.'

'Good-bye. I have enjoyed knowing you here. Taunton Basin is the better for your coming. After all, black powder can be a fumigant... Without committing myself, I can say that I'm confident that anything you may have been charged with, you were innocent of committing. And you take my best wishes!'

'Thank you! They're appreciated. Now— you spoke of McGinsey. He's still in town?'

'After my investigation at the Longhorn, in which he figured, he went back with some of his—ah—employees to the Cattlemen's. If you ride out of town this way, you'll miss him.'

'Thanks,' Drago replied. He lifted the reins and, as Button turned left on the street, to himself he said, aloud: 'And if I ride *this* way, I'll not miss him. I'll try not to!'

Before he came to the garishly lit front of Olin Oge's saloon, he drew in. Again it was impressed upon him that Taunton was an all-night town. Though the killing of the famous Wyoming Dees would keep some men gossiping until dawn of the great 'trigernometry' experts ... But a small knot of men stood under the awning at the Cattlemen's.

He sent Button forward at a lope and was off him, at the hitchrack, letting the reins drop, before a man could turn. He ducked under the bar of the rack and ran lightly across the wooden sidewalk to brush through the swing-doors. He had a Colt in each hand when he stopped in the bar-room with back to wall—though it was doubtful if any man he passed saw him draw them.

Halfway down the room Lige McGinsey half-sat, half-leaned, upon the edge of a poker table. Around him were five or six men, pistol-bearers without exception. McGinsey was talking with jerks of his big hands for emphasis. The listening men nodded. They looked pleasantly at their leader; grinned.

'McGinsey!' Drago called. 'Oh, McGinsey! Let go your wolf, for *this* is payday.'

'It *is* payday!' a harsh voice yelled from the back of the long room. 'But *I* pay McGinsey!'

Drago let his eyes shuttle flashingly to where Tonto Peel, coming up the room with a Winchester at the 'trail' in his big left hand, menaced the group about McGinsey with the Colt in his right.

The men in that room—at the bar; standing about McGinsey—had stiffened with Drago's voice. When Tonto Peel appeared in the other end of the barroom, some looked one way, some the other. But every man with McGinsey dropped hard, experienced hand to pistol-butt. McGinsey, also, drew. He had turned to Tonto; he was lifting his Colt when Tonto fired. It still pointed to the floor when he

292

crashed forward with Tonto's bullet in his face.

The Cattlemen's seemed to rock with the roar of firing. Bar-tenders dropped behind the long bar. Drinkers vaulted it or ran around the ends to take shelter. Men burst through the swing-doors, passing Drago who—face twisted in cold, killer's grin—was firing left-hand, right-hand, with machine-like speed and accuracy—into the last front of Taunton Basin's imported killers.

That group was shredded as by a twisting wind. But from the floor some fired. Drago felt slugs rap his hat, his shirt, his trousers; thud into his body. Then—his skull seemed to explode. Blackness was everywhere; then flame; then dark again.

Then, instantly, it seemed, there were voices all about him; voices lifting from a drone to the high note of anger. But he could understand nothing that was said. It seemed to him that he sprawled upon a thin mattress that heaved and tossed high in space. Those troublesome voices came to him out of the dark emptiness in which he floated.

Then people came with branding irons and pushed the fiery ends against him. He told them over and over again to stop it; he explained very logically—although he could not be sure what he said—that he had been branded for years and that it was foolish to do all this work. But the people would not listen. They continued to poke and burn him.

When they had gone, he swung in black space again for years and years, too weak to roll over the edge of his bed and end it all by crashing down to whatever bottom this black void had. He tried to call the branding crews back; he wanted to ask them to push him over and let him die. But his head was swollen enormously and his mouth was too small, now, to let out words. He could see it—a ridiculous little slit in his huge face, from which came tiny squeaking sounds.

But all this changed, after endless time. He was dumped without warning into a furnace, and Lige McGinsey and Wyoming Dees and the lank Norris and that lithe, dark cowboy, The Breed, moved around him while he roasted. They laughed at him and for pride's sake he grinned at them.

He was not always either in space or lying upon the grid of a furnace. Sometimes he opened his eyes and found walls around him; cool, grayish walls.

Nevil Jacklin rode up to him, at last. Drago thought this an odd thing. He told Nevil that he was dead. But the tall, thin Cross J man ignored him. He sat his black horse, as dark and grim as Drago himself.

'I never liked you,' he told Drago. 'But that trial was just funny. Nobody ever saw me without a gun. It was that fat, white rabbit cousin of mine, Heck, who picked the gun up from under my hand in the alley. You remember that Heck was standing at the bar in the Gold Dollar when I talked to you. I wanted to kill you, but you were faster. And when you went back into the Dollar, Heck scooped up the gun. He dropped it into a hole in the alley by the Dollar's wall and covered it with dirt. But it's not there now...' Drago thanked him. But it was queer, he told somebody, for Nevil to grow a long, gray beard. Then he saw that it was not Nevil, but the old billygoat at the stockyards in Fort Worth, the wise, treacherous billygoat that led the silly sheep up to the killers—and ducked aside when they were at the end of the chute. He watched the goat for a long while—watched him until he lost his beard and grew bigger and became Old Funeral, the stubby, curly-haired outlaw he had ridden in Leandro when he was sixteen.

He rode Funeral to a frazzle-dazzle and got off and collected his bets. He was in a room with all the money in his hands. And the room swelled until it covered all of Texas. He could see it with a wall on the Oklahoma line— Oklahoma was colored green, for it was just a page of Maury's Geography—and a corner down in the Gulf of Mexico. And everybody he had ever known was in the room.

'My Lord!' he said to himself. 'Look at Uncle Tom Drago! This must be the first time in forty years that he's looked happy—even not *unhappy*!'

'Do you want a drink?' Nita Fourponies

asked him.

She put her arm under his shoulders and lifted him.

'You can't afford me,' he told her.

'I'd like to try!' she said. 'Now, lie down and take it easy—nitwit! Lord! You've got a beard like a barbwire fence! Scratched my face...'

When he opened his eyes again and found the walls, it was only a room of ordinary size; a clean, light, pleasant room with bright cretonne curtains at the window.

'Well!' Marjorie Littell said, in a shaky voice. 'So you decided to—to stay with us!'

'Who's been making you cry?' he demanded. 'Your eyes are wet. And you've been serious too much of your life.'

'I'm not crying!' she denied. 'But it's wonderful—you—the way you've improved and—Nita says so and Mrs Bell and—and everybody.'

He looked at her for a long while. It was hard to separate those things he had seen and heard from this present moment. He knew that he had been delirious; he found himself afraid that this, also, was unreal.

'How long have I been here?' he asked hesitantly.

'About two weeks. But the doctor says your particular type of constitution is proof against almost anything. Judging by the scars you have, that must be true.'

He moved his head a little, looking around

the room. Now, in a surge, everything came back to him.

'Hurd? Sime Sarkey, I mean! What—what happened to him?'

'Oh, the Leandro deputy sheriff!'

She laughed—and it was the most cheerful sound he had ever heard from her. He watched her broodingly; she was younger than when he had first seen her. Even lovelier.

'What's funny—about Sarkey? And about Leandro?'

'He came into town that—that night. Somehow, he had freed himself from the bunk and found the handcuffs key. He was right on Tonto's heels. Tonto had come back to the house and heard from Nita all that had happened. He put two and two together and decided that Lige McGinsey was at the bottom of my troubles. So he all but killed a horse getting here and he was in the back of the Cattlemen's when *you* walked through the door on your very noble, very silly, errand.'

'There was nothing silly about it. A certain type of man needs killing, just as a rattlesnake has to be killed. McGinsey was that type. I am a killer. I've proved that, time and again. Nothing but a killer would serve you, here in Taunton Basin. And that was one last thing I could do for you; one last time that a killer's gun was needed. I've been a walking dead man for months—ever since that murder charge was filed against me in Taunton. Certainly I wasn't one to worry about being killed. But—you haven't told me about Sime Sarkey!'

'He wanted to arrest you, set a guard over you, after you were almost killed in the Cattlemen's. Tonto wanted to kill him. I think he would have killed him if he hadn't been stopped. But Sarkey had to take his handcuffs back to Leandro when Dennis Crow appeared with a letter.'

'I remember,' Drago said, frowning. 'He told me he had a letter. But—'

'It was a letter from your attorney in Leandro. It seems that you have the capacity for making friends who never desert you. At least, it appeared from this letter that Judge Attley and a man named Keats Tucker had been trying to discover who *could* have taken Nevil Jacklin's pistol from under his hand in the alley; when they had narrowed their search to that list, they discovered who *had* taken it—'

'Heck Jacklin, Nevil's cousin!' Drago interrupted quickly.

'Yes! Heck Jacklin, but—but how did *you* know that?'

'Nevil told me. But never mind that. They found Heck—'

'And scared him into a confession. He did it on the spur of the moment. He hated you, it seemed. But he confessed and Judge Attley so described the trial and everything to the Attorney General and the Governor that, despite the fact that you were an escaped

298

fugitive, the Governor pardoned you and told every newspaper in the State why he was doing it.'

Drago could only stare.

'You mean that I'm *not* a convicted murderer on the dodge? That—that I don't have to run for Mexico? That—that I can even stay here, in Taunton Basin, if I want to?'

She leaned a little to him, nodding, and he tried to lift his hand. But he was too weak.

'See if my hand's still there, will you?' he whispered. 'I—I can't realize all this; not quickly, easily. I can stay in Taunton Basin, for all the law will do?'

'Of course! You can stay here—and be very welcome—'

'Welcome—to you?'

'Most of all to me! If you'll come back to the 56. If you want to come back—'

He concentrated on his hand, now held in hers. And by sheer exercise of will he moved it, raising it until he held her hand against his face.

'I don't want anything else. I only want to stay on the 56, with you.'

'Then there doesn't seem to be a *thing* we can argue about,' she said smilingly. 'Not a thing...'

And she put her face against his, and kept it there.

We hope you have enjoyed this Large Print book. Other Chivers Press or Thorndike Press Large Print books are available at your library or directly from the publishers. For more information about current and forthcoming titles, please call or write, without obligation, to:

Chivers Press Limited
Windsor Bridge Road
Bath BA2 3AX
England
Tel. (0225) 335336

OR

Thorndike Press
P.O. Box 159
Thorndike, ME 04986
USA
Tel. (800) 223-6121
(207) 948-2962
(in Maine and Canada, call collect)

All our Large Print titles are designed for easy reading, and all our books are made to last.